Kasten
7

D1028616

VOCES

VOCES

An Anthology of Nuevo Mexicano Writers

Edited by Rudolfo A. Anaya

University of New Mexico Press
Albuquerque

Library of Congress Cataloging-in-Publication Data

Voces: an anthology of Nuevo Mexicano writers
edited by Rudolfo A. Anaya.
p.   cm.
ISBN 0-8263-1040-0: $12.95
1. American literature—New Mexico.
2. American literature—Mexican American authors.
3. American literature—20th century.
4. Mexican Americans—Literary collections.
5. New Mexico—Literary collections.
I. Anaya, Rudolfo A.
PS571.N6V63   1988
810'.8'09789—dc 19   88-22705

© 1987 by El Norte Publications/Academia.
All rights reserved.

University of New Mexico Press edition
reprinted 1988 by arrangement with
El Norte Publications/Academia.

Table of Contents

continued...

Table of Contents

INTRODUCTION

It is a pleasure to introduce this collection of prose and poetry by contemporary writers from the Nuevo Mexicano community. In this book the reader will recognize the works of familiar writers who are vital links in the oral and written traditions of the Nuevo Mexicano's literary history: writers such as Fray Angélico Chávez and Sabine Ulibarrí. However, if an anthology is to reflect a wide spectrum of a community's literary expression, it must also introduce talented new writers to the public. It is gratifying to see a new generation of Nuevo Mexicano writers developing and to have this opportunity to introduce them to the public.

A few of the writers are new arrivals to the state, others, such as José Montoya and Leroy Quintana, live in California, but we still claim part of their souls and talents in our familia of writers. It is also important to include in this anthology the works of Mexican writers who now live in New Mexico. The novels of Gustavo Sainz are well known in México and throughout the world, they should be known here as well.

In 1598 our colonial ancestors brought their way of life, their religion and their language up the Rio Grande Valley to establish the beginnings of Nuevo Mexicano culture. It was the daily as well as the poetic use of that faith and language that provided continuity and cohesion to the newly settled Mexicano/Hispano pueblos of Nuevo México.

The Native American pueblos were already settled along the Rio Grande. Their languages and their faith were an integral part of the area which the Spanish and Mexican settlers came to occupy. In the fields, in the daily life of the pueblos, in the kivas, the Pueblo ceremonial ways and

vii

languages were crucial to the spiritual relationship they established with the earth and the cosmos.

The Anglo Americans arrived in Nuevo México in the mid-nineteenth century, introducing yet another language to our land. We have all learned to share the languages and cultures of Nuevo México, even as we continue to preserve our distinct ways of life. The majority of the writers represented here use English, a reflection of the reality within which we live. At the same time we applaud writers like Estevan Arellano and Erlinda Gonzalez-Berry for continuing a tradition, the creation of literary works in Spanish.

I believe we must pass on to the present generation a serious concern about learning to speak the native languages of the state. Traditions rest within the language. At the same time we are compelled to learn English, not only to survive, but to reach wider audiences with our writings. Language is a tool we learn to utilize. We learn to use it to reflect on life, and that reflection becomes our history.

These writers, through their stories and poems, represent the artistic expression of our community. Collectively, these writers begin to define a new literary space. We continue not only in the tradition of the cuentistas and the poets of the Hispano villages, we also create our own present space, a space which defines our reality and our creative impulse.

From my experience in writing, I have discovered that the most important concern for a writer is to identify and develop his most personal, intimate voice. That authentic voice within us is the voice which yearns to create story and poetry. In any community which values creativity, the voice of the poet is encouraged and nurtured. Nuevo Mexicanos have always appreciated their singers and storytellers. The voice of the storyteller and poet passed on history, values, traditions, ceremonies, and jokes as well as prayers. Our writers have always recorded the artistic history of our culture, it is their stories and poems which provide the ideas and images for reflection, but because we lacked access to publishing we lacked wide dissemination of our viewpoints. Now we are at a crucial time in the unfolding of our destiny. Our community is evolving, changing, exploring its potential. Crucial to the development of our destiny and the definition of that destiny, are the voices of the writers and poets, for it is their reflection on the existential questions of our life and destiny that helps define and light the way. Thus it has been in all the cultures of the world, and so it is for our Nuevo Mexicano way of life. If we are to survive, we must not only continue developing our writers, we must also make sure their works are published and disseminated to our community. *Voces* marks one more step in that process.

I thank each writer represented here; each has dared to find and nurture his or her creative voice. This book assures us that the poetic voice of the Nuevo Mexicanos is alive and engaged in reflecting our reality.

I want to thank Cecilio García-Camarillo for his constant encouragement and help during my editing of *Voces*. I also thank Erlinda Gonzales-Berry for reading some of the manuscripts and Teresa Marquez for organizing the Contributors' Notes. The concept of *Voces* is important, it must continue to grow.

Rudolfo A. Anaya
Albuquerque, New Mexico

MY WONDER HORSE

Sabine Ulibarrí

He was white. White as memories lost. He was free. Free as happiness is. He was fantasy, liberty, and excitement. He filled and dominated the mountain valleys and surrounding plains. He was a white horse that flooded my youth with dreams and poetry.

Around the campfires of the country and in the sunny patios of the town, the ranch hands talked about him with enthusiasm and admiration. But gradually their eyes would become hazy and blurred with dreaming. The lively talk would die down. All thoughts fixed on the vision evoked by the horse. Myth of the animal kingdom. Poem of the world of men.

White and mysterious, he paraded his harem through the summer forests with lordly rejoicing. Winter sent him to the plains and sheltered hillsides for the protection of his females. He spent the summer like an Oriental potentate in his woodland gardens. The winter he passed like an illustrious warrior celebrating a well-earned victory.

He was a legend. The stories told of the Wonder Horse were endless. Some true, others fabricated. So many traps, so many snares, so many searching parties, and all in vain. The horse always escaped, always mocked his pursuers, always rose above the control of man. Many a valiant cowboy swore to put his halter and his brand on the animal. But always he had to confess later that the mystic horse was more of a man than he.

I was fifteen years old. Although I had never seen the Wonder Horse, he filled my imagination and fired my ambition. I used to listen open-mouthed as my father and the ranch hands talked about the phantom horse who turned into mist and air and nothingness when he was trapped. I joined in the universal obsession—like the hope of winning the lottery—of putting my lasso on him some day, of capturing him and showing him off on Sunday afternoons when the girls of the town strolled through the streets.

It was high summer. The forests were fresh, green, and gay. The cattle moved slowly, fat and sleek in the August sun and shadow. Listless and drowsy in the lethargy of late afternoon, I was dozing on my horse. It was time to round up the herd and go back to the good bread of the cowboy camp. Already my comrades would be sitting around the campfire, playing the guitar, telling stories of past or present, or surrendering to the languor of the late afternoon. The sun was setting behind me in a riot of streaks and colors. Deep, harmonious silence.

I sit drowsily still, forgetting the cattle in the glade. Suddenly the forest falls silent, a deafening quiet. The afternoon comes to a standstill. The breeze stops blowing, but it vibrates. The sun flares hotly. The planet, life, and time itself have stopped in an inexplicable way. For a moment, I don't understand what is happening.

Then my eyes focus. There he is! The Wonder Horse! At the end of the glade, on high ground surrounded by summer green. He is a statue. He is an engraving. Line and form and white stain on a green background. Pride, prestige, and art incarnate in animal flesh. A picture of burning beauty and virile freedom. An ideal, pure and invincible, rising from the eternal dreams of humanity. Even today my being thrills when I remember him.

A sharp neigh. A far-reaching challenge that soars on high, ripping the virginal fabric of the rosy clouds. Ears at the point. Eyes flashing. Tail waving active defiance. Hoofs glossy and destructive. Arrogant ruler of the countryside.

The moment is never ending, a momentary eternity. It no longer exists, but it will always live....There must have been mares. I did not see them.

The cattle went on their indifferent way. My horse followed them, and I came slowly back from the land of dreams to the world of toil. But life could no longer be what it was before.

That night under the stars I didn't sleep. I dreamed. How much I dreamed awake and how much I dreamed asleep, I do not know. I only know that a white horse occupied my dreams and filled them with vibrant sound, and light, and turmoil.

Summer passed and winter came. Green grass gave place to white snow. The herds descended from the mountains to the valleys and the hollows. And in the town they kept saying that the Wonder Horse was roaming through this or that secluded area. I inquired everywhere for his whereabouts. Every day he became for me more of an ideal, more of an idol, more of a mystery.

It was Sunday. The sun had barely risen above the snowy mountains. My breath was a white cloud. My horse was trembling with cold and fear like me. I left without going to mass. Without any breakfast. Without the usual bread and sardines in my saddle bags. I had slept badly, but had kept the vigil well. I was going in search of the white light that galloped through my dreams.

On leaving the town for the open country, the roads disappear. There are no tracks, human or animal. Only a silence, deep, white, and sparkling. My horse breaks trail with his chest and leaves an unending wake, an open rift, in the white sea. My trained, concentrated gaze covers the landscape from horizon to horizon, searching for the noble silhouette of the talismanic horse.

It must have been midday. I don't know. Time had lost its meaning. I found him! On a slope stained with sunlight. We saw one another at the same time. Together, we turned to stone. Motionless, absorbed, and panting, I gazed at his beauty, his pride, his nobility. As still as sculptured marble, he allowed himself to be admired.

A sudden, violent scream breaks the silence. A glove hurled into my face. A challenge and a mandate. Then something surprising happens. The horse that in summer takes his stand between any threat and his herd, swinging back and forth from left to right, now plunges into the snow. Stronger than they, he is breaking trail for his mares. They follow him. His flight is slow in order to conserve his strength.

I follow. Slowly. Quivering. Thinking about his intelligence. Admiring his courage. Understanding his courtesy. The afternoon advances. My horse is taking it easy.

One by one the mares become weary. One by one, they drop out of the trail. Alone! He and I. My inner ferment bubbles to my lips. I speak to him. He listens and is quiet.

He still opens the way, and I follow in the path he leaves me. Behind us a long, deep trench crosses the white plain. My horse, which has eaten grain and good hay, is still strong. Undernourished as the Wonder Horse is, his strength is waning. But he keeps on because that is the way he is. He does not know how to surrender.

I now see black stains over his body. Sweat and the wet snow have revealed the black skin beneath the white hair. Snorting breath, turned to steam, tears the air. White spume above white snow. Sweat, spume, and steam. Uneasiness

I felt like an executioner. But there was no turning back. The distance between us was growing relentlessly shorter. God and Nature watched indifferently.

I feel sure of myself at last. I untie the rope. I open the lasso and pull the reins tight. Every nerve, every muscle is tense. My heart is in my mouth. Spurs pressed against trembling flanks. The horse leaps. I whirl the rope and throw the obedient lasso.

A frenzy of fury and rage. Whirlpools of light and fans of transparent snow. A rope that whistles and burns the saddle tree. Smoking, fighting gloves. Eyes burning in their sockets. Mouth parched. Fevered forehead. The whole earth shakes and shudders. The long, white trench ends in a wide, white pool.

Deep, gasping quiet. The Wonder Horse is mine! Both still trembling, we look at one another squarely for a long time. Intelligent and realistic, he stops struggling and even takes a hesitant step toward me. I speak to him. As I talk, I approach him. At first, he flinches and recoils. Then he waits for me. The two horses greet one another in their own way. Finally, I succeed in stroking his mane. I tell him many things, and he seems to understand.

Ahead of me, along the trail already made, I drove him toward the town. Triumphant. Exultant. Childish laughter gathered in my throat. With my newfound manliness, I controlled it. I wanted to sing, but I fought down the desire. I wanted to shout, but I kept quiet. It was the ultimate in happiness. It was the pride of the male adolescent. I felt myself a conqueror

Occasionally the Wonder Horse made a try for his liberty, snatching me abruptly from my thoughts. For a few moments, the struggle was renewed. Then we went on.

It was necessary to go through the town. There was no other way. The sun was setting. Icy streets and people on the porches. The Wonder Horse full of terror and panic for the first time. He ran and my well-shod horse stopped him. He slipped and fell on his side. I suffered for him. The indignity. The humiliation. Majesty degraded. I begged him not to struggle, to let himself be led. How it hurt me that other people should see him like that!

Finally we reached home.

"What shall I do with you, Mago? If I put you into the stable or the corral, you are sure to hurt yourself. Besides, it would be an insult. You aren't a slave. You aren't a servant. You aren't even an animal."

I decided to turn him loose in the fenced pasture. There, little by little, Mago would become accustomed to my friendship and my company. No animal had ever escaped from that pasture.

My father saw me coming and waited for me without a word. A smile played over his face, and a spark danced in his eyes. He watched me take the rope from Mago, and the two of us thoughtfully observed him move away. My father clasped my hand a little more firmly than usual and said, "That was a man's job." That was all. Nothing more was needed. We understood one another very well. I was playing the role of a real man, but the childish laughter and shouting that bubbled up inside me almost destroyed the impression I wanted to create.

That night I slept little, and when I slept, I did not know that I was asleep. For dreaming is the same when one really dreams, asleep or awake. I was up at dawn. I had to go to see my Wonder Horse. As soon as it was light, I went out into the cold to look for him.

The pasture was large. It contained a grove of trees and a small gully. The Wonder Horse was not visible anywhere, but I was not worried. I walked slowly, my head full of the events of yesterday and my plans for the future. Suddenly I realized that I had walked a long way. I quicken my steps. I look apprehensively around me. I begin to be afraid. Without knowing it, I begin to run. Faster and faster.

He is not there. The Wonder Horse has escaped. I search every corner where he could be hidden. I follow his tracks. I see that during the night he walked incessantly, sniffing, searching for a way out. He did not find one. He made one for himself.

I followed the track that led straight to the fence. And I saw that the trail did not stop but continued on the other side. It was a barbed-wire fence. There was white hair on the wire. There was blood on the barbs. There were red stains on the snow and little red drops in the hoofprints on the other side of the fence.

I stopped there. I did not go any further. The rays of the morning sun on my face. Eyes clouded and yet filled with light. Childish tears on the cheeks of a man. A cry stifled in my throat. Slow silent sobs.

Standing there, I forgot myself and the world and time. I cannot explain it, but my sorrow was mixed with pleasure. I was weeping with happiness. No matter how much it hurt me, I was rejoicing over the flight and the freedom of the Wonder Horse, the dimensions of his indomitable spirit. Now he would always be fantasy, freedom, and excitement. The Wonder Horse was transcendent. He had enriched my life forever.

My father found me there. He came close without a word and laid his arm across my shoulders. We stood looking at the white trench with its flecks of red that led into the rising sun.

AMELIA

Rosalie Otero

Taos Valley is a wide, flat plain in northern New Mexico, 7000 feet above
sea level. To the northeast are the pine-covered Sangre de Cristo mountains,
looming sharply in a series of probing triangles. To the west the Rio Grande
cuts ever deeper into its narrow gorge as it tumbles its way south. This valley
with its tremendous vista had become home and inspiration to countless
artists. Barbara Stevens was among them. She had come to vacation and
stayed. The Taos scene appealed greatly to her. She responded to the
Spanish people of the area and was inspired by respect for their culture.
Their seasonal, rural rituals of working in the irrigation ditches ("acequias"
Amelia would say), planting, harvesting, and plastering their adobe homes
fascinated her. She also never tired of going to the Taos Pueblo as she had
today. She felt awe and peace sitting by the creek and sketching the
ancient structure.

Hundreds of years before the Spanish conquistadors discovered New
Mexico, the Taos Pueblo was already standing. Its adobe rooms rise one
upon the other in clifflike form. Beams protrude from the wall, their shadows
slanting across the adobe. Ladders and chimneys add detail to these ancient
apartment houses. Gray smoke curls from the chimneys and from outdoor

ovens that are dotted about like beehives in front of the buildings. Every so often a shawl-clad woman or blanket-wrapped man walks with dignity across the packed earth between the pueblo and the creek. This was true today as it was when Barbara first came here ten years before. As she sat there, her gaze would move to the blue and purple mountain rising behind the pueblo. The view was made dramatic by swiftly moving clouds that threw sharp shadow patterns across its face. She thought of Amelia.

It was a mild, fragrant evening in early May, several weeks after Barbara had come to visit an old family friend, Oscar Berninghaus, that she was introduced to Amelia. Amelia was a petite Hispanic woman in her early thirties. Their meeting had been so brief and their lives so different that Barbara could never have predicted that Amelia would remember her or even that they would see each other again.

It was a few weeks later when Barbara had decided on impulse to buy an old adobe house and stay in Taos that she encountered Amelia again. Barbara had gone on one of her usual treks through the hills carrying her black case, sketch pad, and brown lunch bag. She had been too involved in her sketching to notice that a storm was approaching. When she stood up, the rolling black clouds were spitting lightning and rumbling deep guttural sounds. Barbara had to climb over a small hill before she could get on the path that led home.

She came muttering, hunched so far forward she looked like a mountain goat. The storm too came muttering, trembling heaving black clouds forward. Amelia stood fascinated, watching their ominous approach. Barbara came looming larger; her floppy brown hat smashed on her head.

"Hel..." Amelia's greeting was lost in a crash of thunder. The rain was released and in that same moment Barbara was by her side, panting but smiling a recognition.

"Damn! I didn't even see it coming. Come on, we'd better hurry." Barbara grabbed Amelia's arm at the same time that Amelia reached for Barbara. They grabbed for each other and stumbled down the hill. The rain blinded both women so that, although they both knew the path well, they didn't follow it. They zigzagged down like two drunks. The only sound was their heavy breathing and the swishing of rain and wind.

When they finally reached Barbara's front door they were both drenched.

"Please, you must come in. We'll dry ourselves and I'll put on a pot of coffee." Barbara took off her hat and sweater and piled it along with the rest of her things near the doorway and went down the hallway leaving muddy, wet tracks. Amelia stood shivering by the door. In a matter of seconds Barbara returned with towels and pushed Amelia toward the kitchen. She talked the whole time she dried her bright red hair, threw out old coffee grounds, and got a new pot of coffee started.

"What in the world were you doing up on the hill? I met you at Bernie's didn't I? Do you live near here? Storms sure come quickly around here. Don't even warn you that they're coming. Damn, I'm cold. We'd better take off these wet clothes. Come on. You can use one of my robes."

Before Amelia even got one word out, she was ushered into a bedroom. Barbara began to undress. Amelia was struck by the whiteness of her skin contrasted by that wild red hair. Barbara was a large woman; not fat exactly, but she was large-boned and well-padded. Amelia was not accustomed to seeing a naked woman; she had been brought up to be extremely modest. Although she had slept with her cousins when she was a little girl, she had never seen any of them naked. She stood blushing trying to avert her gaze, but her large brown eyes rounded when she looked upon the huge breasts of Barbara and the reddish patch of hair between her heavy, strong legs.

"Come on. Come on. Take off those clothes before you catch a chill. You're dripping all over the carpet besides."

At Barbara's insistent encouragement and example, Amelia began, timidly at first, to take off the layers of wet clothing. Barbara threw a blue robe at her and wrapped a red robe around herself.

Later, sitting at the kitchen table with both hands circling a hot cup of coffee, Amelia found her voice. "You really fixed up this old adobe place."

"I loved it from the first. Apparently it had been abandoned for quite some time."

"The old man died. His only son lived in Santa Fe and just left the old place to sit and rot."

"Well, I'm glad. It's perfect. I'll give you a tour as soon as we're thawed enough to walk." Barbara smiled at her; Amelia felt an immediate pleasure at Barbara's intimate tone. She was grateful for her kind regard, so she replied to all of Barbara's questions, but supplying only a modicum of information: yes, she had lived in Taos all her life, she worked part-time at the high school, it was all wonderfully challenging.

Barbara stood up and strode about the kitchen, filling the room with her presence. She refilled their cups and picking up her cup motioned Amelia to follow her. The tour had begun. Amelia looked at everything like a curious child, examining the rattan furniture, the mismatched tables and chairs, the pale green carpet and the colorful, magestic paintings on the walls. She recognized many of the signatures: Blumenschein, Phillips, Berninghaus. Some were unknown to her. She liked the watercolors done by Barbara.

A week later, having volunteered to sort through an accumulation of years' work ("work and rubbish," as Barbara said) in the vast closet in Barbara's studio, Amelia discovered, unframed, an exquisite little watercolor of the Pueblo. Amelia told Barbara that it was beautiful and certainly worth a great deal of money. Would Barbara sell it to her?

"For Christ's sake," Barbara said, snorting in amusement. "If you like it, take it, take it."

Amelia repeated that she wanted to buy it. Barbara looked at her bemused. "Look, it's pointless to argue. I don't argue. I'd be happy to see the painting hanging in your house, if you really like it."

Amelia's senses were sharpened, her pulsebeat quick, agitated. How bullying Barbara was! But Amelia backed down. She said faltering: "But— are you sure? I mean—I hadn't intended—It really is so beautiful—"

Barbara too relented. She examined the watercolor from a distance of several feet, her head turned to one side. "Well, it's beautiful if you say so.

Amelia took away the watercolor as if she feared her friend's presence might do injury to it. Later she said: "But Barbara, it isn't fair—what can I give you in return?"

The remark hung awkwardly between them. Barbara murmured, embarrassed, "Friendship isn't a matter of barter, is it?"

So it began. Barbara and Amelia appeared everywhere together. Barbara, robust, wild red hair escaping from that brown floppy hat, her loose-fitting clothes; and Amelia, neat, tidy, brown hair drawn straight back into a knot at the nape of her neck. They made an odd pair. Barbara had been taking Spanish lessons and appreciated Amelia's patience when she mispronounced a word or mixed phrases of French with her Spanish. Barbara realized how much she really understood the afternoon she went with Amelia to see Tío Fermín, an old uncle of Amelia's who had been ill—from too much drink people would say.

Tío's house was an old adobe with cracks in the mud plaster. In places the adobes were exposed. Barbara made a mental note to sketch the old place. It would make an interesting watercolor. Amelia led the way through the low doorway into the damp coolness of the hallway. The pungent smell of camphor and tobacco made Barbara wrinkle her nose. She hung back, although by nature she was not the retiring sort. But she felt that she was in a new element. She stood in the shadow of the kitchen door as Amelia walked forward.

"Tío?" — *fighting*

"Entra, hijita. Aquí estoy lidiando con este pinche café." Tío Fermín stood by the stove. His undershirt, stained with tobacco juice, seemed too large for his thin shoulders. His brown trousers were held up by a pair of suspenders.

"¿Cómo está, Tío?"

"Así nomás, como la vaca del pobre." *milked*

"Mal asistida pero bien ordeñada." Amelia laughed at her spontaneous rejoiner. She beckoned Barbara and introduced her to her uncle.

"Come in, come in. sit down. Barbara Estevens?" He said her name with a heavy Spanish accent. "You are an artista? Amelia has talked about you. Siéntate. Sit down. I'll get you some coffee."

Barbara was overcome by the friendly, comfortable kindness of the old man. She smiled at him and sat down.

"¿Dónde está mi tía?" Amelia asked the old man as she took over the coffee-making.

"Pues está hasta los chongos. Ricardo brought her some green chile and today she went to Eduvijen's to roast it. But I don't expect her until late, porque ya sabes esa Eduvijen, tiene una lengua que hasta se la pisa. Y tu tía, ya de que se sienta, se aplana." *straighten/flatten*

Amelia laughed at her Uncle's description and translated roughly for Barbara, but Barbara found that she understood most of what was said.

"Are you feeling better? Amelia told me you had been sick." Barbara joined easily in the conversation.

"Well, you know how it is at my age. Some days good, some days se me cae el cielo encima."

The three of them spent an hour pleasantly talking and drinking mugs of hot, strong coffee. He brought out his prized jar of holy dirt to show Barbara.

"Del Santuario, hija. Tierra santa. Holy earth." Amelia remembered having seen the miraculous hole in the earth that never emptied and where hundreds claimed to have been cured by the power of the miraculous dirt. "People fill it after dark," the cynics said. But for those who believed in its healing powers, this tierra bendita could do wonders. "Do you believe in it?" Barbara asked. She had, of course, heard of Lourdes and Fatima, but never of Chimayo.

"...without the earth all would be lost—old costumbres and traditions," Tío Fermín was saying. "Es la tierra, the earth which nurtures life, hijas. To understand it you have to be able to look at it with the eyes of la gente. Como decía empapá, «The land is our mother. Without her somos huérfanos. Where would we be?»" He slowly shook his head from side to side. Barbara enthusiastically stated that she was going to Chimayo as soon as she could arrange it. And she would take Tío Fermín if he wanted to go. That pleased the old man and he took her hands, "Gracias, hija, pero no quiero prenderme como dolor de muela. You go. You go."

In the weeks and months that followed the two women saw each other frequently. They had lengthy conversations in one or the other of their houses. Amelia was a little dazed, and certainly flattered, by Barbara's interest in her.

"Really—?" Barbara would say, staring at Amelia. "How interesting."

And Amelia began to believe that—perhaps—she was interesting. Their conversations were invariably intense, even strained, lasting well past midnight even on weeknights, leaving Amelia depleted of energy but invigorated as if she had been exercising in the fresh air. The rift didn't happen until two years later. Amelia had gone to her cousin's wedding. She was assaulted by the comments of her neighbors and even family members. She had not even been aware that she and Barbara had been the object of gossip. But this afternoon she came face to face with that reality. Two of her neighbors came up to her and with sneers on their faces asked very politely, "¿Dónde está tu esposa? Why didn't you bring her with you? ¿Que no comen del mismo plato?"

At first Amelia didn't know what they were talking about and smiled a friendly "Hello."

"Hello? Ya se creé gringa la Amelia." She poked her elbow at Cecilia.

"Ya se creé cosa. Soon she will be dying her hair blond."

"No, red." Both women giggled wickedly and left Amelia standing there, humiliated and angry.

Amelia did not visit Barbara for a week. On Sunday she heard that Barbara was ill, so she went to her house that evening. Amelia went in the night to avoid the whispers and the harsh looks of her neighbors. She found Barbara in her studio painting. Her red hair looked even wilder. She stood in a blue robe applying umber rythmically on the canvass. Amelia thought that Barbara should be resting, but decided against disturbing her and left noiselessly.

The rift lasted that whole winter, a dismal winter. The days were cold and even the wet snow too soon became gray and dirty, making the whole world look leaden. The roads were full of pot holes and slimy mud that would freeze at night, making the whole business of transportation practically impossible. Amelia had become engaged to a politician. Barbara read about it in the paper.

Barbara was, or was not, waiting for Amelia to visit her. But it made no difference in Barbara's life, in either case. She had her own life and work. At least that's what she told herself. She filled her days by visiting the Burninghaus's and involving herself in the Taos Artist's activities. She scheduled a spring show and spent much of her time in her studio in preparation. On those few occassions when she stopped by Amelia's house on one pretense or another, she would find Amelia gone, or guarded and quiet.

Spring finally arrived although Barbara had had her doubts that it would ever come. She took advantage one sunny day and once more pulled out her old black case, packed a lunch and walked the quiet paths away from the village. She discovered early flowers beginning to peek out of mud and melt-

ing snowbanks. She didn't paint or sketch, just walked. She enjoyed the out-
ing and found it made her ravenously hungry. But instead of eating her lunch,
she went home to fix a big dinner. She felt ambitious enough to invite a few
friends. The prospect hurried her along. When she reached her front door
she discovered Amelia huddled on the stone steps.

"What in the world?"

"Barbara."

Barbara hurriedly opened the door and helped Amelia into a chair.
Amelia rested. She muttered through tears about how she had been used
more cruelly than she had ever been before, and by a man she believed was
actually in love with her and whom she believed she loved. For the first time
since her mother died she was a child crying.

"What happened?" Barbara's worried and compassionate look made the
tears flow even more effusively. Amelia told her story, between sobs and
nose-blowing. Felipe, the man she had been engaged to, wasn't faithful. He
bragged about all his conquests and abused Amelia physically as well.
When Amelia threatened to forget about the wedding, he had cruelly
reminded her that there was nobody else who would marry her. She was too
old. And she would get married to stop the gossip concerning Barbara
and herself.

"My God! What a cruel man. You musn't go back to him." Barbara
cradled Amelia in her arms and wept with her.

"I'm not. Ese cabrón can go to hell. I don't care what people say. I don't
even know why I cared in the first place." She rubbed her forehead with one
hand, as if to rub out indecision and doubt.

"Shsh...why don't you lie down on my bed and rest for a while. I'll make
some coffee."

Amelia rested. She fought an attack of nausea and faintness. As she lay in
Barbara's bed, she realized what a fool she had been. She had been taken in
by Felipe's charm. Everyone had said they were an attractive couple. As she
re-lived the last few months with Felipe, she came to realize that they
weren't lovers...even friendship was doubtful. He had merely come to her for
feeding and watering. Even sex had not been exciting or tender. He had been
rough and insensitive and often would shame her afterwards by asking how
many there had been before him. Nothing she ever did seemed to please him

except meals. "How? Why had she done that to herself?"

Barbara came in carrying a tray with a pot of coffee, two mugs, and a plate of cookies. "Are you feeling better? Here, this will make you feel better." She poured the coffee. "Have one of my cookies. I baked yesterday. I burned half the first batch—awful! But then I began to get confidence and all went well. I'm sure they're not as good as your biscochitos," she said the word slowly, "but I'll bet we eat this whole plate."

Amelia smiled weakly, "I'm sorry...I shouldn't have come to bother you."

"Nonsense. You did the right thing. I've been worried about you."

"How could I have been so stupid?"

"We all do some pretty dumb things sometimes. At least you realized the truth before you actually got married."

Amelia shuddered to think that she had almost married that...ventajoso. She couldn't, didn't want to think about that anymore. She was safe here with her friend.

Barbara and Amelia ate all the cookies on the plate. Barbara replenished the plate and they ate those as well while they talked. Amelia hadn't even realized she had been hungry. Barbara decided they needed something more nutritious and went off to fix supper. When she returned to call Amelia she found her asleep. She didn't wake her. The supper was forgotten as Barbara sat in a chair and watched Amelia sleep. Then she too crawled in beside Amelia and slept dreamlessly.

It had been unseasonably warm for those early days of spring...this day promised to be the same, a romantic sunrise, clouds edged in crimson just before the sun rose between two banks of soft gray. At half past nine the clouds had vanished, the mountains sat serene, blue. Barbara and Amelia had planned a climb. The one to sketch, the other to read or think. When they reached the top of the hill, Barbara stood exclaiming and pointing as was her habit everytime she was confronted with such a beautiful vista. "This place will never be painted out. It has an infinite variety of moods and types."

"You'd think with all the artists that have come and gone, Taos would have all been painted by now." Amelia also felt awe, but she liked to pretend that it was all old to her.

"Oh, stop the bullshit." They both laughed good naturedly.

"Why don't you paint people?"

"I don't know. I guess I always had trouble really capturing expressions. The other day I was looking at the portrait of Jim Mirabal that Ufer did. Christ! That is powerful."

"Have you met Jim Mirabal?"

"No, but I bet he's a very interesting man."

"When we go to the pueblo next time, I'll introduce you. My father knew him well. They called each other compadres."

Barbara sat down to examine a wild flower. "This remind me that I have to trim that wild rose bush in the back."

"That beautiful yellow Rosa de Castilla? It's supposed to be wild. I remember eating the petals when I was a little girl. They were sweet."

"There's a unicorn in my garden, eating my roses." Barbara laughed at Amelia. "I suppose if the bush begins to look bare, I'll know you've been out there eating away."

The two settled down to their work. They sat in companionable silence. The quiet was undisturbed until about one o'clock when they both seemed to get hungry at the same time. They devoured the sandwiches, talking all the while.

In April of that year, Oscar Berninhaus died. He and Winnie had been good friends to Barbara. She knew Bernie in St. Louis and it was while visiting him that she fell in love with Taos. Talking to Amelia about him Barbara said, "He loved to paint horses, you know. I always liked his studies of Indians and western men in their outdoor settings."

"He was such a gentle man. To see him on the street, you'd never know he was an artist. He looked like a businessman, always dressed neatly in his suit and white shirt."

"Winnie's going to miss him."

"Taos is going to miss him. He was a generous, caring man."

"He was so slight. I used to tower over him. He'd look up at me through his gold-rimmed glasses, bright-eyed and energetic." Then Barbara started laughing. Amelia looked astonished. Barbara leaned forward and speaking in little rushes as she did when she was fully absorbed, she explained, "Oh, Christ! I was remembering the time you watched El Rendón steal Bernie's axe and hide in the culvert. You climbed into that muddy place, recovered the axe and returned it to Bernie. I remember your disgusted look, and Bernie patiently thanked you with a twinkle in his eyes."

"For God's sake. Everyone knew Miguel was a thief. He used to begin his rounds as soon as it got dark. The people had the saying, 'Lock up everything by sunset, hay viene El Rendón.' It amazes me to this day that apparently nobody prosecuted him. But that axe. I was embarrassed and upset that anybody should steal anything from Mr. Berninghaus."

"How did I get involved."

"You probably thought you'd better help this mad woman with an axe asking you to go with her to the Berninghaus's." Both women laughed at the sight they must have been; Barbara in old workman's overalls, red hair flying; Amelia in a neat skirt and white blouse, carrying an old, rusty axe.

One Saturday in May Amelia found Barbara hard at work in her studio. She sat down quietly and watched, fascinated as Barbara executed a few felicitous strokes of a brush. Amelia stared hard, but the shifting angles and planes of paint, the subtle gradations of color, conformed to a structural grid she could not understand. Then she made a mistake. A real blunder. Speaking warmly and effusively, chattering away as, in the past, Barbara had seemed to like her to chatter, she happened to say, "Why don't you stop right there?" Barbara's face turned red almost matching her hair. She was barely able to speak.

Amelia sensed her tactlessness and hurriedly backed down. Of course Barbara knew what she was doing, what she wanted, Amelia knew nothing. Amelia was being intrusive and stupid and very, very sorry. For an immeasurable second the two remained silent. Then Barbara walked toward Amelia and gave her a little smile. All was forgiven.

Two weeks later, Barbara's work was being shown along with works by Dorothy Brett, Helen Blemenschein, and Regina Cooke. Amelia walked into the Harwood Foundation alive with chirping groups of women. Amelia caught sight of Barbara's red hair and proceeded in that direction. Barbara was excited; arm in arm the two looked at many works of art. They talked about what they saw, and were drawn together both by their enthusiasm and their prejudices. They said "uggh" and "wow," and Amelia deferred to Barbara's judgment. Amelia was studying the vibrant colors of one of Barbara's oils when she heard her friend gasp, "How did this get here?"

Barbara was pointing to a small water-color of the Pueblo. Amelia made a feeble gesture of dismissal and Barbara seized her small hand and squeezed it hard.

DEATH MARCH

Ed Chavez

It seemed a defiance of instinct, but a greater drive compelled the lizard to lie on the large, warm, flat rock. Daytime he spent in a cool place in the ground, and at night he came out to find warmth and food. The lizard lay in the open in the light of the full moon, protected by his chameleon-like coloring. And always his patience paid off.

An insect scampered onto the rock and carelessly meandered closer and closer to the lizard. Closer and closer until—spak!—the moth came too close and the lizard lifted him away with a hardly perceptible flick of the tongue.

Hardly, but perceptible enough for another patient night watcher. A shapeless tree branch immediately revealed its powerful wing span and swiftly it swooped down and clutched the lizard in its talons, then sailed back in a wide arc to a higher branch in another tree. It was all a simultaneous motion of a few seconds and the dead lizard was still wriggling involuntarily in the owl's claws when the owl perched on his new branch.

On the ground below the tree a frightened voice whispered, "Did you hear that, Loyd? The owl's sending us a warning."

"Don't be so superstitious, Tony. It's only calling because you're making so much noise."

But Eloyd didn't resist Tony huddling close to him. It was gloomy hiding there in the woods and very spooky for the ten year olds. They were hiding under a juniper, down on their bellies so they could look out and watch the path.

A loud whistle pierced the stillness and Tony hugged Eloyd and buried his face in his shoulder and whimpered, "I shouldn't have come, Loyd. I'll never see my mother again. We're going to die, Loyd! I know it!"

"Ssh!" Eloyd was just as frightened. But he had to know.

"Let's go back, Loyd. We can hear about it tomorrow when the big folks talk. They do every year after Las Tinieblas is over."

"Quiet!" Eloyd cupped his hand over Tony's mouth. Tony calmed down. Then he started wriggling again when the mournful tooting started.

"Be still! It's only the pitero, Tony."

They could see him now. A shuffling figure, all in white, swaying to the lament as he walked up the trail. Soon he would be close enough to touch, if they dared, but they would lay quietly on their bellies, holding their breath in the shadows.

Behind the pitero more figures emerged, some wearing peaked hats under their black shrouds. One of them began to sing, a wailing alabado with pitiful, quavering sounds.

From their place under the juniper the two boys could only see feet now, each stepping to a solemn deliberate pace. Three men walked apart, stripped to the waist. The sound of their whips lashing over their shoulders was a painful counterpoint to the alabado.

It was the scrape of a huge timber dragging on the hard packed trail that caused Eloyd to dare a bolder look. He lifted the lowest branch and saw a lone man pulling the enormous madero on his shoulder. The man slipped and others gathered quickly to help him. He wore a band of chamiso around his forehead. He was shirtless and Eloyd could see where the rough beam scraped the skin off his shoulder. His white calzones were damp with sweat and blood.

Eloyd gasped. He saw what he had come to see. One of the compañeros dabbed the man's face. His father's face!

So many wonderful things had happened in Eloyd's life the past few weeks. His father had returned after an absence of many years and he was greeted in Punta de Agua—in the whole county!—as a hero. As indeed he was. His father had fought in the war in the Phillipines, survived the Death March from Bataan, outlasted the atrocities of the Japanese internment, manfully regained his strength in a California hospital, and now the brotherhood had selected him to be the Cristo. The Cristo!

And why not? To Eloyd the logic was plain. Who else but his father was more deserving? It explained those looks Eloyd had noticed—the serene glow in his father's eyes, the adoring fussiness of his mother, the solicitude of the women and children, and the open respect of the men. It explained the murmurs that evaporated to a solemn hush when Eloyd chanced upon adult conversants in the village. They would gently smile at him, nod, and keep a respectful silence. Their manner indicated they knew something that would make Eloyd proud. And Eloyd knew better than to ask any direct questions. Be he also knew they all shared a special knowledge. Even the most firmly kept secrets have a way of seeping among the people. And now Eloyd confirmed what he had guessed.

The brotherhood had conveyed the distinct honor on his father to be the Cristo in the annual reenactment of the Passion.

Three men helped his father lift the two hundred and fifty pound madero, constructed in the shape of a cross, and then he proceeded, genuine agony accompanying every step.

Eloyd strained for a better view as his father staggered up the loma. Mostly, he carried the load alone, but the Cyreños were there to assist when he weakened.

So overcome was Eloyd in watching his father that he failed to hear the creaking of the cart wheels. Tony stifled another whimper and Eloyd turned, ready to chide Tony, but instead he sucked his breath in horror. There, in a cart, sat a shawled figure with a bow and arrow poised right at him. And deep in the hood Eloyd saw the glowing green eyes of a skull.

"La Muerte," Eloyd whspered.

"Si!" Another voice whispered hoarsely. Eloyd felt long, nimble fingers cup his mouth with gentle firmness and he turned to see the stern face of Dedos. Tony started to scream, but Dedos shushed him and ordered, "Go home! To your mamá!"

Eloyd started to move but Dedos held him back with the same gentle firmness. "Not You! This baby here. Go! And don't look back!"

Tony obeyed and fled. Dedos dropped the venda over his face, took Eloyd's hand and admonished, "Stay with me and do only as I say."

Up the trail they went in the procesión de sangre, behind the Carreta del Muerto, across the camposanto, past the wooden gravemarkers, and up an ever steepening slope. El Calvario.

Dedos led Eloyd to the shaded side of the cart from where he could see without obstruction the continuing live enactment of the Passion. The flaring lights of the torches reflected off the walls of the barranca and lighted the scene.

Eloyd's breath quickened. He heard the sound of a steel hammer pounding on a spike, muffled at first until it pierced the flesh, then ringing more clearly as it was driven into the madero his father so recently carried. Were they actually going to *nail* him to the cross? Three times Eloyd heard the ringing clang of metal striking metal until the job was done.

Why didn't they bind him with ropes? Or had his father actually made this awful promise in Japan? Is this why they were doing it in the dark instead of in the afternoon as in prior years?

Eloyd watched as six men tugged at ropes while another five pushed from behind and lifted the cross to which his father was tied. There was a shuddering thud as it slipped into its hole in the ground. Eloyd observed how the five men quickly tumbled rocks and fitted supporting stumps into the slot to hold the madero upright.

He heard his father cry out, "Por el amor de Dios! Basta!"

He wanted to help. He wanted to scream or run away. He wanted to stop them, but all he could do was remember Dedo's warning to do as he was told. He averted his eyes and stared at La Muerte. She held her taut bow and arrow poised directly at him, as if she were deliberately threatening him.

"Dejame! No puedo mas!"

Something was wrong. Eloyd knew his father would be ashamed of him for getting anxious like a woman, but this was not expected. Real nails? He gulped a long, deep breath and slowly expelled it, the way the priest had taught him to control his emotions before receiving his First Communion, and he thought of Christ. Christ? *Not* Christ! Not now! Concentrate on something else.

Eloyd noticed La Muerte was a real skeleton and not a carved one as he had seen in other processions. Whose skeleton? He wondered. From the old Indian grave on the other side of the lagunita?

"Ten piedad!" His father cried.

Couldn't they hear his father? Don't get anxious. He is only saying the words of the Cristo. They will take him down soon, bathe him, and let him rest. And then, for a year at least, everyone will come to see his wounds, marvel at his courage and at his holiness, and ask him for a blessing. And he will bless them.

Eloyd had seen only one other with the scarred hands, an old man from Las Trampas, and now his own father would show the marks. Because he chose the nails, people would come to him for more than a year. They would come to him for the rest of his life.

It was too magnificent to think about. If only they would hurry and take him down. Eloyd chewed on his lower lip and tried to think of something else.

He stared at La Muerte square in the eyes. What causes that green glow? Yes. It was a real skull alright. Such long teeth. Large and yellow. Some of them missing.

"Hermanos! Ya no aguanto!"

Eloyd was numbed by a deafening clatter of the matracas and a thundering from corrugated tins. The noise boomed and raged louder in the deafening din, and all Eloyd could see were the glowing green eyes. He dared not move or even look away.

Dedos gently pulled Eloyd's arm.

"Is it finished?"

"Sí. Let's go."

"Where's my father?"

"They're taking care of him. Come. We have to go back to the morada."

"Was I asleep?"

"You never closed your eyes." Dedos dismantled the bowstring from La Muerte's hand and dropped the black hood over her skull. "Hurry. They're waiting for us."

"Aren't we gong to walk behind the cart?"

"No. We go behind the pitero now. Vamonos. It's almost time for the sun to rise."

The pitero piped a repetitious, melancholy dirge all the way back. People were already standing by the morada. When Eloyd saw his mother in the crowd, he wanted to go to her, but Dedos would not let his hand go. He wanted to comfort her. Why did she look so worried?

Eloyd entered the morada with all the men and was led to a spot in front of the altar. Above the piping of the pitero he could hear the squeak of the carreta as it entered the chapel, and above all these sounds he could hear his mother wail outside when she saw the hooded skull. Eloyd was ashamed she should carry on so. Didn't she know this was only a drama, a ceremony reenacting the death of Christ? Someone was leading her away and he could hear her fading wail, pleading, "¡Mi esposo! ¿Dónde 'sta Alberto? ¡Alberto! ¿Dónde 'sta?"

Dedos led Eloyd back through the chapel of the morada into a room he had never been permitted to enter before. He could still hear the pitero in the chapel while the rezador launched into a long prayer for the dead.

Only the Hermano Mayor, Dedos and Eloyd were in the secret room. Dario solemnly addressed Dedos. "Sangrador, prepare the novice."

Dedos nodded and removed Eloyd's shirt. He instructed Eloyd to shed the rest of his clothes and to put on the white cotton calzones he handed him.

In the chapel Eloyd could hear the sas! sas! sas! of wet lashes. It was the sound of yucca whips the flaggelants used to scourge themselves. Dedos dipped a similar whip in a mixture of romero herb tea and salt. "Toma!" He handed it to Eloyd. "To prepare yourself as a worthy hermano, you must scourge yourself."

Eloyd could not think of disobeying. He tentatively lashed the wet whip over his shoulder and felt the sting.

"Harder!"

Eloyd heard the rezador intone "Ven pecador y veras," and the voices of the entire brotherhood fearsomely continued the alabado.

Eloyd flailed himself again. In the chapel he could hear the sas! sas! sas! of the bloody wet whips.

"Harder!"

He closed his eyes and lashed himself over the other shoulder.

"Again!"

He whipped himself again.

"Faster!"

At first, the salted solution stung his welted back, but it had a perverse healing affect because of the romero juice. Eloyd kept whipping himself hypnotically without prompting until the Hermano Mayor intervened.

"Basta!"

Exhausted, Eloyd let his whip drop.

The singing stopped in the chapel, but all the while the pitero piped away to a higher and more piercing crescendo.

The Hermano Mayor held out a cigar box and Dedos ceremoniously lifted the lid and selected a sharp flint. Then he stepped back and positioned himself behind Eloyd.

The Hermano Mayor intoned: "Is the Sangrador ready?"

"I am ready," Dedos replied.

"Then proceed," the Hermano Mayor ordered.

Immediately in the chapel the matracas began to clatter accompanied by booming tins. Eloyd did not resist nor did he even flinch because he knew there was no stopping the inevitable. Dedos deftly made six gashes on Eloyd's back, three on each side. It took considerable skill to be a sangrador, to know how to cut without severing a nerve or causing any permanent disability.

Eloyd cooperated without a whimper, fully conscious of the entire rite, until he felt the warm trickle down his back. Only then did he swoon.

"Que niño tan valiente," was Dario's only comment as he steadied Eloyd so that Dedos could finish his work. Dedos took a cloth soaked with romero brew and bathed Eloyd's wounds until they were clean and stopped bleeding.

"He is so young for the rite, Dario. Why so soon?"

"First, as the Hermano Mayor and the Maestro de Novicios, I decide who is ready. Also," Dario's tone became more soothing, "there has been an unbroken line, in his family, of membership in the hermandad ever since this morada was founded. I know Alberto—que en paz descanse—" Dario added, "would be pleased to know his son has not let the chain be interrupted. And finally, as an hermano, this young man is bound to secrecy. Or suffer the ultimate penalty."

Dedos nodded in agreement. "He should rest."

"Yes. Let him rest. The diggers should be finished. Only they, you, and I shall know Alberto's Gethsemani. He shall be buried upright to guarantee his salvation. The confradia will continue the sudario until we return."

Eloyd was very proud of his initiation at so young an age and he could not understand why his mother deplored it. That his father died as the Cristo was an extreme honor surely to guarantee his own, and their, salvation. But all she did was weep.

It was no wonder to Eloyd that women were not permitted to enter the brotherhood.

THE ADVENTURES OF
SALVADOR DOMINGUEZ

(from a novel in progress)

James Gonzales

In our neighborhood of Barelas in the city of Albuquerque there lived a man by the name of Salvador Dominguez who was the proprietor of a small variety store where he sold anything and everything, new and used. He was exceedingly fat, for throughout his fifty years of life he had always eaten well and exercised little, and he exerted himself mainly at night when it was his custom to take a walk and then return home to read his books. Oh, but I must mention that these walks usually took him to the Fat King Cafe where he usually supped regally, so that if the walk contributed toward helping him reduce in weight, the toning down was either totally cancelled out or seriously undermined by the heftiness of the meal he consumed.

Salvador Dominguez had large black eyes; a large full-lipped mouth (it always seemed loosened by a sort of wonderment); curly jet-black hair (it sprang tensely from all sides of his almost perfectly circular head and he kept a fluff of it about his forehead); a wide, almost creaseless forehead; and a rather large knobby nose in the style of the Spaniard who has many relatives in France. This fabulous nose was wide and fleshy and it visibly quivered at the smell of food, of which Dominguez always kept plenty on hand since the

27

fare at the Fat King was limited to New Mexican dishes, and he loved a variety of things. He loved his food and he loved his books. But it must here be mentioned that our hero read only books dealing with detectives, fiction and nonfiction, and he gave himself to this endeavor every chance he got. And while he read, he ate, be it baloney sandwiches or whatever. There was always something edible to go with his story. Psychologists say that when two activities are frequently performed simultaneously, one activity automatically brings to mind the other. Because of this fact, eating and reading were quite inseparable to Dominguez and even the names of detectives conjured up thoughts of food. Maigret reminded him of coffee laced with brandy, hot croissants, and delightful little things with French names such as crêpes á la bordelaise; Simon Templar (the Saint) of lamb curry and other spicy dishes from exotic lands; and Nero Wolfe of shad roe creole and chablis. Even Martin Beck—who cannot really be termed much of a gourmet—brought to our hero the idea of steaming coffee, perhaps because of the perpetual chill of Sweden.

Now you will immediately discover—if you are a good detective yourself—that the abovementioned men are all fictitious sleuths. Dominguez did not see them as such. At least I can't find anything in my research to attest to that fact. Before me I have a stack of journals kept by him (and later by his personal secretary, Transito Cadena); on almost every page two or three detectives are mentioned and, taken randomly, 95% of the time someone like Sherlock Holmes pops up. And yet there are also real detectives mentioned. For example: Albert Seedman, whose book *Chief!* gives an account of his work as Chief of Detectives for the New York City police force, is mentioned. But then right alongside Seedman, Dominguez makes a notation concerning Kohlberg who appears in the Martin Beck novels! This and many other examples have brought me to the conclusion that Dominguez made absolutely no distinction between fiction and nonfiction. Then there is the fact that when he talked to Transito, his man, he always said things like: "I consider the Saint a much better shot than Martin Beck, yet I respect them both for the simple reason that they are good detectives."

It might be deduced that Dominguez suffered from the same condition that afflicted Quijote. I disagree. People all over Barelas will tell you: "He was like Quijote. He was exactly like el Caballero de la Triste Figura. Dominguez lived in a deluded state. He was crazy." Nothing is further from the truth. Dominguez held a firm grasp on reality and managed his daily life, for the most part, quite sanely and judiciously; it would be erroneous to say he underwent the same transformation as Quijote. "Vino a perder el juicio," writes Cervantes of Quijote, and Samuel Putnam translates: "He went completely out of his mind." This does not apply to Dominguez. He allowed fantasy and reality to intermingle and nurture each other, but there always existed for him a distinction—though at times tenuous—between the two.

Salvador Dominguez was like Quijote in two ways only: he believed what he read, held the written word as being incarnate and, to repeat, made absolutely no distinction between fiction and nonfiction. He was illogical that way but managed to keep his mind functioning quite properly with regards to all other aspects of life. Books were his undoing; had he never laid eyes on the books of those bedeviling writers of detective stories who tell all sorts of intriguing pretty tales where everything goes wrong and then right, he never would have been a fit subject for these memoirs, for who would want to read about a fat man who simply does nothing. I certainly wouldn't have troubled myself with writing this book had Dominguez simply been a shopkeeper. Who would want to read the adventures of a shopkeeper? No, we all want to know about men of action, men of words and deeds and all sorts of exploits. Dominguez is one of those men.

Detective stories helped Salvador Dominguez conceive the notion that some day similar adventures might fill his future, and he patiently awaited such a time.

The time came suddenly.

One of his tenants was a woman with large, quick black eyes and peevishly-angled black eyebrows by the name of Federica Montantes, more commonly known in Barelas as "Federica de los Peines" because she danced flamenco so violently that the hair and combs on her vibrating head frequently parted company; also known as "la estremecedora," she nightly practiced her steps while her male friend, Juan Lechuga, with hectic clumsy fingers, accompanied her on the guitar. On the same fateful Sunday night that everyone in Barelas remembers because murder is difficult to forget, Dominguez was reading one of his detective stories. He heard the usual stacatto thumps of Federica's impassioned dancing. There was no guitar to be heard; there was only the "ti-ri le-re" of her quavering gypsy outburst as she swept out of her room and stomped rhythmically away and over the wooden floor of the porch and then onto a continuation thereof, more wooden planks leading to a communal bathroom behind the house. She went "lerelerelere—ayyyyiiieee...." Then she was immobilized by what she saw.

There was hardly a sound for one whole minute except the noisy scratch of her record player as it struggled to emit a Spanish refrain that rose crackly through the air like the sound of a cat with its snout in a can.

Then Federica cried murder and Dominguez felt his skin crawl. But then just a second later his heart thrilled. He flew out of his armchair, his loose red tie tossing up over one of his large ears, and barreled down the stairs as fast as his fat legs would carry him. It should not be exactly like this, he thought as he saw the red necktie flapping on one side of him; if it's truly a murder I should be much calmer and not be stumbling down like this. I should appear on the scene like a cool James Bond, ready to tackle anything—even the murderer if he is about—and very deftly clip him on the chin and lay him out. But—

Dominguez ran out to where Federica stood and, as she was frozen with terror, he ran instead in the direction of the dancer's outpointed arm, toward the wooden gate that opened onto the alley, and discovered the limp dead body of Emilia Cortez.

She was fully clothed, her head turned to one side, and in one hand there was a broken neck chain that looked expensive.

My God! thought Dominguez. Can it really be that here, under my nose, a true-to-life murder has occurred? And indeed that was the case! In his mind he began casting back in thought, and images came to him of how Sherlock Holmes or Charlie Chan or Martin Beck might handle such a situation. He stood there thinking, then he recalled that these detectives always acted quickly, knowingly, decisively, and so when he saw Juan Lechuga, Federica's guitarist, just then very sneakily coming down the alley, he shouted: "Cabrón! Haven't I told you to stay away from here! Eh? Never mind! Look, I have a corpse on my hands. This woman has been murdered. At least it looks that way to me. Vete por el callejón and see if anyone suspicious-looking is out there. Hurry! I'll call the police."

It's now the following evening and Dominguez can sense a new and exciting chapter in his life beginning. Everything looks different—even the railyards across the way seem permeated with the smoke and atmosphere of Istanbul rather than that of Barelas, and he almost expects the Orient Express to fly over the rails with James Bond connivingly esconsced in one of the compartments awaiting the next intrigue; there is a different smell—as if the Barelas sewage plant no longer exudes its foul stench and now, instead, a mystic incense hangs over it; and there is a different feeling inside him.

In his soul, ever since he could remember, Dominguez had always felt he was not destined for ordinary things. Knowing this and, moreover, feeling certain now that he was a unique and very splendid individual for having helped the police with the murder at hand, he smiled to himself and felt his innards gurgle joyously. He began feeling a desire to commence his detective work forthwith, but also he began to project his career into the future and saw that one day he would be a person deserving of fame. Yes, more than anything, he now longed for that day of superlative greatness when all the glory of life and all earth's cherished praise would break upon him like a shower of stars. From that day on he would have an undying name and the story of his illustrious existence—like a unique flower—would blossom and grow eternally.

In his soul he knew he would be great and he also knew this: that upon reading about all the great and mighty things he had accomplished and upon seeing him tower above all other detectives when it came to sheer brilliance, heads would turn, eyes would open with excitement, and chroniclers the world over would vie for the honor of recording the merest utterance from his lips.

That night he felt such a tremendous desire to begin putting all the knowledge he had accumulated from his readings to work, that he thought of how he might begin. It seemed very necessary to physically appraise himself. In later years his chroniclers might wish to describe him in detail and it would do well to see for himself exactly what he looked like at this particular moment; so, with somewhat of a severe gleam in his eyes, he drew back and examined himself in the mirror. He adjusted the knot of his bright red tie and his jowls seemed to grow in size. His face assumed a dignified expression. It bothered him that he was extremely fat but an inner voice told him, be it noted, that this corpulence lent him an air of distinction and that it further signified to the world that he spent his time on intellectual matters rather than on tedious physical exercise. Yes, he would not worry about it for it was his sagacious plan, once he was a full-time battler of criminals, to shun physical contact in bringing them to heel. Against any given villainy,he told himself, he would retaliate with sheer intelligence, responding only with that certain quick cunning he knew he possessed. There was a challenge in that—to go out on the chase, without a gun, fearless, equipped only with a keen professional mind, superior in every respect to those who fought against him. Which meant he would not be much like Simon Templar (whom he greatly admired), knocking heads here and there, kicking in mid-air, slamming judo chops at some ugly opponent; no, instead he would be more like the cool Swede, Martin Beck, who usually displayed a sparing show of force and achieved his greatness mainly through brilliant deductive reasoning.

One evening as he walked through the barrio of Barelas his imagination flew away with him. He envisioned himself first here: peering down through a microscope, comparing blood samples; then there: going down on one knee to examine a dead body. When it came to murder he would immerse his investigative brain into the case and delve deeply into the mystery of it all. Others might dismiss the case at hand as, perhaps, a suicide or accidental death, but he would not. Remembering the words of someone (he could not recall who) he told himself: "It's a policeman's job to suspect murder!" And the same applied to detectives. Painstakingly, shrewdly, he would indeed evince such a fact, leaving his colleagues dumbfounded. Now in his imagination he was again here: turning the tables on a bigtime dope dealer; and then there: dexterously extricating himself from the snares of a lovely moll hired by thugs to set him up for a post-copulative execution. Scenes like these ran through his utterly enthralled mind, and he was the focal point in each one. Headlines streamed through his mind—

Then Salvador Dominguez suddenly disappeared from sight. It happened that as he was looking up at the sky, his thoughts all in a whirl, his mind conceiving all sorts of fantasies, his steps took him beyond the path he had been following and he absentmindedly wandered off into someone's backyard.... O that step, my dear friends! O that step, I say:—mortal foe to a grand adventure! Dominguez went forward, his big foot went out, came down, but there was nothing to support it, and down it went through the darkness, our great detective quite naturally following, into a dank hole big enough to fit a horse. That day someone had done what was mandated by city code: an outdoor privy had been razed to mollify those of us who are unable to tolerate the thought of a natural necessity being performed anywhere but indoors. The older people of Barelas at this time were always joking about this. 'Ha! ha!" they laughed: "In the old days we used to eat indoors and make caca outdoors; now we cook outdoors and make caca indoors." But be that as it may, this foul-smelling cavity before us had been left uncovered over night and so before Dominguez could even blink, he went down in a clap of arms, head and ears over into the stinkiest mush a person can ever have occasion to swim in. Of course, being quick and cunning of mind, he managed to flail his arms in such a way as to keep himself afloat; but this was much later, after he had gone under once or twice. His red tie now floated up and he managed to lean over at an angle and grab at the root of a tree. There he hung on for the life of him.

Instinctively he yelled: "Help!" Then he quickly decided that this sort of outcry was not in keeping with his courageous spirit and so he quickly contained himself. He told himself in a low voice as though someone might be listening: "It might later be said of me that I weakened. Ha! ha! The great detective, Salvador Dominguez, once fell into a shithole and yelled his lungs out for help." No, that would not do. It was all very simple; he soothed himself with the thought that now his fearless dog would come to his aid. Certainly this was a very distasteful predicament he was in, but detectives always got into some jam or other and always figured a way out. Now he was glad he had brought Becerrico and, luckily, the dog had not fallen in. He called the dog's name to establish his whereabouts.

"Becerrico!" The dog would surely respond like a champion....And now—yes!—there he was at the rim of the mushy crater, sniffing, coming closer. "Becerrico, come boy. Come here, my good fearless dog. Come to me, my dearest dog."

But Becerrico merely sniffed. Then the dog sneezed and backed off, looking like an English butler opening the door on a beggar.

"Becerrico!" shouted Dominguez, infuriated at this lack of loyalty in the dog he had raised from a pup. "Cabrón, come here!"

The dog still disobeyed, his glittering eyes turning away. He backed off even more and finally was so far away that Dominguez, no matter how much he stretched and craned, could not get a clear eye on the infernal hound. Now with his eyelids laden down with fecal matter and having reached the end of his tether, his composure gave way. He had cudgeled his brain to obtain a solution to the problem and he finally came up with:

"Help!" Over and over he shouted while he sloshed here and there. Even a detective, he reasoned, needs assistance from time to time. "Help me, someone! Help me! Help!"

BITTER DREAMS

(from a novel in progress)

Elida Lechuga

Nightmares frightened Denise. Especially nightmares that she could remember so vividly. Most of the dreams she remembered flashed in bits and pieces through her mind like trout in a mountain stream, she could never catch the entire scene from start to finish.

Denise Martinez, home from college for the first time since Thanksgiving, lay in her bed unable to sleep. She had been trying unsuccessfully to forget the thoughts of the baby she was carrying and now they were invading her sleep.

Closing her eyes and shutting out the darkness, she remembered the dream. After a long walk up the snow covered path, Denise reached a dark house. Only a yellowish light emanated from her grandmother's window. Denise peeked in. The drapes were open and she saw her grandmother sitting in the far corner of the large room fingering the beads of her rosary. Two lights, a tall candle and a roaring fire cast unnatural shadows about the room. Denise saw all the familiar things of the room and then looked at her grandmother. She seemed very old, older than Denise remembered. The old woman was so covered with shawls and scarves that only her tanned hands and face were visible. Large lucid eyes reflected the firelight and seemed to look right through Denise.

Denise was about to knock on the window when her father walked into her grandmother's room. The tall, broad shouldered man moved with unusually hesitant steps.

"Buenas noches, Louis. What brings you here at this hour?"

"Buenas noches," Louis answered. "You asked me to come see you after supper. Don't you remember? Have you finished with your novena?"

"My novena is never finished. Don't stand there making my room look so small. Here. Sit by me," she said and motioned for Louis to sit on the couch beside her chair. He sat uncomfortably on the edge of the worn couch as his mother continued to stare intently at him.

"Is something wrong?" Louis asked. The old woman shook her head and fixed her gaze on the middle of the room. Denise started to knock on the window again when she saw a cloud of smoke begin to appear in front of her grandmother.

"Dios mío!" Louis exclaimed and started to stand, but his mother signaled for him to stop. He fell back heavily into the couch.

A figure began to take shape within the cloud. Soon Denise could see that it was a woman. The woman was kneeling, her hands covered her face, she was crying. A bright ring of fire burst around the woman. Suddenly the woman stood, her hands outstretched. Denise gasped as she recognized herself. She was the woman within the ring of fire. The fire rose higher and higher until it consumed Denise completely. But as the vision disappeared, a voice could be heard. "Save me! Save me, Daddy, I didn't mean to hurt anyone. I didn't mean to kill you. Save me, Daddy," the voice pleaded.

Silence. Then the fire crackled and broke the spell. Louis covered his face with his hands and moaned, "Ay Dios! What was Denise doing here?" He looked at his mother and demanded, "What is it? What does it mean?"

The old woman stood up and moved near the candle, "You saw, you heard" she answered, "there is nothing more."

"But can't we do anything?"

"Nada."

Louis ran out of the room. Suddenly Denise was at the front door, first ringing the doorbell then pounding the door till it was opened. She fell into her father's arms. He hugged her then quickly released her as if he had been burned by her touch. She fell to the floor.

"Get away from me," he whispered viciously. "Get away from me." He rushed out into the cold.

"Daddy," Denise cried as she lay on the floor. Slowly she picked herself up and looked out the door. The snow was falling heavily and had covered his footprints. Her father was gone.

Denise made her way down the hall to her grandmother's rooms. Without knocking she pulled open the door only to be confronted by darkness. The coals of a once-blazing fire radiated the only light in the room.

"Mother," Denise called out. "Where are you?"

A match was struck on the other side of the dark room. The old woman moved slowly to the candle and lit it. "Que?" She asked.

"I won't hurt anyone," whispered Denise, suddenly feeling very excited. She wanted to shout. She did shout. "I won't hurt my baby," she said.

Denise's grandmother smiled, "Now I understand. It is more than your father saw. Those visions. They mean you will kill your unborn child."

Denise was shocked. "Your're lying," she whispered. "You don't know. I won't kill my baby."

"You will kill and you will burn in hell for it," the old woman whispered, narrowing her eyes.

Unable to restrain herself, Denise reached for her grandmother, throwing off the old woman's shawls, shaking her like a rag doll, all the time screaming, "No! I'll never kill my baby! You hear me, never!" After a few moments, her grandmother's eyes closed and her head fell backward, blood trickling from her nose and mouth. "Oh God," Denise exclaimed, releasing her grandmother's body. She fell slowly to the floor, falling gently on the shawl.

Denise opened her mouth and screamed because suddenly she was being shaken. She, too, would soon die. "No," she screamed, "I didn't mean it." Then she woke up and realized it was her father who was shaking her awake, bringing her back from the dead.

Denise remembered heaving against her father's shoulder. She cried harder than she had ever cried before, wishing she could stay forever in his arms, never going away again, never betraying his trust in her, never seeking the shelter of another man's arms.

THE LAST WALK

Joseph M. Olonia

As I stepped out of the house, I took a deep breath of the cold and smokey night air. I shivered and my breath trembled when I exhaled. I had worn only my patched levi jacket, with its red embroidered streak across the back, as protection from the winter chill.

I paused on the porch step and turned to look at the light that penetrated the curtained living room window. Vague shadows moved across the curtains, silhouttes whose ghostly sobs threatened to pull me back into the house. Mamita was trying to console Margaret, my girl, and was not succeeding. What a useless act, I thought. Who can console grief. Margaret had begged me not to go, for our love's sake. But I had not changed my mind. If I would not stay for love's sake, then what else might she have said to convince me. Nothing. The summation came quickly and mercilessly, like Eligio's brand of mercy, like my old *sin piedad*. I cursed into the night, and it responded with an abiding chill that cut through my thin jacket.

Why Margaret, I demanded of myself. Before tonight, I had always called her Margarita, and whenever I drank tequila, I thought of her. Margaritas were my favorite drink. But why were my thoughts full of Margaret and not Margarita? Perhaps it was for the same reason that I could not bring myself to put on my red headband, why it was still tied to a belt loop on my pants.

I had betrayed mi jefe, Eligio, to the police. Now he had escaped and was looking for me. And he would find me. So instead of running away, as Margaret insisted, I would go to Eligio and save him the trouble of the hunt.

I turned and walked across the yard, but when I reached the sidewalk I stopped. Eligio had always liked my walk, smooth and unhurried, and he had tried to imitate me in this. My body stiffened, and I moved toward my awaiting destino, my fate. I felt like an old man whose every bone hurts.

I betrayed Eligio because of the gringa he raped and killed. I had tried to stop him, and when that failed, I turned him in. When the police showed, I tried to explain it to him, tried to tell him that we who had been raped and murdered by the gringo world had no right to turn around and do the same thing. But I failed. It was like trying to pry understanding from a gravestone. All he could say was that I had grown soft like las mujeres de las casas who cried when someone broke their windows. In a way he was right. But I had not grown soft. I could never take violence as casually as Eligio. That is not to say my hands were clean. Fighting was a way of life here—he who did not fight became a victim. And I had killed once, though my soul has been sickened by the memory ever since.

Mostly I was a thief. I preferred the stealth involved to violent confrontations. As a result, I was good at stealing. There was no one better except maybe my buddy Pañuelo, and his skill was exceeded only by his pride.

I remembered Eligio calling me a gringo. It was a bad insult, the worst that anyone in my neighborhood could receive. Some told me afterward that Eligio had paid me back with that insult. They, of course, didn't think Eligio would escape. I knew better. Before the police shoved him into the back seat of their car, Eligio managed to twist around and look me in the eye.

"You're dead, Martín," he said calmly, without doubt or reservation.

"You're not going to be doing anymore killing for awhile," one of the police answered and shoved him into the car.

Me and Eligio, we knew better. Neither one of us doubted his words.

I crossed the street then, and regretted it, because I would be walking with my back to traffic. A moment later I laughed aloud. Before I had left

Margaret—still Margaret—I had told her that I was already dead. It was true. And as I let the thought burrow in deeply, it occurred to me that a swift death from behind would be preferable to facing Eligio's revenge. But a back stabbing wasn't likely with Eligio. He liked killing too much, and he liked the fear, the desolation in his victims' faces when they knew death was certain. Eligio would look me in the eye and wrench the life from me.

As I passed the San Miguel Church, my shivering increased, as if the cold stones of the church wall expelled icy pins. I hugged the wall nonetheless. Instinct kept me close to all the deep shadows, even though, I knew Eligio and my Compañeros of the Red Band knew the shadows every bit as well as I did. In the sloping churchyard I was exposed to the lights from the street. I felt stripped of my human nature, like an animal moving to its death, when it should be fleeing. Animals are stupid creatures. So am I, Holy Gaucho, so am I. I knew I could not go any further like this. There had to be some dignity left inside, a vestige of lost pride. All I could think to do was untie my head-band from its belt loop and slip it onto my forehead. Once, I had fancied the red strip of cloth as a crown of sorts, worn by the Spanish nobility my Tío Manuel used to tell me about before he died of drinking. Now, however, it felt like a different sort of crown, a sharp and cutting crown of death. But it set well, wrapping, staunching my bleeding thoughts, even as it reminded me of the old days with my gang.

Across from the church was the old school. Last year the teachers and students had moved to a new school. But the building remained. Its windows were boarded up, as were its arched doors. Nonetheless it was occupied by old hatred and old violence.

Eligio and my Compañeros of the Red Band stood near the doors of the school. Some leaned against the wall, while others sat on the steps, huddling around the ineffectual warmth of cigarettes. Only Eligio stood oblivious against the cold. His straight, proud body faced in my direction, and as I entered the schoolyard, I could see him stir, shifting his weight from one leg to another. He did not move after that, but waited for me to come to him. I did.

I was drawn to him, as I had always been, hopelessly, irrevocably. I was his. Either as friend, or servant, or victim, I was his. I was no one elses, not even Margaret. Eligio's hold on me ran deeper and was far older than love of a woman, or even God.

I came to stand at the bottom of the steps. Eligio remained standing on the top step. He said nothing. I could see the street light reflecting a terrible intensity in his eyes, a blood lust that caused me to tremble. I stuck my hands into my pockets and hunched my shoulders. I looked away from Eligio even as he descended the steps. Meanwhile, My Compañeros of the Red Band all watched me through cigarette smiles. Pañuelo, who sat on the steps to my left, did not smile. We had been friends before, and it was he who had taught me what I knew of theivery. In Pañuelo's face I could read mixed loyalties, and as he turned his eyes up, I could also read a strange kind of respect for my having come to meet Eligio.

"Take your hands out of your pockets, Martín." Eligio stood on the bottom step, still taller than me. For a moment I remained unmoving, not understanding his demand. Then I removed my hands from my pockets to show him I was not armed. "OK, ese," Eligio smiled, and from a sheath at his belt he drew forth his bone-handled hunting knife. The gringa had died at that knife's point, she whose death was about to cost me my life.

As the word *gringa* entered my mind I felt a sudden distaste, and I could not figure out why. The word had always felt natural, had always fit easily into my vocabulary. Now it was bitter in my mouth and in my head. Then I realized that my guilt over having betrayed Eligio was not the reason why I had come here to face death. I was not punishing myself for turning in one of my compañeros to the police, I was punishing myself because I had not had the guts to keep Eligio from raping and killing that woman. Yes, I had argued with him, tried to persuade him, to cajole him, but the violence that would have occurred had I gone any further had frightened me. Eligio had frightened me. His coldness, like winter on the Sangre de Cristo peaks, was unapproachable, at least by me.

"You know," Eligio said, musing, delaying for his own pleasure the violence he longed for. "The Compañeros spoke for you tonight. They asked me to forgive you. One even begged for you."

Begged? I could not believe it. There was nothing Eligio hated more than begging. My eyes wandered. Gil, red-headed and nearly as blood thirsty as Eligio, stood near the school doors with Timón and Gordo Rojo. They were passing a joint between them. I could hardly imagine any of them begging, least of all on my behalf. As I looked at them, their expressions betrayed nothing, their thoughts hidden behind immovable masks. Felipe and his younger brother,who we called Rojo Chico, sat on the steps just above Pañuelo. I had gotten along with them. Perhaps they had stood up for me. But begged? I didn't think so. My eyes moved and met Pañuelo's gaze, and I knew instantly by his wry smile that it had been he who had begged for my life. He's a good amigo, I thought, though I hoped that Eligio would not punish Pañuelo for his lack of pride.

Eligio raised his arm then and pressed the sharp blade of his knife against my throat. A trickle of blood ran down my neck. I shuddered, knowing that I was about to die. It was not the thought of death that scared me though, it was the pain which would fill me and torment me antes de mi muerte. Neither would Eligio let me go quickly. My mind went numb, my pulse quickened.

My fear took away my resolve to accept whatever punishment Eligio had in mind. Now I wanted a quick death, and so I spoke. As I did, the knife cut deeper.

"For the life you owe me, hazlo pronto!"

Eligio's hand suddenly dropped away. He stared at me in disbelief. Perhaps he had forgotten, or had chosen to forget, that I had once saved his life. There was a time when Eligio was not the jefe of the neighborhood. There was another gang. Los Hombres del Muerte they called themselves, and Hernando was their leader. When Eligio began contesting Hernando's position, Hernando went after him. He and three of Los Hombres trapped Eligio in an alley on a cold night. They would have killed him if I had not showed up. I hardly remember what my thoughts were when I saw the fear in Eligio's eyes. All I can recall now was the fury that rose in my blood at seeing someone I had thought without fear, trembling and pleading for mercy. Then, unlike now, I had my switchblade with me. I drew it from my pocket without conscious thought as I came up behind the closest hombre. I drove my knife into his back and before the others could react, I knifed another. Then it was too late for the remaining two. Eligio sprang at Hernando while the other ran. I stood, my fury suddenly drained, and I watched the fiercest struggle between two men that I have ever witnessed. Eligio won out. With a triumphant joy he slit the jefe Hernando's throat.

After that Eligio swore that I could ask anything of him and he would do it. That favor had always gone unasked for. Now, though I was not proud of those deaths, I called on the memory of that oath.

I could see the conflict in Eligio's face, and I could tell that he wanted to dispense with that old promise. Yet the shame would have destroyed his position as the leader of our gang. A man like Eligio, who rarely made promises, could not afford to break them.

Abruptly, Eligio grinned.

"You're a smart boy, ese." He nodded with a solemnity I had never before seen in him. But an instant later it was gone. Blood lust returned to his hard, cinder-like face. "Too bad I have to kill you." His arm shot into the air and hovered.

Eligio's eyes shot to the left as red lights suddenly flashed over us, like blood from several deep wounds. I turned away from Eligio and looked to the street where a squad of police cars had pulled up.

All I had to do to preserve my life was to run out of reach of Eligio's knife. But I didn't. He would only escape again and I had used up the promise. I took an involuntary step toward Eligio, and even as the police exited their cars and called to Eligio to give himself up, the knife pierced my back, slicing flesh, and muscle, and bone, and deeper. I fell forward and struck the cold ground. Shots rang in my ear, while warm blood flowed and soaked my back. Then darkness covered me and I felt neither cold, nor warmth.

The police shot and killed Eligio. I learned it from Pañuelo when I was released from the hospital. I nearly died too. It was with confusion and surprise that I found myself alive. I had survived Eligio, who had never before missed his mark.

Pañuelo came to visit me when I got home. We were still friends, more so since that night he had begged Eligio to spare me.

I thanked him for what he did.

He shrugged his shoulders, but at the same time he grinned, as if Eligio's death was adequate payment for humiliation. "Anyway, it doesn't matter now. We're free of him."

"We'll never be free of him," I said in anger, not at Pañuelo, rather at dead Eligio.

Pañuelo nodded. "Gil's the leader now."

I thought Gil was a good choice. He would feel comfortable in Eligio's place. Whether Gil could command the same fear and respect, I couldn't tell.

Then Pañuelo asked me about Margarita, and I shook my head in answer. It was adequate for him, but not for me. No answer seemed to satisfy, or staunch the emptiness inside when I thought of her. Mamita had told me it was she who had called the police. It had been her last act of love toward me. I had tried calling, but she refused to come to the phone. And this morning when I woke up I found, on my bedstand, the ring I had given Margarita nearly a year before. It was Margarita's answer to the hurt I had caused her. Margarita's lost, and I wondered, now that she was no longer a part of my life, why once more I referred to her as Margarita.

I took out a pint of tequila. Pañuelo and I drank, without toast or dedication. I drank for the bitterness and false warmth.

"I thought I was dead," I told Pañuelo. But the fact that I was alive did not make me feel very good. "Mi anima se siente pesada."

"Don't worry, it'll pass," Pañuelo said.

Surprisingly, Gil came by. He said that he wanted me back with the Compañeros of the Red Band. "I need a thief with balls," he said.

I told him no. I no longer wanted to steal, or rape, or murder. He laughed, as if I were joking. Pañuelo joined in and I could see the side of him that made him right for the Compañeros, a side that I once possessed—quizas—but which I was losing in spite of my wish not to.

Gil left, then Pañuelo. I haven't seen mis Compañeros much since then, because our paths no longer cross, separated beyond our strength to reach out to each other.

I've also thrown away my jacket. It was bloodstained, as red as the embroidered streak on the back. Once, that blood, whether mine or someone elses, might have made me proud. Now the sight sickens me. Still, I've kept the headband. I don't seem able to let go of that part of me.

EL JUEGO DE LAS
RELACIONES ELEMENTALES

(fragmentos de una novela en preparación)

Gustavo Sainz

¿Me oyes, papá? ¿Estás despierto? Acabo de llegar, fui a dejar a Tatiana. ¿Me oyes? Hubieras ido con nosotros, fuimos a Xochimilco y compré una orquídea. ¿Me estás escuchando? Los aztecas no concebían una fiesta sin flores. Fuimos con ese muchacho que vive en la calle Temístocles, en su coche, y de regreso manejé yo, porque bebimos pulque y a él se le subió. No me gusta el pulque ¿sabes? Es pegajoso y dulce y pesado. Estábamos sentados muy tiesos arriba de una chinampa, o creo que chinampas son nada más esas balsas de caña cubiertas de tierra, algas y flores cuyo olor no logra resaltar, bueno, pero estábamos arriba de una góndola, Tatiana y yo tomados de la mano, y una banda de mariachis nos acompañó durante buena parte del paseo. Hubieras oído qué falsete se aventaban. Siempre he querido gritar así. Pero Temístocles le dijo algo a Tatiana, y yo escribí en el fondo de una cajita de cerillos si quería ser mi novia, y cuando empezamos a fumar le extendí la cajita y ella leyó la pregunta y sonrió, y me miró con complicidad, y hasta una sonrisita giocondesca. Lo único que me gustó aparte de esto fue la abundancia de flores. Las bugambilias se enredan en los postes de teléfono y corren por los cables. El agua era espesa y negra, casi lodo, y

45

había muchos niños semidesnudos en el mercado, un perro muerto, y
zopilotes sentados en las ramas más altas de los árboles. Y se podía ver el
volcán. ¿Hace cuánto que ya no hecha humo? ¿Hace cuánto que no desciendes al cráter? Y los limosneros se acercaban cada vez que parábamos el
coche, tan desvalidos como amenazadores. O más bien amenazadores, más
que cabrones, ajenos a nosotros. Una viejita vendía orquídeas. Hubieras
visto qué flores, casi extraterrestres. No pude resisterlas y le compré una
para Tatiana. Los tres veníamos en el asiento delantero y de vez en cuando
Temístocles le agarraba las piernas a Tatiana, sin importarle nada que yo
estuviera manejando, y por evitarlo la segunda o tercera vez, de regreso,
atropellamos a una serpiente, es decir, la atropellé, pero fue sin querer, y por
todo el camino nos siguieron los zopilotes, pesados, negros, malévolos y
aburridos. Afuera debe estar uno esperándome, estoy seguro, si es que no
hay uno en la cabecera de mi cama. ¿Me oyes?

Al final del primer capítulo de mi novela en proyecto debo pasar lista en el
salón de clases. Predominarán los nombres de doble sentido. Seleccionar
entre:

> Tulio Vergara
> Hugo Vélez Ovando
> José Boquitas de la Corona
> Bartolomé Topene
> Tanyecto Mokito
> Guillermo Costecho
> Tomás de la Veiga Fuerte
> Lola Meraz
> Martín Cholano
> Agapito Melórquez
> Etc.

Tatiana rompe mis cartas de amor en pequeños pedazos, los atraviesa con
un cordón y se los cuelga como collar antes de bajar a la fiesta. Bailo con ella,
respiro sobre los pedazos de papel. Los reconozco. Ni siquiera he tenido que
mirarlos con atención. Me detengo. ¿Y si yo fuera un cabrón, un reverendo
hijo de la chingada?

Liberalia: fiesta de la liberación. Nada se prohibe.

Fui como pude ser en la juventud; hay un momento el la juventud en que todo es posible, en que todo es poco en la inmensidad de nuestra vida. Adolfo Bioy Casáres: *Clave para un amor.*

Miro a Tatiana y le digo:
—Estoy desperdiciando los mejores años de *tu* vida...

Cito a Tatiana en la esquina de Herodoto y Ejército Nacional, junto a la tienda de mi madre. Se retrasa. Entro en la tienda y advierto:
—Si vienen a buscarme avisen que estoy en el departamento...

Voy al departamento, están los viejitos húngaros que hospeda mi madre. Hago diversas llamadas telefónicas, pero sobre todo, espero la de Tatiana, que no llega.

Voy de nuevo a la tienda, recorriendo las paradas de autobuses, mirando a un lado y a otro de las calles. En la tienda la vendedora me dice que la vió, que la llamó por su nombre e incluso se preparaba a describirle el camino al departamento cuando ella dijo:
—Ya sé por dónde ir, señora, muchas gracias...
—Y también conocía el número de teléfono, joven, deveras...

Corrí de nuevo al departamento. A mi madre le extrañó mucho.
—¿No la encontraste? Acaba de estar aquí...

Los viejitos me miraban con asombro.
—¿Cuántos tiene?—preguntó la anciana, refiriéndose a mi amiga.
—Trece—mentí...
—Ah,—rechinó—, si tuviera quince ya estaría buena...

Tengo miedo y vuelvo a correr hasta la tienda, pensando que los viejitos húngaros son unos asesinos y la han capturado. Quizás Tatiana estaba encerrada en el clóset y oyó nuestro diálogo. No ha vuelto a la tienda, y la vendedora y un muchacho repiten cuidadosamente todo lo que le dijeron. Desesperado vuelvo una vez más al departamento y la busco en el clóset, pero no está. Entonces tomo un taxi a su casa y la encuentro viendo televisión y se pone contenta cuando le cuento que tenía miedo de los viejitos.

Recordar: la pared en el cuarto de la tía de Tatiana, cubierta con imágines de los 365 santos del año.

Me cuenta Francisco Tario que la mordedura de los Niños (especie de grillos voladores con diminutas manos humanas) es tan atrozmente ponzoñosa que ningún medicamento conocido puede salvar de la muerte a su víctima. Y agregó:

—Solamente con la cura de los violines se obtienen buenos resultados...

Que consiste dulce y generosamente en hacer sonar un violín durante tantas horas como sean necesarias a la cabecera del moribundo.

Al parecer la música debe ser tierna, insignificante y sin prisas.

Himeneo meo, dijo el gato miau...

Piedad para nosotros que combatimos siempre en las fronteras de lo ilimitado y del porvenir, piedad para nuestros errores y nuestros pecados...

Apollinaire

El Rey Salomón, que era un sabio, poseía 700 mujeres y 300 concubinas.

Yo sería sabio con menos.

Probable episodio para la novela:

En casa de Tatiana, Sofócles trata de componer el tocadiscos cuando llega el señor Medallas rebosante de hijos que corretean, gritan y tropiezan con los bulbos desperdigados por el suelo...

—¡Escuincles del demonio, get aut!—grita Sofócles...

Pronto los llevan a la calle y el padre de Tatiana los acomoda en la amplia cajuela de la nueva camioneta. Sofócles ayuda a la tía polaca a caminar, casi la carga para subirla al interior del vehículo. Suben doña Esther, el señor Medallas, Sofócles, el padre de Tatiana y Tatiana, que con estremecimientos notables se sienta sobre las piernas de Sofócles. Nadie protesta e inician la marcha. Los niños gritan en la parte de atrás, riendo, y la tía polaca recita:

—Creo en Dios Padre, creador de todas las cosas, visibles e invisibles, y en Jesucristo, nuestro señor, su único hijo, y en el Espíritu Santo, que del hijo y del Padre procede, que con el Padre y el Hijo es glorificado...

Sofócles va adelante, junto a la ventanilla. Tatiana se reacomoda sobre sus piernas, pregunta si pesa y él dice que no, pero no tarda en mojarse el pantalón a la altura de la bragueta. Se lo dice a ella, muy quedo, y ella ríe con franqueza.

Cuando llegan al lugar de la fiesta, Sofócles se esfuma durante más de una hora para aparecer después, con ropa nueva y los cabellos revueltos. Tatiana corre hacia él, trastabillea con el lenguaje:

—¿Dónde estabas? Me dejas aquí, abandonada a mi suerte. Casi te aborrezco. Un escuincle se agarró de mi falda, fue odioso, mira nada más, qué sangrón, me preocupaba horrores que no llegaras y luego hasta llegué a pensar que te había pasado algo...

—Déjame hablar ¿no?

—Sí, pero es que fíjate, chíngale y de repente no estabas...

—¿Me aborreces?

—No.

—Acabas de decir que me aborreces...

—Sí, pero no. Lo que te pregunto es que dónde estabas...

Sofócles pasa una mano por su cabeza alisando los cabellos hacia adelante.

El padre de Tatiana le dice algo parecido.

—Caray, ya ni la amuela, nomás se fue al salón de belleza y pegó la carrera pa acá...

Sofócles se restriega los ojos llenos de tierra.

Dicen que durante el viaje eyaculó porque llevaba a Tatiana sobre las piernas, se ensució el pantalón y la trusa. No traía kleenex y buscó el baño, pero estaba ocupado. Entonces se escabulló en busca de una cantina o una fonda y ya en la calle (se atrevió a contar), cruzó frente a una casa grande y lujosa, vio a dos sirvientas y oyó decir:

—En serio, no los espero sino hasta mañana por la noche...

Se encaminó resueltamente hacia ellas.

¿No están mis tíos?—preguntó.

—¿Y usted quién es?—increpó una de las sirvientas.

—Eso iba a preguntarle a usted...—respondió Sofócles—. ¿Desde cuándo trabaja aquí?

—Pos hará algo de cosa como de dos meses... ¿Y eso qué tiene qué ver?

—Necesito entrar en el baño. Soy sobrino de sus patrones.

—Entonces ya debía saber que no están. Se van los sábados y los domingos a Valle de Bravo. Regresan hasta bien tarde...

—Sí, ya sé. Pero eso no quita que sean mis tíos.

—Ya déjalo pasar, tú...—dijo una de ellas.

—Con su permiso...

Y la otra:

—Pos ahi como usté quiera, joven—y dejó pasar a Sofócles que no se intimidó ni un momento y subió automáticamente por las primeras escaleras que encontró.

—Ahi te lo haya...—alcanzó a oír, en la voz de una de las sirvientas.

Encontró bastante decentes las recámaras, y tuvo la suerte, además, de hallar ropa casi de su medida. Arrojó el pantalón y la trusa malolientes en un cesto de mimbre y se bañó. Terminaba de vestirse cuando el timbre primero y después el sonido de la puerta al abrirse, lo sobresaltaron. Oyó cómo un hombre preguntaba por los dueños de la casa, y cómo una de las criadas, la que le había franqueado el paso, respondió que no estaban, como era su costumbre, pero que podía hablar con su sobrino...

—¿Felipín?—curioseó el hombre.

La sirvienta dijo que no sabía cómo se llamaba, porque era nueva, y que su amiga tampoco, estaba de visita, no trabajaba allí, etcétera.

Sofócles terminó de vestirse y con sigilo caricaturesco inició el descenso de la escalera. El hombre desconocido lo descubrió.

—¡Felipín!—dijo en un espasmo, ofreciendo sus brazos abiertos—: ¿No te acuerdas de mí?—Y en cuanto pudo lo apresó de los hombros...

—No—susurró Sofócoles, completamente a su merced.

—Claro, cómo te ibas a acordar, si estabas muy chiquito...Soy tu padrino...¡Ah, qué Felipín! Te conozco desde que tenías dos años...¿Te acuerdas cómo nos íbamos de pinta a Zihuatanejo a pescar y a jugar tennis? ¿Eh, maldito? ¡Acuérdate, acuérdate!

—¿A jugar tennis?

Y en el mismo tono entusiasta siguió diciendo cosas a las que Sofócles respondía siempre que sí, hasta que las sirvientas anunciaron que iban llegando los señores.

La que abrió la puerta a Sofócles escapó calle abajo, y él, por su parte, aprovechó un descuido del hombre amable para soltarse, fingir caminar hacia el garage adonde entraba un caravelle remolcando una lancha con motor fuera de borda, y en realidad correr desaforadamente, correr de prisa, cada vez más aprisa, hasta comprobar que nadie lo seguía.

—Nomás te peinaste y te veniste—dijo alguien, cuando llegó a la fiesta, parece que Tatiana.

Sofócles sonrío con su mueca Terry Thomas y se llevó una mano a la cabeza para sobar el cabello hacia adelante con vigorosa insistencia.

Entonces ella notó la ropa diferente, la camisa nueva, el pantalón desconocido, la mirada significativa, y pidió saber todo, cuando a él las palabras ya le brotaban de la boca, ensalivadas y de una manera casi automática...

EL TREN DE LA AUSENCIA

(fragmento de una novela en preparación)

Erlinda Gonzalez-Berry

No te sentí entrar. Es que estaba durmiendo y soñando. Espera, me está volviendo. Mi abuelita, sí, estaba soñando con mi abuelita. Me estaba haciendo un traje, una blusa de encaje y una falda amarilla, como cuando era niñia y vivía con ella. Siempre me hacía vestidos. Desbarataba los suyos y los cambiaba y los hacía pequeños para mí. Entonces me decía, anda mídetelo. Cuándo me veía con el nuevo traje se le encendía la cara de placer. Ven, déjame peinarte. Luego me peinaba y me ponía maquillaje. Nunca tuvo hijos. Es que era mi tía abuela, no mi abuela. Era tía de mi papá pero como no tuvo hijos, le pidió a su hermana—sí, la que se casó con su primo— que lo mandara a vivir con ella y siempre fue como su mamá. Así que por el lado de papi tuvimos dos abuelas, una abuela, y la otra, tía que llamábamos abuela. Cuando yo tenía diez años le pidió a papi que me dejara vivir con ella porque mi abuelo trabajaba en un rancho y sólo venía al pueblo los fines de semana y ella se ponía muy triste. Así que me fui a vivir con ella. Al principio fue muy raro. Yo estaba acostumbrada a mis hermanas y la bulla y el desorden que siempre había en casa. Con mi abuela todo siempre estaba arregladito y se hablaba en voz baja. En casa todas siempre hablábamos a la misma vez, y gritábamos y chillábamos y siempre era un carnaval. Donde mi abuelita todo era distinto.

Después de vestirme y peinarme me decía que si no quería ir a visitar a mi mamá porque ella tenía dolor de cabeza y quería dormir un rato. Así que me iba yo feliz de la vida con guantecitos y con una cartera de cuentas de colores que era de ella. Al llegar a la casa de mis padres, mis hermanas siempre estaban con los quehaceres de la casa, lavando platos, limpiando el piso, planchando, barriendo el patio. Entraba yo, muy princesita y me miraban con cara de ay qué asco y apenas me hablaban. Yo iba a hablar con mamá y las podía oír cuchicheando y riéndose de mí. Antes de irme, me arrinconaban y empezaban a pellizcarme y a jalarme el pelo. Cuando llegaba donde mi abuela ya yo venía toda desgreñada y con el traje nuevo roto. Y cada vez que podía, regresaba con ilusiones de que esta vez me tratarían bien y jugarían conmigo, pero ni modo. Siempre era igual. Después de unos años volví a vivir con mis padres y todo se olvidó y volví a integrarme a la familia. Creo que esa experiencia tuvo un efecto muy profundo en la formación de mi personalidad. En primer lugar siempre causé como motivo para manipular a mis padres. Les salía con que ustedes no me querían y me regalaron a la abuelita como a cualquier huerfanita. No, la verdad es que yo estaba tan feliz de estar una vez más donde había señas de vida que muy pronto las perdoné. A veces nos acordamos y me llaman la princesita y yo las llamo las cenicientas y nos da mucha risa.

Pues mi abuelita murió el año pasado. Ay Sergio, fue la cosa más horrible y deshumanizante que jamás podrías imaginar. Después de hacerle una operación la conectaron a un montón de máquinas. Estuvo así durante diez días con tubitos en la boca, en la nariz y por donde quiera. La piel la tenía amarilla y llena de moretones. Nunca abrió los ojos y nunca supimos si estaba consciente o no, y las malditas máquinas forzándola a respirar. Mami y papi se pusieron muy mal, pues ya te puedes imaginar viéndola así. Papi peor porque a él le había quedado la decisión de sí o no hacerle la operación. Si no se la hubieran hecho, habría muerto a las pocas horas, pero al hacérsela siguió viviendo en ese infierno mecánico y claro, él se sentía culpable.

Conocimos a otra familia; bueno mi hermana ya la conocía porque eran de su pueblito. Un hijo de dieciocho años había chocado en su moto en frente de la casa de sus padres el día de su graduación de la secundaria, y también

estaba como verdura conectado a las máquinas. Era una familia enorme de
diez hijos, y esposos, y niños y los viejitos. Pues esos diez días los pasaron en
el hospital. Arreglaban camas en el piso del corredor y allí dormían. Traían
comida y en fin, vivían en el corredor. Cada hora, permitían entrar a uno o
dos familiares a ver a su paciente. Los dos, el joven y mi abuelita estaban en
condiciones iguales. No se movían, no hablaban, no abrían los ojos. Nomás
se oía el siseo de la máquina respiradora. Y a cada hora del día y de la noche
entraba alguien a verlos así, por tres, cinco o diez minutos. Nos quedábamos
allí nomás parados mirándolos sin saber que hacer. Papi por fin ya no
aguantó y se rehusó a entrar a verla porque le causaba tanta agonía. Así que
nos turnábamos las hermanas y mamá.

    La décima noche entré con mi hermana, la que hace tiempo se metío a una
religión aleluya o qué sé yo. No me lo vas a creer pero cada aspecto de su
vida está ligado a su religión. Antes de entrar habíamos estado hablando y
todas habíamos quedado de acuerdo en que era absurdo que la tuvieran viva
a pura fuerza de las máquinas. Que lo que merecía era morir con dignidad en
su casita. Los médicos, olvídate, que es nuestra responsibilidad moral
tenerla así mientras sigan funcionando tres órganos vitales y quién sabe
cuántas más pendejadas nos decían. Pues esa noche eran como las once
cuando entramos a darle vuelta como habíamos hecho durante diez días.
Como era la primera vez que entraba con Luz, me quedé sorprendida
cuando empezó a hablarle. Los demás de la familia no decían nada; nomás
se quedaban allí mirándola llorando y todo los demás. Pero Luz de una vez
se puso a hablarle como si nada. Le decía que Dios la esperaba con los
brazos abiertos, que ya era tiempo que le diera su alma, que no se resistiera a
su voluntad, que el cielo era bellísimo, que había jardines y huertas por todos
lados, que el abuelito la esperaba en el cielo y no sé cuanto más. Y la abuelita
seguía como siempre, inerte, sin dar señas de oír o de comprender nada.
Pero, sabes, de pronto empezó a ocurrir la cosa más rara. A medida que mi
hermana le hablaba, acariciándole siempre la frente, empezaron a cambiar
los números en la máquina que le registraba el pulso. Cuando entramos
estaba a 140. Poco a poco empezó a bajar: 135-134-133-130. A medida que
le bajaba el pulso a mí se me aceleraba y se me hacía difícil respirar. Pues,
fíjate que jamás había visto a nadie morir y se me hacía que allí a mi ladito
estaba la calaca, tú sabes, personificada y todo eso. Cuando por fin marcó

94 la máquina, se detuvo, pero seguía el siseo de la respiradora. Pronto entró la enfermera a decirnos que era tiempo de salir. Salimos al corredor, Luz la misma estampa de la serenidad, yo totalmente histérica. Ella me abrazó e inmediatamente sentí una ola de calma extenderse a través de mi cuerpo. Así estábamos abrazadas cuando salió la enfermera a decirnos que había muerto la abuelita.

La escena que presencié esa noche me dejó verdaderamente impresionada. Y todavía todo ese episodio de la muerte de la abuelita—el horror de las máquinas, la frustración de verla así ni viva ni muerta durante tanto tiempo—me obsesiona y me agobia. A veces logro olvidarlo por algún tiempo, pero hoy volví a recordar. Quizá quiera que rece por ella y por eso la soñé. Es lo que dicen cuando uno sueña a los muertos, ¿no?

¿El muchacho de la moto? Murió esa misma noche, a las doce.

VISIONES OTOÑALES/AUTUMN VISIONS

A. Gabriel Meléndez

Tan chingones que nos creíamos, as we prowled the streets of the Valley on our nightly encounters, esculcándole los forros a la vida, searching our nuestra adolor-esencia. Yo junto con toda la bola, even though my jefitos would keep me busy all summer working con la Mrs. Bagely o el Mr. Samuels, keeping faith to their conviction que asina se enseña a trabajar y no va a andar de anducio en las calles sin quehacer (o sin qué hacer) y haciendo males. But Fall was otra cosa, my jefitos settled cozily into their routine of work and the new T.V. season; an existance occasionally punctuate by a compulsory attendance at the Rosario de un conocido o algún vecino del pueblo.

As September edged into the deep round glowing days of October, our clica at school began to form; una bola de camaradas desparejos, odds and evens, rotos y descosidos; each of us different, but too young to understand in just how many ways.

Our days were half-heartedly given to el escuelín, where we were con-tinually admonished by the coaches, the principal, the homeroom teacher, the counsellors and even the janitors, concerning the pitfalls that awaited us in adulthood "soon after graduation." We wanted so much to be adults and forever badly imitated them. Pero, ¿qué había pa nosotros? The future was as blank and silent as the spiral notebooks we carried from class to class.

Each year in High School we became bolder in the liberties we took at home, demanding nuestra independencia, using whatever ploy or línea pa desprendernos de las naguas de las jefitas: —Mom, I'm going to play basketball, see ya. —¿Otra vez? ¿Pues que no tienes paradero? ¿No tienes que estudiar? —No, ma, I'm finished, ya me voy...—Bueno, (then sternly), pero muncho cuidao, (then forcefully), y no vayas a venir muy tarde, ¿entiendes?

We were off and running. Sure we'd play a few games of basketball, but we were young, chingones. Two hours of basketball and then we'd slip out of the gym sweating, heads wrapped in towels, melding into the chill breeze of the otoño nights. Una bola de descosidos, teasing, cajoling, cateándonos, pataleándonos, haciendo pedo, anything pa fregar la paciencia, to make each other laugh, to make ourselves laugh. Laughing, pa descargarnos la viga, que ya maliciábamos nos tenían aprevenida.

The heat from our bodies would fog up the car windows and inevitably someone would write something cute or obscene with a finger: —Hey man, cut that shit out, ass. Whose car is this anyway? —Bueno, no te arrugues.

We'd take to the streets, we'd kick back and cruise, becoming the huevones chavalos our jefitos would comment about:

—No tienen oficio, no hacen más que andar pa'arriba y pa'bajo.

By the time we were Juniors, there were two of us that could pass for rucos, two bigotones that lower their voices, then cooly and nonchalantly would hit the driveups: —Let me have a six of Bud, ese...—¿Botes o Botellas? —Bottles man.

Later on nearly everyone at school advanced to adulthood, when Ricky Cisneros, started selling fake drivers licenses for ten bucks apiece. As it turned out, Ricky had this movida because his cousin worked with this vato whose brother operated the camera at the state Motor Vehicle Department. Things worked out for Ricky for a while till chavalitos who could barely peek over the dashboards of their jefitos' carruchas began appearing all too regularly at the drive-ups. Porporting defiant looks and aliviánate súplicas, didn't help, bar owners feeling the heat of an alerted jura automatically refused service, no matter how unscrupulous their reputations were known to have been previously. And not long after, al Ricky lo torció la ley.

Our clica was blessed, fared better than most. Our two prematurely ruco camaradas kept us cruising, alivianaos y contentos. Benny was el de cincho, the ice man. He had already established himself as a regular at El Berrendo, the Band Box and our old standby at the A & P. The only problem with el Osito as he was affectionately nicknamed, was his undependability, a trait not owing to his design, but to the crafty scrutiny of his aging, but truchas, abuelita. Osito was an only son to a widowed mother and an only nieto to his saintly, devotísima abuela. He was strapped by dependency and immobilized by guilt feelings that keep him home most nights of the week. Although he would never admit it, we were sure his abuelita had him praying el Rosario, cuando no, una novena, or pouring our refrescos for visiting parientes more nights than not.

Larry, Lorenzo Onésimo López, on the other hand was less successful than Osito, but certainly more available. He was tenacious, always willing and never undaunted by failure. Where it would take Osito one shot at his favorite neighborhood package store, it would invariably take Larry several miss fires to score some pisto. It was not uncommon to find him leading us into the next county, to Corrales or Algodones, where no once cared whether you had an I.D. or not anyway.

There were a hundred ways to get pisto, how much time was lost in securing it was another matter altogether. Seldom discouraged, this clica ran dry only as a matter of choice o por la falta de lana.

So cruising became for us on shadowy autumn nights an aberrant social interaction (no se asusten mis queridos orejones, it was before us and it still is) an interlude to adulthood, that hurled us with a self charging momentum, pa'rriba y pa'bajo, down blue-lit boulevards, country callejones, passed the well to do, the doing well and the ain't nothing doing here crowd; up to the Heights (imagínense) and through the forgotten vecindades del Valle, across dusty mesas, and past the twinkling lights of a cityscape gridded across the horizon: a sun-belt pueblo of dreams and penas nailed to the desert floor.

The caminitos and the boulevards, the side streets and the country lanes were all connected. Only the barriers were invisible, you could never see them, never touch them, but they held you and you could sense them. Streets turned into callejones, pavement broke off into ruts and barrio bumps, freeways exited into dust. We would follow the roads and our otoño visions and were seldom deterred by ominous dead ends or sleepy vega caminitos where other vatos anducios had sworn to have seen burning bruja fireballs hurling through the night.

There were nights given to la movida, nights for seeking out the hot chavalitas that every anducio had a fishing story about. Fridays and Saturdays when Chicanitas wrangled an older carnal's Monte Carlo or the jefitos' Dodge Polara and merged into the left lane of a "Hi...What's your name?" "Tírales el loco" groupie trip. And although genuinely enraptured by the giggling effervesce of these mamacitas, a vato could only take so much rejection and we would circle wider and return less often to water in that love cruise illusion. (Nos gustaba el pedo, pero nos agüitaban los negochiations.)

Occasionally a caminito would entice us to follow it, taking us by alamolined pasturas, over and past gurgling acequias deep with the bittersweet aroma of jarales and yerbabuena, and through hundred year old arboledas to some year old development where four or five custom adobe homes huddled around a softly lit cul-de-sac. De cincho, this enclave of sophisticated rancho style gentrification bore in true Ralph Lorenesque developer perception a colorful, picturesque, Southwestern Spanish traditional name like: *La Villa Escondida del Caminito Angosto del Bosque Grande de la Vista Hermosa de las Montañas Azules de El Dorado.* Through the luminescent atrium windows appeared sculptured walls and curving stairways, hand hewn vigas and Tewa sarapes nailed to white tabiques. Ristras de chile, trenzas de maíz and chamiso wreaths that hung by the massive hand carved wooden doorway, were illuminated by brightly colored patio lights and in the glow a plaque that read: "El ranchito de los Kirkhams'."

We would naively comment, "Someday, I'll have a chante like that, vato," surprised by the irony of our remarks. We took note, made observations, threw some puntadas and exchanged imagined descriptions of the people we thought the inhabitants of such inverted and beguiling quaintness. The jefito was surely a doctor or a lawyer, a professor at the "U"; the ruca a slim muscle-toned güera eternally basking at pool side, a brick thick novel in hand, a gin and tonic at her side; the chavalos, two spoiled rich kids wheeling trail bikes through the bosque or selling lemonade and cookies on the front lawn.

We were half-impressed, half-escamaos by the symmetry and order of gabacho neighborhoods. We had no patience for the confining nature of sculptured hedge, landscaped lawns, deep-wide cement driveways, endless and unbroken curbs, and while we coveted the shiny Vets parked next to the wood paneled station wagons, the motionless mortuary parlour world into which they were juxtaposed seemed as insipid to us as store bought bread.

In our barrios nothing remained the same, forms abruptly, rudely clashed or broke off in jagged edges. Symmetry and uniformity were foreign and absent. Collage, pastiche and discontinuity were the functions of our want and our miseria. Cerquitos de tablas ran into cinder block walls that gnawed at pale yellow street lights through gaping holes where back yards tumbled into vacant lots. Cuartitos were added onto cuartitos, chantes de adobe adjoined mobile homes, store fronts became residencias, residencias became beauty shops or a card reader's parlour, remiendos de enjarre loomed in the dark and old "Enjoy Coca-Cola" signs replaced broken windows, carros arrumbaos were tied to barking dogs and shadeless lightbulbs were recessed deep in the bastidores of timeless adobe walls.

We would follow the barrio caminitos and backstreets that raced and rattled over train tracks, that edged between junk yards and warehouses, that sped by dairy farms and slaughterhouses or rose precipitously and followed the grenaje, past a contractor's dompe full of concrete, of jarrería and broken glass that shattered the October moon over yards and yards of useless trash. Red reflectors nailed to ancient alamos forwarned anducio vagamundos of paciente and deceptive curvas that hunched in the dark. Grey wooden crosses, flores de plástico, vasos de velas, una estampa de la Virgencita de Guadalupe at the trunk of such an alamo, gave testimony to las penas y congojas de una madre, that waited en vela por su hijo parrandero que no volvió, as surely as our jefitas would wait for us.

Tan chingones man, as we floated and grimaced in the dark by the edge of the bosque when it was time to take a piss: —Aliviánate vato, I heard they've seen la Llorona around here. —Who you trying to kid?....Chale man, there's no such thing....Hey but don't turn off the headlights, I'll only be a sec....And tarde o temprano we'd opt for home. "Dale pa'l chante loco...." porque even though we were chingones nos daba sueño, un sueño como de pena, un sueño inculcado por una ansia desconocida, una ansia agitada por los espectros y las realidades de nuestra anducia, por lo que sabíamos y por lo mucho que nos quedaba por andar.

THE BIRTHDAY PARTY

Michelle Sedillo

Fifteen more minutes to go before the bell. Manuel sat at his desk struggling with his arithmetic assignment. The long division just didn't seem to work out correctly, and Mrs. Ramirez was busy helping someone else.

Manuel looked to the back of the room where the class pets were kept. There was an aquarium containing several types of fish, which had been brought in over the years by Mrs. Ramirez' students. In other glass cases, lizards slept under flourescent lights on rocks and sand, while frogs plunged into the warm pond in their artificial environment. On another counter lay the cage containing snakes, which fascinated all the children, except Manuel.

With a malicious grin on his face, Manuel sneaked to the aquariums, taking the long way around the snake enclosure. He snatched a slimy frog from the pond. Making sure Mrs. Ramirez was still occupied, he placed the frog in the top drawer of her desk. Satisfied with himself, Manuel took a Hershey bar from his coat pocket and slowly unwrapped it, so Mrs. Ramirez would not hear the paper crackle.

Mrs. Ramirez glanced at the clock and walked back to her desk. A few children snickered as she sat down.

"All right, children, get your things together, it's almost time to go home."
Mrs. Ramirez began gathering a few pens and pencils which were strewn
across her desk.

"Does everyone know who's birthday it is today?" she asked.

"George Washington's!" a small boy yelled from the back of the
classroom.

"No Jimmy, not George Washington's birthday," Mrs. Ramirez
answered. Manuel raised his hand, squirming in his seat.

"It's mine! My birthday!" he yelled through a mouthful of chocolate.

"Yes it is," said Mrs. Ramirez, and we're all going to sing Happy Birthday to you, Manuel." As she said this, she opened the desk drawer and
placed the pens and pencils inside. The frog leaped out of the drawer and
sailed directly into Mrs. Ramirez' blouse, which opened in a V in the
front.

"¡Cabrón!" she screamed as she thrust her hand in after the frog. It eluded
her probing fingers and worked its way further down.

"Aaaaaaaagh!" she screamed again, this time nearly in tears. The class
roared with laughter, and Manuel nearly choked on his Hershey bar.

"Who's responsible for this!" Mrs. Ramirez twisted around the front of
the room trying to grasp the frog, which was now squirming around to the
back of her blouse. Tears streamed down her cheeks, and her face was crim-
som from embarassment.

Just as the bell rang, Jimmy yelled, "Manuel did it!" Still clutching at her
back, Mrs. Ramirez lunged at Manuel, but he was already out of his desk and
running for the door.

"I'm calling your mother! You're not getting away with this!" she yelled
as Manuel fled into the playground and out of sight. The other kids laughed
as they hurried away from school, but although several walked home in the
same direction as Manuel, none cared to accompany him.

As he walked home, Manuel thought of his tenth birthday party that afternoon. Oh, it would be wonderful, he thought, his classmates would bring him
mountains of presents. Manuel did not really like his classmates, but had
invited them for the gifts they would bring. He had made certain to send
invitations only to the kids who would bring him the best presents.

He smiled in satisfaction as he bounced down the side of the dirt road and gave a whack to each of Mrs. Ortega's surviving flowers. It was late September, the twenty second to be exact, and Mrs. Ortega's well-cared for azaleas were in full bloom. The old lady spied Manuel from her kitchen window and began to yell and shake her fist at him. He merely smiled and thrust up his middle finger at her, knowing her old legs could not catch him. All the kids at school could catch him, though, probably because he was chubby from shoplifting candy bars at the local grocery store and devouring them so he would not have to share them with anybody.

Manuel thought of old Don Ramón, whose home was next to Mrs. Ortega's. Manuel had often tormented the old man by opening the gate and letting Don Ramón's goats run free, or by taking the chicken's eggs and splattering them one by one on Ramón's old horse Pita, which everyone secretly called Puta. Once, Manuel had lifted the parking brake on Ramón's ancient truck, and the truck had rolled right into Ramón's melon patch, splattering most of the nearly ripe crop. Manuel smiled, remembering how furious the old man had looked as he hobbled after him, cursing loudly, and waving his fists in the air. Yes, he thought, it would be fun to pester Don Ramón today.

He peered through the trees at Don Ramón's two-room adobe house which stood proudly at the center of the lot. Behind it there was a small barn which housed the chicken coop, a grave-yard for delapitated vehicles, and the sectioned off, half acre where Ramón kept his five goats and Puta. Manuel was glad that Don Ramón's old hound, Pendejo, had run away last summer and had never come back; Pendejo had made Manuel's adventures difficult.

The boy crept toward the barn, making sure Don Ramón was not outside toiling with his old cars, or feeding his animals. Today, Manuel thought, I will let the goats and Puta out of their pens. He opened the gate to the goat-pen, and laughed as they bounced away, relishing their unexpected freedom. Grinning fiendishly, he crept around the other side, thinking of how angry Don Ramón would be. Puta only gaped at him when Manuel poked her on the rump with a stick to urge her on. She merely turned her head and snickered, infuriating Manuel, until he screamed at her, "Your mother was a mule, and your father was a wart-hog, you stupid old horse!" Hearing the clamor, Don Ramón grabbed his shotgun and hobbled through the front door, barking obscenities at the boy. Seeing the gun, Manuel panicked, and in his haste to escape, backed into Puta's drinking trough and fell in. The old man's rage turned to laughter.

"Now let's see what your mother says when you come home smelling like horse-spit, cabroncito!" As Manuel struggled out of the stinky trough, Ramon cocked his gun and aimed at his behind. The shotgun was loaded with salt and Manual knew that a well placed shot would sting like hell. He also realized he had gone too far, so he bolted down the road as fast as his chunky legs would go. He could hear Don Ramon's laughter in the distance, and he cursed the old man for having a gun.

Later that evening, Manuel watched his mother prepare his three-layer chocolate birthday cake and hang purple crepe-paper decorations from the vigas on the ceiling. The entire house was filled with the swirling aromas of home-made cake, and red hot chile from the enchilada dinner his mother had prepared for the family.

Manuel sat on his ample behind and enjoyed the privileges of being a birthday boy. He had explained to his mother that the bully's from school had pushed him in a ditch on his way home, and was immediately rewarded for his misfortune by receiving twinkies and ice cream before dinner. The horse odor emanating from Manuel's wet clothes was overlooked.

Satisfied with his mother's trust in him, Manuel wandered into his little sister's room, spotted her doll on her bed, and decided to hide it. Stuffing the doll under his shirt and sneaking into the garage, he opened the large freezer and hid Samantha under a large frozen turkey, taking care to hide any exposed parts of the doll with bags of frozen vegetables. Extremely satisfied with himself, Manuel marched into the house and plopped down on the easy chair to watch "Gilligan's Island" with his mother.

Margaret entered the room in a flurry, stopping to look under the couch and in a large vase.

"My dolly's gone!" the five year squeaked as she peered under the coffee table.

"Where was the last place you remember taking her, sweetheart?" Manuel's mother asked.

"She was on my bed sleeping. The fatty took her!" Margaret's accusing eyes turned on Manuel, who immediately put on his most innocent facade.

"Don't you call me fatty, you ol' wart-hog! Mom tell her not to call me fatty, she's mean!" sobbed Manuel as he thrust his tongue out at Margaret.

"Cool it you two!" his mother exclaimed. Agitated, she grabbed Margaret's hand and proceeded to search the bedrooms once more for Samantha.

Chuckling to himself, Manuel turned to the television, but he was repulsed as a documentary on reptiles showed an enormous python swallowing a defenseless ferret. Manuel loathed snakes more than anything in the world. Several years before, on a family camping trip, he had wandered off alone and decided to explore a small cave nestled against a hillside. The opening was just large enough for him to become wedged in, head first. There were snakes in the cave; he could hear them, and he could see them slithering in the dim light. Manuel let out a horrifying shriek. He struggled insanely, cutting his forehead and scraping his hands on the floor of the cave. In one last desperate thrust, he freed himself and ran back to camp, sobbing hysterically and bleeding from the many scratches on his face and hands.

His cuts healed within two weeks but the snake nightmares continued for months. That was six years ago, shortly before his father had left them. Manuel could still remember the security and warmth of being comforted in his father's arms after his bad dreams.

Manuel shivered as he hastily changed the disturbing program to something more appealing. In the next room the telephone rang and as he listened to his mother's muffled words, he vaguely wondered if it could be Mrs. Ramirez calling about the frog. His mother didn't mention the incident so Manuel decided maybe Mrs. Ramirez had forgotten the prank.

Later that afternoon, after Margaret had cried herself to sleep over the loss of Samantha, Manuel and his guests played musical chairs, and spin the bottle, and they took turns hitting the piñata with Manuel's baseball bat until it burst open, spilling candy all over the living-room floor. The highlight of the party occured while playing pin the tail on the donkey. Jimmy Sanchez, the shortest boy in the whole fourth grade, pinned the donkey's tail on Manuel's mother's behind. She let out a surprised shriek and reached for the offended area. The children bellowed with laughter and Jimmy pulled off his blindfold to see what the laughter was about.

"I'm sorry," he stammered. "I didn't mean to do it. I really didn't." His eyes filled with tears when he saw the angry look on Manuel's mother's face.

"It's alright. It was an accident," she said, fighting her embarrassment. "Let's all have some cake, then we can open the presents," she said.

At the mention of cake, everyone including Jimmy forgot the donkey's tail and scrambled to get a place at the table.

"Manuel has to blow out the candles!" his mother shouted above the noise.

Manuel watched proudly as his mother lit the ten candles, and one to grow on. Drawing a deep breath, he fiercely blew out the candles and, at the same time, blew spittle all over Jimmy and his plate.

"Chingao!" Jimmy cried. Turning to Manuel's mother he bawled, " He spit all over me. I want another plate, this one's gross." His lower lip nudged out and his eyes filled with tears.

"All right Jimmy, here's another plate, and a napkin to clean your face." Manuel's mother nervously wiped Jimmy's face with the napkin. "Now I'll cut the cake."

Following the party-meal, Manuel reminded everyone about his unopened presents, which were sitting on the coffee-table in the living-room.

The children looked on eagerly as Manuel opened his gifts. There were the walkie-talkies and a winter jacket from his mother, a checkers set, money and various other playthings, including a large gift from Jimmy, which Manuel saved for last. He greedily shredded the colorful paper off each present, until only Jimmy's was left.

The children crowded around, eager to see what Jimmy had given Manuel. His mother quietly watched from the kitchen door. His fingers were shaking in anticipation as he ripped through the brightly colored paper. When he lifted the lid, his excitement turned to horror. He saw it, coiled and ready to strike. Manuel screamed in terror and jumped away, wide-eyed with dread.

Everybody laughed. "It's not real," Jimmy said and picked up the rubber snake. He held it out to Manuel. "It's just a fake," Jimmy laughed. The others joined in the mocking laughter. Jimmy threw the rubber snake on

Manuel's shoulder. Manuel gave a terrified moan and stumbled to the safety of his mother's arms.

"Chicken!" Jimmy teased, "Manuel's a chicken!"

Sobbing with shame, Manuel ran to his room, locked the door, and crawled under the covers of his bed in a effort to hide from his embarrassment. His classmates had laughed at him for being afraid of a rubber snake. He closed his eyes and held the pillow over his face to shut out the wretchedness he felt.

"Honey, please come out," his mother called, "It was just a joke. Nobody thinks you're a chicken."

His mother made a valiant effort to bring Manuel out of his room, but he would not budge. Although he tried to hold them back, the tears filled his eyes and soaked into the pillow covering his face. He didn't ever want to see his friends again. Suddenly, he thought of Mrs. Ramirez with the frog down her shirt, and all the children laughing at her; he understood how she had felt.

Later, after everyone had left, his mother knocked once more.

"Sweetheart, it's me. Please let me in, so we can talk about this."

Reluctantly, Manuel arose from his rumpled bed and opened the door for his mother. She swept him up in her arms and silently rocked him, while fresh tears gushed from his swollen eyes. After a moment she spoke.

"Honey, Mrs. Ramirez called me earlier and explained what you did to her. That wasn't very nice."

"It was just a joke," Manuel sobbed.

"Jimmy's present was just a joke too, sweetheart, but it wasn't very funny to you, was it?" The irony of his mother's words began to make sense to Manuel.

"I'm sorry, mom. I know how she felt, really I do. Everybody laughed at me." Manuel rubbed his hand across his tear-stained cheeks.

"You're going to have to apologize for what you did, and never do it again, alright?"

"I guess so Mom," Manuel reluctantly agreed. Mrs. Ramirez was just such a witch, Manuel thought, but his mother would punish him if he did not apologize.

"Well, goodnight, honey. Everything will be okay." His mother's gentle voice soothed his hurt pride. Hugging his tear-stained pillow, Manuel called out "Goodnight" as she flipped the lights out and left the room. He felt a hollow pain inside, like the time in the third grade, when Eddie had punched him in the stomach after Manuel had eaten Eddie's lunch and replaced its contents with the classroom's pet hamster, which had died the night before. Manuel thought of Mrs. Ortega's flowers, of Don Ramón and Puta, and of his father. He vaguely wondered if his father had left the family because Manuel was such a pest. He felt sorry for what he had done and at the same time, also sad. He thought of Margaret who had cried herself to sleep over losing Samantha and had missed the party. Manuel felt mean because he had hidden her doll.

Determined to ease his conscience, he shuffled into the garage to retrieve Samantha from her arctic prison. He lifted the freezer door, extracting the doll.

"Time for sleep," he said to the doll as he walked into Margaret's bedroom. He placed the frigid doll next to Margaret and watched her sleep. In the past he would have poured a bottle of ketchup on her face and awakened her by shouting, "You're bleeding! you're dying!"

Now he smiled at her and said, "Goodnight little sister." Manuel walked to the door and paused. Something just did not feel right, but what could it be? A mischievous grin crossed his face as he walked back to Margaret's bed.

"What the heck," he said as he pulled Margaret's blankets and shoved the icy doll into her warm arms. The five year old awoke with a cry. Frightened of the cold thing in her arms, she pushed the doll away and let out a cry for her mother.

Now that was better, thought Manuel as he hurried to his room. Although he knew his mother would be angry, at least his pride was restored.

LA LLUVIA

(*from* Nambe Year-One)

Orlando Romero

"¡Qué lluvia tan desgraciada!"

Marcos García's words echo in the fathom mist of this unnatural rain on the first week in March. His partner and compadre, Fermin Gonzales, stoically sits beneath his oiled and rainproof rawhide rain slick. Both their horses' pace is caught in the same magnetic pull that traps my dreams and sleep. They barely move in fog that is so rare in Nambé. They hope their horses will lead them to their warm beds and the loving affections of their young brides.

Marcos is disturbed by the eerie mist.

"What time do you think it is, Fermin?"

"God only knows. All I know is that we're somewhere in Nambé and it's 1830." From under his slick he pushes a bottle of homemade wine.

"Here, Marcos, have a drink. It may not keep this chill and mist away, but it will help you ease your worries."

The horses move and they wearily stir in their saddles. With the chill that fills their bones, the longing to be with their women is intensified.

"You know something, Fermin? Every time I'm coming down from those Sangre de Cristo's I get the feeling I'll never see my Juanita's green eyes again. I don't care if it's just a week or a couple of days; every time you and I go up there looking for the big bucks I feel that when I get home she won't be there."

"No seas pendejo, Marcos, she's devoted to you and everyone in the village knows how much she loves you. Do you know that my wife caught her picking wild flowers in the fields one day when you were gone to Santa Fe. She told my wife how much you loved flowers and that she wanted to smother the house with flowers when you returned."

In the unnatural, incessant mist and chill the horses neigh. Their second fears are more intense as Fermin is almost rocked out of his saddle when his horse's hooves claw the mist in fear. Marcos extends the candlelight lamp. No one is seen, yet someone approaches.

Less than two feet away, like a ghostly apparition, a figure becomes visible by the dim light of Marcos' lamp. They are stunned beyond belief. The figure is shrouded in a black leather cape. A hood covers all of his face except two bluish specks of light that seem to come from his eyes. They are not sure if he even has eyes. His horse is the blackest horse they have ever seen. Even in the saddle, his height towers above them. Yet, the figure is not as wide as if a man's body lies within the cape and hood. His horse comes between Marcos and Fermin, as if they were not even there, and smoothly glides and eases his way between them. They both notice a black cock, with his bluish-black rain-resistant feathers, its bloody red crown peeking from under his master's cape. The rooster seems to be sitting between his legs. The chill they both know before has turned to beads of perspiration, and the mist becomes suffocating.

Speechless and almost motionless, Fermin slowly reaches for Marcos' dim lamp. As if in a state of sleep-walking he dismounts. He brings the lamp close enough to the ground to touch it. Fermin's fears find words.

"Dios Mio, Marcos, there are no tracks on the ground!"

Fermin returns to his saddle and hands the lamp back to his friend. In the dim light, Marcos' face has turned to ice white. "Marcos, companion, what's the matter? You look as pale as death."

In Marcos' confusion he retorts only because he believes he is alive.

"I am sick, my friend."

Marcos hastily dismounts and stumbles in the thickness of the mist. He tries to remove himself as far away from Fermin as possible. Fermin waits, he too is in a state of suspended confusion. From the depths of that foreboding mist and thicket of black dreams he hears his friend in convulsion.

"Marcos, Marcos, ¿Qué pasa?"

Marcos' heaves are as dry as the moon itself. He lies close to the bank of a ditch, close to his own vomit of fear. Even the life-giving gurgle of the acequia cannot comfort him. Distraught and weak he manages to scoop up a handful of water to wash the filth from his face.

Moved by the concern for his friend, Fermin leaves his horse to search for Marcos. They almost collide in the dimness of their lamp. Marcos speaks out of necessity.

"Never in my life have I known such helplessness and fear. You know I have faced wild beasts and ridden the meanest horses, and at times up there, in those Sangre de Cristos, lived in the shadow of death, but never, never in my life have I come so close to something that appears out of nowhere and is so totally incomprehensible."

The echo of Marcos' words pierce the mist, but it does not help conquer the fear that came out of the darkness as unexpectedly as the fog itself.

As if they were alive or their horses could never forget the way home, the trail to the village became the visible path that the stubbornness of the mist had to surrender to its maternal owner,Nambé. It must have been around two in the afternoon when they came to the bend they both knew so well. The shadow of a barren, pre-Spring apricot tree threw its silhouette branches around the riders and their horses as if snakes were part of a new mirage.

The pack horse carrying the butchered elk strains as the ascent begins. They know that at its top their adobe houses will be coming into view. The mirage appears wavy in the intensity of the blue backdrop that surrounds the village. The desire to be with their women becomes obsessive.

Fermin turns to Marcos, mumbling words he wishes had concrete reality.

"There it is Marcos, Nambé,and soon my beautiful Florecita."

"Sí, compañero, and mine too!"

As they take the upper road that cuts the village in half, a small child and his dog come close enough to be trampled by the slow movement of Marcos' horse.

"Did you see that Fermin? A small child ran in front of us as if we weren't even here."

Fermin only sees the eternal numbness of his soul and is weary of doubt and confusion. He can smell the cheese melting in his wife's kitchen.

Marcos puts persistent doubt out of his mind only to dream that in a few feet the edge of his fields will become reality. He sees himself milking his favorite cow. Then he sees himself dancing a very slow and intoxicating waltz with Juanita. As if his thoughts have congealed into bad dreams, he sees his neighbor, Tomás Archuleta step in front of him and knock on the door that he was about to open.

The aged Tomás Archuleta has had this task before. In this kind of situation, he can almost anticipate the facial and emotional reactions in people. That is why he is always chosen to announce that death has arrived.

"Buenos días Don Tomás, how is your wife? Let me fix you a cup of coffee and some biscochitos!"

"No, Juanita, you'd better sit down. Juanita, understand child, we don't know the way the world works."

"No, Don Tomás, don't say it. I'd rather pretend it's not true. Here, let me take your hat. Sit down and have a cup of coffee."

"Juanita, you must know the truth!"

"Don Tomás,...please...have your coffee first. I already know."

The smell of freshly brewed coffee becomes nauseating to Don Tomás. This type of situation is unusual to him. In most cases people break out in mournful lament and wails reach such a peak of hysteria that he too would accompany them in the tearful agony of loss. But this young girl was somehow caught in a fixed mood of serenity and calm.

"I know because last night I had the sweetest and longest dream I've ever had of Marcos. He embraced me and we danced until the sun came up. I know because after my dream I heard knocking at the door and when I answered there was no one there. I know because I helped ease the torment of fears that always followed him around. I know because he was the son of mountain people. Up there, even this village seems like lowlands compared to the way he felt for those altitudes."

While Don Tomás finished his coffee neither spoke another word. The silence became so oppressive that Don Tomás was determined to break its hold. As if his bladder was about to burst, he stumbled forward with sincerity.

"Juanita, let me butcher one of my cows for the wake. Please, child, I love you and your husband deeply, it's the least that I can do!"

"Don Tomás, where did they find him?"

"Both Fermin and Marcos were found down a deep crevice. It seems as if they never saw it and rode their horses right into it. They think they had been there about a day before they were discovered. I don't know."

Leo Romero

Not Knowing What To Say

Casamirio
    I don't know what to say
    after the silence of years

Casandra
    Say that you are a still pond
    and that I am the stone
    that has broken your repose
    Or that I stir within you
    the memory of tides
    Of sudden urges

Casamirio
    I don't know what to say
    after the silence of years

Casandra
    Say that your heart has grown
    shy and timid
    and is easily startled
    Say that you thought
    as you grew older
    you would grow more hardened
    But that instead you feel brittle
    As brittle as the thin ice
    that coats winter grass

Casamirio
    I don't know what to say
    after the silence of years

Moon and River

Casandra, seeing the moon
reflected in the river
I am reminded
of who we are

We know that what
we are seeing
is only a reflection
We know that the river and moon
are many thousands of miles apart

And yet we see them both in one
Nothing in nature is changed
by this occurrence
Except we notice

And I am reminded
of who we are
Transient, beautiful light
Shimmering within a body

I Opened My Window

Casamirio, I opened my window
to let in the cool air
and the smell of rain

A soothing breeze parts
the warm air in my room
and bathes me, caresses me
like oil massaged over my skin

I am refreshed, Casamirio
Sitting before my window
Seeing the gray sky through branches
Enjoying the company of a rain swept day

Casamirio, I know others have said
that I am living alone
But that's not true, I live
with my window open to the world

Loves and Lives

Casandra, we speak of the present
But as we kiss
the kiss is already lost
As we touch
the touch is already lost

To become conscious
is to think of what is past

How often we look back
at loves and lives
that had seemed so distant
or had been unexpected

Yet no time
seems to have passed
Who we were and what we did
is all behind us
as if it was always behind us

Casandra, how can we convey
who we are or where we are
We can only say
who we think we were
where we think we were

When Love Leaves

Casamirio, what do you remember
of my love for you

> That it was like sunlight
> on a branch
> Luminous and warm

Casandra, what do you remember
of my love for you

> That it was like a classroom
> of children going for a walk
> with their teacher
> Straggling and boisterous
> but full of joy

Casamirio, what do you know
about sorrow

> That it is like the dark trunk
> of a pine tree
> deep in a dense forest
> where sunlight never penetrates

Casandra, what do you know
about sorrow

> That when love leaves
> sorrow takes its place

Jimmy S. Baca

Martin, *part VI*

At dawn
rusted field iron
stock tanks and gates
smoldered mist.
Beyond the railroad tracks
engine echoes hummed in deep shafts of grey silence
then whirred away

Father Padilla
tugged the bell rope,
clapped the bell's iron tong
down on black head veils
of viejas,
mumbling spanish prayers
as they walked
down field paths
meandering to the church.
The bell shook
like a horse
shuddering dew off—
the dew clinging to head veils and flowers.

The distant groans from St. Francis church
reached you mother
as you scraped seed out
of the feed sack, slopped supper
green to chickens,
and pailed windmill water to calves and pigs.
From where the bus left you,
you'd walk the tracks back home.
You gazed at the llano—
wind blew
blue-knife day,
sharpening its silver edge
on Manzano crag rock,
chipping red grit
like a santero
carving a pre-historic God—
a scar-scaled reptile
bordering the distant horizon,
breathing a sigh at dusk,
whirling sand at your doorstep,
rustling cornstalks
and water in troughs.
Leisure hours
you hung out at the local gas station,
dreaming of being a calendar pin-up girl,
flipping through Sears Catalogue
and Romance magazines,
imagining yourself in a bathing suit,
embraced by a matinee idol.

At 13
step-father climbed the stairs
to your room one night,
and his fingers stroked between your thighs
and warmed your blood.
Outside, the leaf skinned snake,
slithered in arroyo silt grain
to warm itself
in the stored sun's heat.

For two years
step-father drew his dull life out
like a knife from sheath
and found happiness in the wound.
You vowed
never to be vulnerable again,
after you left home.

For two years,
after he left your room,
you stayed awake
learning cunning,
from coyotes that prowled
scrap-wood corrals,
learning endurance,
from the windmill's pipe and blades,
grunting and creaking constantly,
and you learned to dream
in the darkness,
as the night train pulled you
onto its rattling boxcars,
toward California.

One evening, reading scripture
from his black bible,
his hands gripped the wooden chair arm rests,
his haggard face whitened
like a black haired ear of corn in morning mist,
as you told him
you were carrying a backseat baby.

His silence carved
stone doors in the air,
you walked through, slowly closing the doors on him.
Cruising out of Willard
in a new black Ford, with Danny,
your heart gave its first free wingspread,
soaring along the edge
of your body, that had been field prey,
and now felt like a nest.
You thought of me,
planted in the soft furrow of your body,
knowing I too would be,
field prey.

A few days after I was born,
you filed for divorce,
left me at grandma's door,
and ran away to California
with another man.

This act of abandonment
was God's Will,
and it left no scent, no view, no mark,
others might find.
In Santa Fe,
you let your old life fall like a black branch,
your new life sparkled over like snow frost.

I was never told
where you were
or what you were doing,
or if you were alive or dead.
My thoughts of you
filled the air with a vast space of lights,
softly glowing in the darkness,
and not until your return years later,
when I was a man,
did the snow crust melt,
and your hands drift in like yellow flowers
I plucked,
and your face floated up like a mask
I wore.

Time had spun a white veil
around the dream you were to me.
Now your words were moths
eating through the white veil,
as you told me of the frayed-skirt life
father had given you.

Your indifference and apathy toward me
had become aged stone
unbudged for decades,
erected in the ruins of a baby's scream,
rubbling over the dirty linoleum tile
on which the baby crawled
in an adobe shack
with an army blanket door.

I didn't like who you were
and never spoke with you again,
until several years after our meeting,
a telephone call came around midnight.

"Your mother, has been shot,
and she won't make it through the night."

Her own two children hadn't come
to see her. Swollen mass of bruised flesh,
a mangled half-face inhuman thing
tubed and monitered on the bed,
wrapped in gauzes soaked in blood.

"Unplug the machine," I told the doctor.

She was polishing her nails
in the kitchen, when she looked up,
and her husband fired four bullets
at point blank against her skull.

The four bullets
gave four chill tings,
like a botique shop door tin bell,
opening the door of her life
to interminable darkness,
she walked in,
over the meat scraps and bone fragments,
deep into her own being,
over the rock-slag scrub-brush farmland
she grew up on,
to a fireplace with a woman rocking her
in warm arms.

At the suicide-murder scene,
I found her diary
laying on her dresser. I read it.
                    "I want to die,
                    I want to die,
                    I have no one in this world,
                    I want to die..."

written hundreds of times.
Her daughter, my step sister, rushed in,
ripped the diary from my hands,
and burned it in the fireplace.
I had already read
how they had gone on for months
without talking,
how mother had spiraled into love affairs
with young men,
her daughter had been in love with,
how they dived into the river bottom of pleasure
flowing high between mother's legs,
and how mother wanted to destroy a marriage,
to become who she had never been, herself.

On the refrigerator,
written in lipstick, he scrawled,

                    "You will never leave me!
                    You will never go out
                    on me again!"

Then he took his own life.

A long time ago
he thought he had saved you,
from your own culture, your own language,
from the dust and tumbleweeds of Santa Fe,
and had promised to make you
his leading lady.
He drove you across the llano,
to grassy valleys of California,
placed the photograph of you
on his fireplace mantel.

When you wanted to seize
your freedom again,
take the big game trophy of your photograph
and shatter it,
he shot you.

I felt sad for you mother,
that your life ended so lonely and desolate—
a smokey dancehall
closed after midnight,
where misery glows
in garbage cluttered streets
under dim streetlamps,
where voices cough with sickness
and growl with tragedy,
while young children sit up all night
watching an old Wild West film,
yearning to be the handsome cowboy
who abducts the young girl
from an Apache tribe.

Jaime Chávez

El Camino Viejo

I.

Las ruedas del 68 El Camino
caminan rumbo a Carnuel
piedra antigua de pueblo,
que cuida, sola, al inocente,
será un desconocido,
amigo o visitante
dice un hombre viejo
cantando en la resolana.

II.

Cuantos años han pasado
bajo de mi ventana
el perro se estira al suave sol
que llama la primavera,
los pinos se deshacen
de la última nieve invernal,
y el graznido lejano de gansos
se oye en busca de la playa norteña.

III.

Tu nombre, Bartolo Baca
se asienta en mi garganta
come parado primaveral
brotando del piso del bosque
bajo las hojas y liso palpar,
te veo vagar en el poblado,

cantando canto de viento en puertas
abiertas como olas que golpean la antigua piedra,
Bartolo Baca.

IV.

Maya nació en marzo,
el día seis, si, me acuerdo,
con plumas de perico pendientes de sus trenzas.
M'ija, oyeme llamar tu nombre
de cuevas vacias buscando
a tu nana, Mayatún,
oyeme profundamente en tu corazón
afinando las cuerdas de la existencia.

V.

Hoy un espíritu llama
dentro de la piedra partida de Tijeras,
montaña piedra y canto del rio,
tu pueblo de zoquete constuido
y las vigas, algún día se tetornarán
al polvo de donde has surgido
bajo las espigas de la luz del sol
en la voragine silenciosa del monte.

VI.

Y quien hubiera creido
que llegaría a ser testigo a la cavadura
de los caminos enpolvados de Arenal
del vientre y la matriz del Valle
un sueño desmembrado de santos derrocados
en los campos exhibidos
como piezas de museo.
Un canto decrepito, un alabado quebrado.

VII.

El Camino color sinsontle
aguanta los filerazos del viento,
ya no vuelan las aves de barro
de las jualas metálicas ni los cajones
guardados en pomos mentales
esculpidos de la memoria desolada;
un viento frío se devora el camino
y se forman pétalos de hielo en mi ventana.

(Translation by Juan José Peña)

San Ysidro

San Ysidro watched from the portal.
Dream like pictures
unfold in my eyes
and the tin roofs reflect
the silhouette of my nana
chanting, her fingers lifted
into the air, apache like,
speaking in tongues
painful to the imagination;
the earth trembled.
She seemed so far away,
lured by corn
and other secrets
not of this world.
Her children touched her feet,
pay tribute
in the blood of each seed
and name
that resounds within me.

Windows Of The Heart

I open windows
of the heart
to the survivors
of this journey,
harvesting dreams
in the breath
of an old man
telling stories
about this land,
forged in the flora
of truth,
where santos emerge
smelling of pine
and distant rains
and pueblos carved
in the bone of sunlight.
The passing years
nurture the spirit
in the shadow, ageless.
New visions
born in pain and song
unravel each thread
of light within me.
It is the Day of the Innocent!
I walk cloaked in herbs
drinking from the waters
giving unto the earth;
each season fills
the tracks of this journey
claiming life
among simple things
starved in the hope
and promise
hidden in the land.

Cleofes Vigil

Hermoso Árbol de Piñon

Y soy el Chicano poeta
que vivo en las montañas
trovando canción alegre
gritando viva mi raza.

Aquel monte de piñon
que es mi árbol perferido
de bajo de él me crie
y allí es donde resido.

Ay laderas encantadas
revestidas de piñon
ay montes elevados
donde está mi corazón.

Traciende piñon al viento
tu aroma de buen agrado
en estas laderas vellas
fue donde nací y criado.

Paraiso son mis montañas
que se cambían de color
cuatro veces en el año
las reviste el criador.

Aquellas flores hermosas
que traslucen en los campos
que el sol desde el cielo
las embriaga con sus rayos.

Ay cormena que te chupas
la dulce miel de las flores
en la tierra del encanto
criada por Dios para amores.

En este paraiso vello
vajo el árbol de piñon
encontre a mi amada
y sellamos nuestro amor.

Juan José Peña

Las Vegas

Camino por tus calles
de vez en cuando
y veo las casas
de otro tiempo
y veo los árboles
grandes y fuertes.

Por tus calles
caminó la historia
de mis ancestros
y de mi pasado
y me acuerdo
de tu dureza.

Barrio de gringo
nos tocó a nosotros
y al indio
pero conocí también
los barrios
de la Raza.

La calle cuatro
era bella
con sus prados
y sus árboles
bien cuidados
y la escuela.

Ahí conocí amistad
con los gringos
y con mi raza
y también lo cabrón
que puede ser
mi raza.

Caminaba por la calle
desde ya muy chico
por no estar en casa
hasta el Ford
y a la Case
cerca de la plaza.

En primer año
en la clase de Gallegos
de la escuela
yo me fuí
a buscar a mi abuelo
para ir al Sapelló.

Conferina Bustos
siguió con mi educación
en la Castle Elementary
que parecía castillo
que mi abuelo
construyó.

Nos cambiaron
a la escuela de ladrillo
donde me enamoré
de una peliroja
y donde me pelié
con Garner y su gavilla.

En la noche vendía
el Optic en la cantina,
mocosito y frío,
porque las rutas
eran de gringuitos
y la esquina paga poco.

Me acuerdo de primavera
siempre bella y fresca
y la lluvia de verano
que venía a tiempo
para el sembrado
y para el otoño.

La nieve era alta,
pero ya se fue,
ya no nieva
como antes
y el verdor
ya se fue.

Me acuerdo del Hi Di Ho
donde se compraba chicle
sabor de jabón
y las granadas
que comían las muchachas,
pero no le hallé sabor.

En el callejón
de la casa
se agarraba la raza
al puro jodazo,
y las pachuquitas
de las greñas.

Me acuerdo del Snack and Freeze
y del Spic and Span
y del embarcadero
o los "stock yards"
y los chingazos
y las carreras.

En los deportes rifaban
East y West Las Vegas
al chingazo en el campo
y también la cancha
pero en el fútbol
siempre les ganamos.

Que bellas calles
y que linda tierra
era la de Las Vegas
en la prepa y universidad
jugando y peleando
con ese gran placer.

Pero luego vino la guerra
y todo se cambió;
todo se puso serio
y la lucha se emprendió.
Por todo Las Vegas
El Movimiento se lanzó.

Nos organizamos
y marchamos
protestando la
injusticia
de ser controlados
por los de afuera.

Salimos de Las Vegas
para todos lados
para conocer los compas
de Texas, California,
Illinois y Colorado
para el Movimiento

Y la belleza
se entorpeció
con el rudo
estampido
de la raza
y de la chota.

Cambiamos el Presidente
de la universidad
y el Superintendiente
de las escuelas
con CASO y Raza Unida
y Chicanos Unidos.

Pero luego vino
la grave enfermedad,
la yerba mala
y el polvo blanco
que envenena
a la conciencia.

Y la lucha siguió
desde Las Vegas
al estado
junto con Río Arriba,
Bernalillo y Otero
y los otros estados.

La nación de Aztlán
se organizó
con el Teatro de Norte
y El Grito de Norte
y de muchos otros
todos parecidos.

Boicotiamos la uva
la lechuga y la Coors
y marchamos
en solidardad con América Latina
y la Raza Cósmica.

La Lucha sin fronteras
queríamos empezar
para ser una sola raza
del Bravo a la Patogonia
con la nación de Aztlán
empezando de Las Vegas.

Poco vi a mi pueblo
esos largos días
de lucha y viajar
pero ahí llegaba
solo para descansar
y nutrir el alma.

No veía la belleza,
solo un borrón
al llegar de noche
en carro o el camión
pero tenía ahi mi nido
mi esposa y mi hogar.

Pero la entrega fue total
a la causa de la raza
que la lucha
nunca se iba a acabar
y que la derrota
jamás iría a llegar.

Pero como el tiempo
cambia y todo envejece
asi también nosotros
llegamos a caer
como el cerillo
que no vuelve a encender.

Unos se fueron
a casarse o trabajar
pero Las Vegas seguía
como pueblo radical
con el núcleo
que no quiere descansar.

Le seguimos
hasta la derrota total
en que fuimos abatidos
hasta en lo personal
porque era mucha
la fuerza gubernamental.

Ya no hay marchas
por las calles
y todo regresó
a su estado de antes
del político
y de patrón.

Solo marchan
las fantasmas
de la Raza Unida
con las Gorras Blancas
y los Caballeros de Labor
y la Liga Obrera.

Las calles son bonitas
y llenas de verdor
pero estan cambiando,
y esto da pavor
de ver tanto gringo
que nos esta invandiendo.

Me voy a Las Vegas
y me siento
como extraño
por mi tierra
de ver tanta
gente desconocida.

La casa esta igual,
aunque un poco despintada,
y la calle cuatro
todavía está cuartiada
y los mismos árboles
crecen todavía.

Parece como el viaje
de Don Genaro para Iztlán.
Los veo y me ven,
pero no puedo llegar,
no me dejan ya quedarme,
ni aún a descansar.

Y lo añoro y lo anhelo,
el verdor de mi juventud,
pero no la veo llegar,
porque sin mi hijo
ni mi esposa,
solo encuentro soledad.

Y aún quiero volver,
espero que no
se me haya de negar,
vivir en mi casa
y en la tierra
y mi historia ancestral.

Ando por fuera
y no me gusta
esta sociedad
que va ya de caída
y no sabe respetar
el anhelo de la tierra.

Lorenzo Valdez

Viernes Santo
(Un hombre muerto
esperando la resurrección)

Un quebranto de dolor
lágrimas cristalinas un viernes santo
el salamandra anciano bajo agua clara
ondulando entre tela musgosa, gris verde
las ranas suenan matraca
el cuervo negro responde en la distancia
viento, el pito chifla, un rayo de luz brillante

Imagenes de una tranquilidad espejosa, bailan
en filo de agua y sol reluciente
retratos y sentimientos de los antepasados, raíces
como entrañas, enredados en un baile inmobil

Una contemplación del vientre del momento
ese momento que pasa redepente y dura horas, días
meses, y años
promesa de cariños, campos verdes, y las voces de niños

El vientecito de semana santa llega frío por la espalda
se arriza el espejo sobre el agua
los imagenes deshilándose en las orillas de las olas

Sólo el viento queda, chiflando triste
tiñieblas por la tarde

E.A. Mares

Once A Man Knew His Name

(dedicated to the memory of Popé,
great leader of the Pueblo Revolt, 1680)

My name was ripe with summer,
a cornucopia overflowing with food
for the Pueblos.
My name was the summer
and my name
gathered together the life giving maize,
the ripe squash, beans, and chile
that fed the people of Oke Oweenge
and all the Pueblos along the Rio Grande.

As a child
I ran along the banks of the river
and nibbled on the sweet grass that grew there.
I knew the blue grama, the little blue stem,
camomile, and the sunflowers,
the rainbow colors of the earth.

As a child
I learned the stories of the Tewa.
We came from beneath the Sandy Place Lake.
Our first mother was Blue Corn Woman,
the Summer Mother.
And our first mother was White Corn Maiden,
the Winter Mother.

All is sacred in our world:
Shimmering Mountain to the north.
Obsidian Covered Mountain to the west.
Turtle Mountain to the south.
Stone Man Mountain to the east.

All the hills are sacred.
All the shrines are sacred.
All the plazas are sacred.
All the dances in the plazas.
All the directions and their colors.
All, all are sacred for the Pueblo
the Spanish called San Juan.

The Spanish said our spirits were devils,
their faith the one true faith.
In the name of God, they destroyed our kivas.
In the name of God, they burned our katchinas.
In the name of God, they forbade our dances.
In the name of God, they flogged our caciques.
They took our Tewa names away.
Our mouths filled with the dust of our loss.

As a young man
I knew all the colors of life.
I followed blue to the north
and my authority returned to me.

I followed red to the south,
yellow to the west,
white to the east,
and my authority returned to me.

I visited the sacred hills and mountains.
I knew the Summer People.
I knew the Winter People.
And I knew we were one.
I knew my own name
and I was with the people.
I knew my own name.
My authority returned to me.

Then the Spanish took me.
They flogged me
but they could not take away my name.
My authority returned to me.

At Taos Pueblo, in the kiva,
I invoked the highest spirits to guide me.
I knew my name
and my authority returned to me.

In the kiva at Taos Pueblo,
I invoked P'ose Yemu,
he who scatters the mist before him,
and my authority returned to me.

Then the war leaders came to me.
I sent forth the runners
with the knotted cords
to the two dozen Pueblos,
to the six different languages,
to all the directions and their colors
from Taos to the Hopi villages.

When the time came
and the last knot unravelled,
we struck everywhere and all at once.
We raked a fire across the sun.

We let those Spaniards go
who had lived with us in peace.
We drove the rest away.
We let them all go.

When they came with an army
marching towards Santa Fe,
the Rio Grande rose
and their soldiers were scattered
with the mist.

We broke their arrogance
like bits of dry straw.
We drove them away.
We let them all go.

They came back
a better people
to become our compadres, our comadres,
as the people of all colors
come back together
and we are one.
We shine with the brilliance of stars.

I knew my own name.
Within and around the earth,
within and around the hills,
within and around the mountains,
my authority returned to me.

I knew my own name.
I knew my own name.
I knew my own name.

Discourse of the Severed Head
of Joaquín Murieta

(excerpt from the play, **The Ballad of Joaquín Murieta,**
first performed by La Compañía del Teatro de Albuquerque)

From the waters of my mother's womb
I fell swiftly into time.
I walked the land and came to know
The great beasts of the earth
And also the lizard scurrying across sandstone,
The eagle and hawk in the sky,
And always the presence of the buzzard.

Again, I fell into the murky waters,
My head severed like a ripe fruit
Torn from a tree in full bloom,
To be dropped here in this cold glass jar.

My head swirls in this filthy tomb.
I see the bleary eyed drunkards at dawn.
I weep tears unseen in these waters
As I see myself in the eyes of drunkards.
I reach out with their leaden arms.
I stumble about on their uncertain legs.

By the time I was twenty, I could ride a horse
As well as a Comanche. My head thrown back,
My jaw open, I sucked in the wind
Until my lungs took on a wild ecstasy.
Now only dark waters flow in my mouth
And out again to this cloudy sea.

With Carmelita I came to California
To work the mines and the land.
There I found men more beasts than men.
Their blows drove me to the deep canyon
Where all rivers gathered and waited for me.
Now only dark waters flow into my mouth
And out again to this glass bound sea.

My head turns and turns in this filthy jar.
I see the bleary eyed drunkards at dawn.
Once my eyes caught the sun's fire
Burning through pine on a mountain ridge.
When Carmelita laughed, leaves shimmered
And birds took flight in a fluttering of wings.

Driven to the deep canyon,
I became a wild mustang,
My hooves slashing through the California night,
My red-rimmed eyes firing the unerring bullets
Into the grim haters of life.

Thus I came to know the grim haters of life
Who drove me from the land and the mines,
The grim haters of life who took my severed head
And let it fall like some broken bird
Into this miserable jar where it circles
Round and round through the dark and moldy sea.

Demetria Martinez

An El Paso Street by Night

Bronco Ballroom
Black Garter Lounge
Bueno Video
Wetbacks who scrounge
through two rusty trollies
laid up on the tracks,
touch this city's wet cheek,
you'll never go back.

Benzine dreams,
sweet sewage air,
blue motel sinkholes
choked with blonde hair,
in the next room a man
with another man's wife,
on this side of the border
she will recast her life.

She ends daylight savings,
turns back the hands,
an extra hour to fake
with this porcelain man,
Help Wanted, he promised,
then took her backstage,
a Juarez extra scrubs sinks
at slavery wage.

Crossing Over

"...a sanctimonious band of renegades
who advocate open violation of the law"

> —Southwest Regional Commissioner for the
> U.S. Dept. of Justice, Immigration and Naturali-
> zation Service on the sanctuary movement.
> (*Albuquerque Journal*)

Somebody threw a baby
into the Rio Grande.

We scrub the scum off him
in the back of a station wagon
as we leave El Paso.
We tuck him, sleeping,
in a picnic basket
as we near the check point.
Officers see our fishing rods
and nod us through.
At midnight south of Albuquerque
we invent a name, a date of birth,
singing rock-a-bye-baby in English,
burying the placenta of his past.

2.

When grandma left the Catholic Church
and joined Assemblies of God,
they dipped her in the Rio Grande,
she stood up and cried.

Grandma, grandma, the river's not
the same. Sweet jesus
got deported, this baby
bruised and hungry,
my nipples red and pained.

3.

Who's throwing babies
in the river?
What bastard
signs the release?

Who will break
the bastard's brains
and let this baby
keep his name?

Catherine Vallejos Bartlett

Ojo Caliente

for Pat Mora

The story goes that,
while her husband slept,
she lay on the warm desert sand
with another
and wove healing songs
around his heart.

In return,
the man who came
with a tear rolling down his cheek

> cradled her in his arms
> offered her precious metals
> burned her image onto his soul

before he returned to Blue Mountain
before she curled with her husband
again in the desert dawn.

(He did not understand that she meant to carve out his
   heart.)

On calm mornings,
while her husband tended the village store,
she chanted
and danced
and prayed for her lover's return,
though not before she carefully hid

blinding silver and gold
        underneath the mattress
and learned to stare straight ahead
past the mumblings of village women.

Her husband was at first too tired to notice
her longing for red prickly pear and
rocking,
rocking,
curves of her body swaying
with quiet desert rhythms.

Slowly
he grew suspicious
when her body trembled
and her eyes shone gold
in the still nights
without his touch.

She grew careless.
He followed her one night
into the waiting arms
of a Blue Mountain man
and desert,
tears,
hot green
and
dripping,
dripping,
onto the hard earthen floor.

Later,
alone together,
he lifted the mattress,
blinding both by white and gold light.
His gifts are rare, he spat.
I told you nothing was good without me.

She wept,
beat her chest,
begged forgiveness.
I want what he has, he demanded.
She wanted her husband.

(He did not understand that she wanted to live.)

Days spent weaving
black dress from cobwebs,
studded with silver moon, gold stars
brought them
wordless
loveless
to a man from Blue Mountain,
hands cupped and full,
waiting.

She lied.
He found her husand
behind a rock
and in place of the Blue Mountain man
only
water
blood-warm and acrid
bubbled up at them,
engulfing her breasts,
laughing...
                    ...so the story goes.

Leroy V. Quintana

1st Day, 101st Airborne, Phan Rang, Viet Nam!

(from Interrogations, Viet Nam Poetry)

The wounded back from the hospital
readying their rucksacks to return to the line
Line doggies coming out of the bush
the lost year done
Worn rosaries around their necks
Christ nailed to a tree
A man prayed so out there
So many trees out there
So many nails

Restaurant

A restaurant in Munich
Something in the summer afternoon—
the sadness of a day in fall
The sadness of these men who became men
in a war the year I was born
These the men who bore weapons of steel
blue as their eyes for the fatherland
Eyes that stalked men, perhaps my uncles
in the sights of their rifles
They laugh manly laughs, tease the homely waitress,
raise tall glasses of beer golden as their hair
Somewhere in this country there stood a bridge,
was dynamited
Grandfather's nephew broken as the good bread
of this noon

Doña Marina

There was always a sadness in the joy
of Doña Marina's visit. She was grandma's friend,
the vecina from across the street
Over coffee they would mention the weather,
a death on our side of town
but always the talk turned to their sons
A picture of grandma's son on the wall behind her
the Stars and Stripes waving proudly in the background
her eyes moist as she mocked MacArthur in Spanish
It was easy for him to say he would return
He was a general and never suffered
They'd sit for a while in silence, console one another
The mothers Pedro Infante sang about in that sad song
about a young man, sad that he must leave his mother
entrusting her to la Virgen de Guadalupe
as he goes off to prove he too can die for his country
Doña Marina's son never knew combat
Came home one summer on leave from Basic Training
impressed us doing chinups on his front porch
and just as quickly gone and Doña Marina always
after that telling grandma about the sparrows playing
on the ledge of the hospital window the day he died

Bomber Pilot

He had been a bomber pilot in his war
the year I was born
and now was accompanying me to mine
as far as Seattle
From there his vacation in Alaska to hunt bear
He had known fear
and the fear of being afraid that first time
under fire. One thing
he kindly told me you'll come to know
when that time comes
You think you will be the only one
but always
there will be someone who is so much more afraid

Enriqueta L. Vasquez

Grito of Hope

You, woman in the streets;
    cool dude with el 'toke,'
        eduquense,
        learn to live again,
        learn to care,
            por tu gente
            los necesitamos;

You, the one in the big wheels,
    the corbata,
        el sute,
            y todo;
    the one that 'made it'
        pa' donde vas?
        no te olvides de donde vienes,
            tu gente,
            la lucha,
                te llama

And you, the nervous one,
    the one that cooks, cleans la casa
    and raises the chiquitos;
        anda, relax, go to the community
        meetings,
            take the family
            pay attention,
            con tu corazón tan grande
            stake a claim, in the future;

Y usted, the madre viejita,
   with the faded gold star still
           hanging in your window,
           a folded flag in your trunk;
  Ya basta de suspirar;
     anime la familia,
        you can lead the way,
        by what you say;
  Tell the anxious youth
     what pain, sorrow and war is about,
     usted bien lo sabe;

El coro de voices rise;
  the past con banderas de independencias,
  revolutions y sangre,
  wars of the world,
     with aaaee bombs de muerte,
     Vietnams, in agents of orange;

and the whispers of the past become
  gritos of sorrow,
     rage.......and hope;
      Si, hope, tambien,
      porque we must always have that,
  Hope that there is a better way,
     the one that says that we do not
     have to
       destroy the world in order to
       save it.

Marcella Aguilar-Henson

Womanhood

Subjected to the
everyday strain
    of living
Tears of
    joy and pain
have marked
    your way

Struggling to live
    your life
the way you want to
and yet
    so afraid
    of being judged
    by a world
    that doesn't
        understand.

TRAPPED
in a pre-fabricated
mold
    of womanhood
TOLD
by an imposing

  Society

who and what to be

    silently
    you fight
    for the right

    to
    just be

Cecilio García-Camarillo

El Ex-Pinto Todo Contento

wáchalo
here he comes
todo contento
con una sonrisa de oreja a oreja
que parece una rebanada de sandía

viene todo contento
wáchalo
con su chuco walk
los brazos swinging in rhythm
to a subconscious polka

here he comes
wáchalo
por la isleta en el southwest valley
en su barrio
vacilando in his cosmology
y tirándole good vibes
a las barrio queens
with indian faces
and tight jeans
that cruise by

mira
wáchale
los tatoos de aquellas que trai el bato
en el brazo derecho
en technicolor y toda la cosa
trai a la virgen de guadalupe
y en el izquierdo
a la fregada
wáchale
pero cúrate bién

el ex-pinto trai a la gran huesuda
la muerte que se wachea
bién proud and defiant
and she's holding una víbora de bastón

y te das cuenta
que los tatoos
pos they're covering
the needle tracks of the wasteland
where he lost his self-respect
me entiendes como

and the purple scar that's shaped
like a new moon
allí detrás de la oreja izquierda
pos allí fué donde le descargó
el flashlight
that fatal night
an overanxious rookie cop

y de allí lo descontaron pa la pinta
wounded y todo el pedo
pero ay viene ahora wáchalo
todo contento
sporting an emiliano zapata bigote
above the never-ending chorro
of good-hearted carcajadas

nació en el barrio
sufrió en el barrio
torció en el barrio
y aquí viene otra vez
wáchalo
todo contento

pero cúrate como mira
wáchale como usa los ojos
simón que sí
ay está la movida y transformación
el bato mira con ojos concientizados
porque en la pinta
se le prendió el foco
como hombrecito sin miedo
se agarró a chingazos con la realidad
de su vida
y platicó con prisioneros políticos
y leó del movimiento chicano
y el camarada snapped forever

y ora ay viene
wáchalo
todo contento
por la isleta
saludando paca y paya
feeling the sun darkening his skin

he kicks a beer can
a few times
with his mexican guaraches
y se ríe con ojos concientizados

wáchalo
ta en su barrio
donde hay que vivir y trabajar

wáchalo como ahora trai hambre
so he goes into a restaurant
and sits by the window
and orders menudo

wáchalo
como mira pa fuera
scanning his barrio que conoce tan bién
knowing onde stá el desmadre
y la fantasía loca
wáchale
como mira el mundo

ta todo contento
el ex-pinto
ta todo contento
por estar libre con ojos concientizados

José Luis Soto

Esta Lluvia Que Cae Sobre El Mar
a Georgette

importará el instante
el rumor persistente del vuelo del insecto
lo que ve la paloma
esa orquesta nocturna de tres gatos pardos
los rincones del mueble donde se anida el polvo
                            el resorte de la
memoria los poemas
las doce campanadas del reloj
la pasión que se eleva como la cresta de la ola
esta lluvia que cae sobre el mar
importará
      mujer
la lluvia interminable que cae sobre el mar

Recuento

ahogándote de tanta luz, sabes que morirás sin haber
      alcanzado la otra orilla y que te maldirán el río, el árbol
como último recurso, esperarás una muchacha con
      un misterio escondido bajo el párpado y el corazón
      entre los muslos tibios
pero a los treintacinco flaco y miope, arcilla
      solamente, algo como un fastidio te rendirá ante el ocio
entonces cerrarás la puerta tirarás la llave, para
      entregarte atado y sin recuerdos

José Montoya

La Yarda De La Escuelita

La escuelita al pie del monte
Es chica, así es que
Los niños vienen en varios tamaños,
Unos pequeños y ya en el libro ocho
Otros altos, galgos
Y apenas en el tercero.

Alrededor de la mestra
Acurrucados de miedo—como pollitos—
Se amontonan los del baby room
Asustados desde Septiembre,
Y asi permaneceran hasta Junio
Cuando pasen al libro primero.

La escuelita al pie del monte
Porque esta en las sierras
Que dan tan poco
Los niños se visten p'al frio
No pa' verse bien
Y el ropaje corre desde
Botas mucho muy grandes
A túnicos hechos a mano
Que han venido pasando
Desde cuando de hermana a hermana
Así que las medidas
Son de por ahí del medio.

Y la mestra

Estolido monumento de seguridad—
Cambia su compostura
Mil veces al día—pa' cada mal
Un genio negro, pa' cada bien,
Una sonrisa y un aprecio.

Y cuando no está segura
Lo esconde bien—como cuando
Paso lo de Rosendo—acongojado
Rosendo, con las cejas fruncidas
De miedo—esperando lo peor
Por ver dejado la pelota
Salirse del cerco—Ay, po'recito
Mu'chito—y el que nunca
Se mete en males y por que
No podría haber sido uno
De aquellos otros canallas
El que dejo salir esa maldita pelota?

Así es que ahora la mestra
Se encuentra incierta
Y los niños que se le prenden
De la cintura
Ni cuenta se dan
Y ya para entonces
Los traviesos le llaman
La atención
Porque por allá por los escusados
Cerca de los pinavetes
Les andan abajando los bloomes
A unas mu'chitas que pretenden
Escandalo!

            "Boys! Boys!"

Y en lo que la mestra trata
Con ese cuento de nunca acabar
Rosendo brinca el cerco
Sobre la bola—No me vido! No me vido!

Y entre regañadas, la Miss Chavez
Da gracias a Dios y chequea
Su pulsera y el chico
Del libro seis que ha andado
Brincando con anticipación
Porque el es el que suena la campana
Y ha estado esperando
Con mil ansias esa
Momentosa ocasión desde que
Se empezó el resés
Ahora al fin, recive sus ordenes—
La campana!

Y al instante lo domina
Un ataque espasmoso
Y con las dos manos
Suena y brinca
Brinca y suena!

Y el sonido repicante suelta
Una imploción que ahoga
El budicio
Y de todas partes de la yarda
Convergen los niños a matacaballo
Riendo y gritando
Gritando y unos llorando
Trompesandose y puchando,
Acabando con todo.

Unos traen flores
Y puños de piñon
Y otros el bate y la pelota

Y los mas grandes, con calma
Apagan bachas de Golden Grain
Y escupen ploga—los mas
Verdes con caras verdes
Y los otros carcajeando.

Y en la liña la mestra
Organiza sus columnas

    Boys there!
    Girls here!

Tony, get rid of that frog!
"Ora lo veras cuando mire
A tu mom!"

Limpiense el soquete
Before you come in!

Y todos en filas chuecas
Pasan pa' dentro
Y antes de que
Se cierre la puerta
Llegan otros dos que andaban
Por aya correteando
La llegua
De Don Sosten y apenas
Entran a tiempo

Y se cierra la puerta
Y descansa la yarda
De la escuelita de la sierra—
Gentil cuna de los vicios
Y de la virtú—
Descansa, y al rato
Se empiezan a oir los sonidos
De aquel alrededor serreño
El chiripío de los chontes
Los lamentos de las tortolitas
Y los alaridos de una cabra.

Y por alla por la placita
Ladra un perro
Y el ruidoso trigal
Al otro lado del cerco
Suelta un suspiro
De compasión—O será
De alivio—Quien sabe?—pero canta
El silencio al pie del monte.

La Jefita

When I remember the campos
   Y las noches and the sounds
Of those nights en carpas o
Bagones I remember my jefita's
   Palote
   Clik-Clok; clik-clak-clok
   Y su tocesita.

(I swear she never slept!)

Reluctant awakenings a la media
Noche y la luz prendida.

   PRRRRRRRRINNNNGGGGGG!

A noisy chorro missing the
Basín.

Que horas son, 'ama?
Es tarde me hijito. Cover up
Your little brothers.
Y yo con pena but too sleepy,

   Go to bed little mother!

A maternal reply mingled with
The hissing of the hot planchas
Y los frijoles de la hoya
Boiling musically dando segunda
A los ruidos nocturnos and
The snores of the old man

Lulling sounds y los perros

Ladrando—then the familiar
Hallucinations just before sleep.

And my jefita was no more.

But by then it was time to get Up!

My old man had a chiflidito
That irritated the world to
Wakefulness.

Wheeeeeet! Wheeeeeet!

Arriba, cabrones chavalos,
Huevones!

Y todavia la pinche
Noche oscura

Y la jefita slapping tortillas.

Prieta! Help with the lonches!
Caliéntale agua a tu 'apa!

(Me la rayo ese! My jefita never slept!)

Y en el fil, pulling her cien
Libras de algoda se sonreía
Mi jefe y decía,

That woman—she only complains
in her sleep.

Robert Gallegos

Rain Dream

in a rain dream
i smell the scent of earth
cold water to drink
from lips of clay

there was this acoma olla
that you sipped from
and the waterfalls' fingers
held your body

i saw the mirage of a river
come flowing through the window
and the sudden kiss you gave me
moved like a flash flood in the desert
only to drown us
in each others arms
and to carry us back
to an ancient sea

Letter To Vanessa

dearest vanessa
it's a twilight dream
in which we love
forward with our heads
pointed toward the sangre de cristos
to the east and through a window
where we'll wake to see ansel adams'
moonrise, hernandez, new mexico

For My Lover's Tears

your bright feathers fall to the floor
and thirsting flesh is waiting for a breath
i kiss your lips and then your breasts
my tongue deliberately takes its time
to find coral in a sea of gems

in a smolder
we hold each other
until the circulation of blood
has completed its meandering trek

i sleep but it seems brief
and through a maze of dreams
its always the cry of la llorona
calling her lost children
that echos off the darkness
of the night

when the veil is lifted
the dawn comes with a new song
like today when i found you weeping
tears of morning dew

Desire

for now
desire is a dust devil
that cuts through the desert
leaving a trail of bleached bones
scattered across the painted bed
and the taste of your dark skin
stays on my tongue
hours after you're gone

i'm hoping that implosive whirls of want
will bring you to my arms
when your hunger
for the flesh
is what wakes you most

El Hermano Mayor

Davíd Fernández

Antenoche, ya a las dos de la mañana, estaba yo leyendo el libro de Pizarro, *Descubrimiento y Conquista de los Reinos del Perú,* y en haber leído de la manera perfidiosa y traicionera en que fue tirado al suelo la gloriosa vida de los Incas, me pegó una agitación que no se quitaba, porque me pareció claramente que lo que pasó a esa noble gente es también lo que ha pasado a nosotros aquí en el Norte de Nuevo Méjico.

No pude leer mas. Salí de casa y caminé por el lado del Río Pueblo, con mis oídos llenos del sueño de los aguas corrientes y con mi mente llena de pensamientos inquietos, y con mi corazón pesado por la pena que ha sufrido la gente natural del mundo.

Allí me senté en el banco del río, entremedio de la obscuridad de medianoche y el gran soñida de los aguas benditos de nuestro país, un sonido que llevaba mis pensamientos al gran mar de la conciencia.

Rolé un cigaro y fume por un rato, notando a las cenizas vivas volando por unos segundos hasta que se extinguieron en las tinieblas de la noche.

Pero mi visión interior veía la calamidad del fin de Tenochtitlán Azteca, destruido por la traición de la Malinche y la debilidad de Moctezuma; y el asesinato del Inca Atahualpa; y la violación de nuestra Madre Tierra aquí en el Norte.

Pensé de las palabras, "Nuevo Méjico, hasta cuando duraran sus descon-
suelos, con sus hijos tirados en los suelos, y el extranjero mandando."

Las estrellas volaron por los cielos, y la luna era un cimitar dorado que
cortaba la noche negra, hasta se dividió el horizonte y se abajó atras de los
volcanes al occidente.

Y de repente noté que algo venía a mi rumbo, desde ese grande cortada en
el firmamente, muy a lo lejos, pero acercandose rapidamente. Yo ví al
momento que era la figura de una persona, moviendo con pasos largos, y que
me acercaba derechamente. Y en unos pocos minutos estaba allí, en frente
de mi. Y me hablo.

"Saludes, hermano Davíd, quiero hablar contigo." Le respondí
naturalmente, "Pues, por favor, sientese conmigo. Aunque me hace que te
conozco, digame quien eres y de donde vienes."

"Me llamo Luz de Todosantos, y vengo de donde estoy hasta donde me
llaman las animas oprimidas. Tengo prisa ahora mismo porque viene mucha
obscuridad sobre el mundo, pero quiero hablarle de lo que ha pasado a tu
gente y a tu país. Voy hablarte de lo que han perdido y de lo que todavia
tienen para poder ganar mucho mas. Escucheme bien, y mas tarde volveré
para discutir mas. Por mientras, puedes difusir este mensaje a tus compañeros. Es importante.

"Entiende primero que a cada civilización llega su fin, sea la gloria de
Roma o el Sol de Tenochtitlán, o la tecnocracia de America. El mas grande
Imperio tiene que caer en algún día. Y después del caido se empieza todo de
vuelta. En este mundo ya han existido centenares de imperios, y se ha
acabado el mundo ya varias veces. La prueba esta por dondequiera. Al poco
tiempo acabará este ciclo de civilización, y se necesitará alguna gente buena
para reconstruirlo de nuevo.

"Ustedes tenían una vida muy bonita y especial, aquí en el Norte. Tus
antepasados eran muy valientes y muy industriosos para poder establecer la
vida del Norte. Los actos violentos cuando primero choquearon los
Españoles y los Indios fueron recompensados por el amistad que creció
entre los dos poblaciones durante los siglos siguientes. De las cenizas de
destrucción de un mundo creció otro mundo.

"Ustedes tenían sus tierras en forma de los mercedes. Sus aguas en las
acequias. Su religión, su creencia especial en Dios. Yo mismo establecí el

orden de los Hermanos de Luz, que les mantuvo en vida pura y simple. Entendían la verdad que la tierra del mundo les daba vida, les sostenía, y les aceptaba después de la muerte. Conocían bien quien eran, cada uno, y a cada otro. Era una vida temporalmente dura, pero en mis ojos también era una vida pura y fina. Sin tener riquezas materiales como mucho oro, tu gente tenía una moda de vida muy gloriosa.

"Las tierras y las mercedes se perdieron a los ladrones y a los abogados. Las aguas en las acequias solamente te queden como recurso natural propio, y valemas que los protegen y que los preservan, porque los aguas son forma material del espíritu. El Hermandad todavia existe en algunos lugares donde se halla la propria Fé. Su lenguaje esta en peligro de perder. Y los extranjeros están en punto de mandar completamente. Todo esto es el malo.

"Lo bueno es esto: Tienen el Espíritu. Tienen los aguas. Tienen todavia el nucleo de la Hermandad. Cuando se acaba esta civilización ustedes van a ser escogidos para ayudar en formar un mundo mejor. Ya tienen la estructura, y las tradiciones necesarias, que vienen de tres y cuatro siglos pasados.

"Piensan bien en estas cosas. Hablo seriamente. Necesitan de tirar los envidiosos, los traicioneros, los que ya no tienen ninguna Fé. Por todo lo que existe hay razón. La razón de la existencia de la gente del Norte es simplemente para ayudar la salvación del mundo.

"Yo los protejo y les ayudaré. No mas quiero que me reconocen quien soy—lo quien verdaderamente soy: Luz Todosantos, el Hermano Mayor del Hermandad Cósmico de la Luz. Y créeme cuando te digo que soy mas poderoso que el "Big Brother" de la tecnocracia de 1984, que pronto se va caer. Pero: Mantengase la Fé. Te digo y es dicho.

"Bueno. Ya tengo que ir. Vendré pa atrás al rato. Y ya vete pa la casa, Davíd. Es la hora de las brujas. Allí te veo ahorita."

A Romeo and Juliet Story in Early New Mexico

Fray Angelico Chavez

Santa Fe in 1733 was a very old town already, a small cluster of low adobe houses around a plaza and the much taller church; but the great mountain behind it lent it considerable impressiveness both winter and summer. Albuquerque was but a quarter of a century old, hence much smaller as to the number of dwellings and the size of the church; in summer it was almost lost among the cottonwoods on the flat riverbank, but the sharp outline of the high range to the east was near enough as to give it character also. Traffic between the two settlements was of the barest, due chiefly to primitive modes of travel over difficult winding trails. Yet both came close together in that year to provide the scenes for a real-life drama having the more pleasant features of Shakespeare's *Romeo and Juliet*—and some of the heart tragedy, too, even if there were no deaths or carnage to mar or prevent a happy ending.

It was the old story of a boy and a girl in love hounded by parental disapproval, the plot found in folklore and written classics all over the world. We owe the New Mexico version, however, not to some professional or amateur purveyor of romances who wished to regale posterity with a delectable scandal, but to a court clerk down in Mexico City who sandwiched the incident, as a case in point, between dry and drawn-out legal proceedings regarding ecclesiastical jurisdiction. Other ancient archives from Sevilla, Mexico City, and Santa Fe, help us in identifying the chief persons of the play. Manuel Armijo and Francisca Baca were the lovers. Their romance was as tender as that of the Veronese young couple, and they were just as handsome and sweet in each other's eyes, no matter how they might have actually looked. The dun adobe walls and rough vigas of Santa Fe and Albuquerque were a far cry from southern Europe's bright-tiled roofs and graceful colonnades, but the great Sangre de Cristo and Sandia ranges made marvelous backdrops nevertheless.The elder Bacas and Armijos, with knives stuck in their sashes under homespun capes and leering at each other from under low-crowned wide sombreros, were the silken-hosed,swordwielding gentry of other times and other lands.

Why Francisca Baca's family objected to the match is easy to see and important to know. The girl's parents are singled out first because the Armijos are not recorded as having interfered. It was a matter of family pride among the Bacas who claimed direct descent from a First Conquistador; for Don Antonio Baca, a captain in the local militia, prided himself in being the great-great-grandson of the original Baca, Don Cristóval Baca, who had come to New Mexico in 1600. He furthermore believed himself to be, though mistakenly, a descendant of the already legendary Nuñes Cabeza de Vaca. Antonio's wife, Doña María de Aragón, was relatively a newcomer who had arrived with her parents in 1693 at the time of the Reconquest of New Mexico by Don Diego de Vargas; this lent luster to her own family of the Aragón and Ortiz clan, over and above the important fact that, like the Baca, it passed for pure Spanish, although previously established in the Valley of Mexico for some generations.

The Armijos, on the other hand, were not only late-comers, having arrived fully six months after the glorious retaking of Santa Fe from the Indians by Governor de Vargas, but they very casually admitted that they were mestizos from Zacatecas. Of the four grown sons who had come with their parents, Antonio Durán de Armijo was the only surgeon in *"El Reyno de la Nueva México"* at the time and for many years to come, and was very dexterous with the pen as well as with the scalpel, quite an envious distinction in a crude little world of cattlemen and of part-time militiamen who could not sign their names for the most part. But at the time of this story neither Antonio Armijo nor his brothers José and Marcos had any son of marriageable age by the name of Manuel. At least there is none on record. The fourth brother, however, Vicente Durán de Armijo, had not only one but three sons with the same name: Manuel *el Primero*, Manuel *el Segundo*, and Manuel *el Tercero*. So the odds are three to nothing that Vicente was the father of our hero. The first Manuel had been sent as a boy to Guadalupe del Paso in order to learn a trade as a tailor's apprentice, and there, it appears, he married and established himself. The second Manuel married a Lucero de Godoy girl in Santa Fe (a year after our story), and later moved down to Albuquerque to fill that lower part of the Rio Grande valley with Armijos. Then it must be Manuel III who was stirring up the coals of trouble in the exclusive Baca hearth.

But if Don Antonio Baca objected to Armijos in general, he had greater reason for refusing to have Manuel Armijo for his son-in-law. The boy's mother was a María de Apodaca who had been born in a pueblo of an unknown Tewa father and a Spanish or part-Spanish girl who had been captured by the Indians in the Great Rebellion of 1680. Moreover, María's unfortunate mother, after she had been rescued with her child by the conquering De Vargas forces twelve long years after, later married the Governor's Negro drummer. The fact that Manuel Armijo's mother was a Negro's step-child did not better his chances at all. But now to Manuel and Francisca.

In early Spanish civil and church law, when a youth and a maiden fell in love but the latter's family refused to give her hand in marriage, the boy could appeal to the courts and have the girl deposited in a neutral home for some time, where she was supposed to make up her own mind without the interference of relatives on either side. Any such interference brought on the penalty of excommunication on those breaking the law. Manuel Armijo knew his law, at least in this regard, and better than his foes had bargained for. When he appeared before the Lord Vicar and Ecclesiastical Judge to plead his case, he took along two witnesses, an itinerant shoemaker and a farm laborer from the Río Abajo district who happened to be in town. These "friends to Romeo" were to prove invaluable aids in overcoming the many obstacles thrown in Manuel's path by the very court which ought to have been an unbiased arbiter.

Don José de Bustamante y Tagle was the Vicar at this time. As the legal person of the Bishop of Durango twelve hundred miles away, and as a member of the late Governor's family, his sway in Santa Fe was considerable. This priest was an intimate friend of Don Antonio Baca. What is more, two of Don Antonio's brothers had married into the Bustamante social group, and a first cousin of his was the wife of the prominent Captain and merchant, Don Nicolás Ortiz, whose aunt was Don Antonio's mother-in-law. All in all, it was a welter of affinities and consanguinities in higher circles that formed a formidable bastion between poor Manuel Armijo and Francisca Baca. Of necessity an integral part of this barrier, the Vicar could not approve of such a marriage. But here he was confronted by the young swain himself and his two witnesses in due legal form. It may be that he tried to dissuade Armijo from his purpose, or offered him a bribe to leave the north country and join his brother at Guadalupe del Paso. That sort of thing has been tried before, and ever shall be. At any rate, Armijo remained resolute, and the Vicar had no other choice than to carry out the law, although with some reservations that were already ticking in his mind.

First, he interviewed Francisca Baca privately, but she proved just as headstrong as her lover. This vain attempt over, he had her solemnly conducted to the home of a certain Don José Reaño y Tagle. There she was to think seriously upon the matter and, after weighing the disadvantages following a marriage with Armijo, return a negative answer. But her reply was still most affirmative when she was questioned some time later. Then the anger of Santa Fe's society broke loose upon her little head. Her uncle and cousins, not to mention her local aunts came secretly to the house, despite the threat of excommunication, and tried to dissuade her from marrying Armijo. Her own father threatened to kill her with his own sword. Young blades among her relations were ready to do away with Armijo himself. Even the Vicar, avoiding the church penalty by appearing personally, sent her a message. Even if she were pregnant, it said, everything could be taken care of nicely and quietly. Now was the time for sorely beset Francisca, had she ever read Shakespeare, to lean out of the window and cry:

"O Romeo,Romeo! wherefore art thou Romeo?
"Deny thy father and refuse thy name."

Crazed finally by these incessant visits and threats which gave her no rest, or, what is more likely, to gain some respite for her tired mind, Francisca bowed at last to her kinsfolk's wishes; only then was she taken home from the Reaño residence which to her had become a madhouse. Really, it had not been a "neutral home." Don José Reaño was also a Bustamante on his mother's side. His wife was a Roybal, another family of that close-knit society; her brother Mateo was already engaged to Francisca's sister Gregoria; she was, moreover, a sister of the Vicar who had preceded Bustamante and who was to succeed him when all this trouble was over. Both Reaño and his wife had given Francisca no rest in the intervals left her by her more immediate relatives. In the end, it all had turned out into a pitched battle between the Spanish-born Bustamantes of the mountains of Santander and a lone youth from the hills of Santa Fe with more Indian than Spanish blood in his lovelorn heart. And Spain had won, apparently, forgetting for the nonce that all her songs and tales give true love the victory in the end.

Back in her father's house, Francisca recanted, to her credit and our admiration. Don Antonio Baca began fuming anew, and this time resorted to a different strategy. He put his daughter on one of his best horses and sent her under armed escort to Albuquerque "twenty-four leagues away," a tremendous distance in those days of travel by horse or ox-drawn *carreta*. She was to be deposited in the home of her aunt, Doña Josefa Baca, who owned a prosperous hacienda at Pajarito.

How often did not Francisca look back during that first day's journey, as the horses trudged down the dusty road towards La Ciénaga under a bright July sun, blended in the distance with the ochre earth of which they were made. The last to fade away was the great adobe Parroquia of St Francis which she had always imagined as the biggest building on earth; she had not been baptized in it since it was not finished until five years after her birth, and she had not been born in Santa Fe anyway, but she had often dreamed of kneeling at its high altar blazing with candles, and her Manuel at her side placing the ring on her finger and pouring the *arras* into her open palms. Only the great blue and green mountain, called the Sierra Madre in those days, remained in sight all day long, seeming to raise herself even higher the further away she rode, as if telling her like a fond mother that she would not forget.

But as the horses began picking their painful way down the black volcanic boulders of La Bajada, the Sierra Madre regretfully turned away and out of sight, and the Jémez range appeared in front, all purple in the glory of the crimson sunset behind it; but to Francisca that hue and the rough contour of the ridges were more like the sad purple cloth thrown over the images of saints from Passion Week until Good Friday. It was dark when they reached the pueblo of Santo Domingo; there the party spent the night in the houses of the Alcalde Mayor, the only Spanish home in the entire district. Next morning they started out again along the lush groves of the Río del Norte, a monotonous but easier trip now that the familiar landmarks were well out of sight. At noon they stopped to rest at the post of Bernalillo, her parent's hometown where she herself had been born almost twenty-one years before, but she did not remember the place nor many of the vast Baca relationship which came to greet her. The Sandía Mountain, shaped like a mammoth watermelon when viewed from the north, now kept her interest as they rode along its precipitous western flank all afternoon, her eyes scaling each succeeding sky-scratching cliff all the way down the broadening valley, until nightfall found them approaching the ranch of Doña Josefa Baca.

Although Don Antonio Baca knew his sister Josefa well, he had not reckoned with her strong-willed nature, much less with her own views on love problems such as the one he was thrusting upon her. Alone and unmarried, she had developed her inheritance into a prosperous hacienda and had borne and reared six healthy children besides. One can take it for granted that Aunt Josefa quickly won her niece's confidence. She most certainly got a different version of the Santa Fe maneuvers, not only from the girl's lips, but from the Albuquerque men who had gone with Manuel Armijo before the Vicar. What Aunt Josefa did to solve the problem in true playwright fashion may be detected in an unforgettable (yet long-forgotten) incident that took place in the Albuquerque church sometime later.

It was the tenth day of August, in the year 1733, the Feast of the martyr St. Lawrence. This feast day was celebrated by the Spanish population all over New Mexico in memory of those many Franciscans who had been massacred by the Indians on this very day in 1680. While the Bacas and Bustamantes and the rest of the Santa Fe folk were putting on their finery and repairing to the great Parroquia for Mass, the people of the lower valley were flocking to the nearest Mission, those around Albuquerque to the smaller church of San Francisco Xavier (today San Felipe) which faced the Sandía from the plaza by the river.

Doña Josefa Baca came with her children from Pajarito accompanied by her niece who drew all eyes to herself—and also whispered comments among the bystanders—for her frustrated romance had become well known by now despite the difficult means of communication. Francisca and her aunt looked particularly devout that morning as both took their places far up in front near the altar. Had the congregation seen their faces during the chanting of the Mass, they might have caught a nervous twitch of apprehension now and then or a faint smile of anticipation. No sooner was the Mass over than the people began milling and pushing their way out the front door, to watch the play of Moors and Christians and the horse races that were to follow. They had not noticed that the priest had remained at the altar instead of repairing to the sacristy as usual.

Doña Josefa nudged her niece and they both arose and walked close together towards the open sunlit door. As they reached the front, a young man stepped out from behind the door, grasped the young lady by the arm, and swiftly marched her up to the altar where the Padre was waiting. Soon the church filled up again when word got outside that Manuel Armijo and Francisca Baca were being married. The ceremony went on without interruption, either because everybody was so completely taken by surprise, or because there were no men present of that impious stamp who would dare to profane the holy place with violence.

Fray Pedro Montaño, the Franciscan pastor of Albuquerque who ended this true drama happily without the aid of fatal herbs and poisons, later wrote up the case for his Superior so that the latter might present it to the Viceregal Court in the City of Mexico as an illustration of the secular Vicar's abuse of authority. In doing so, the friar makes it appear as though the incident in church was entirely spontaneous and unrehearsed; that, confronted by this unexpected action of the groom, and having questioned the parties concerning the whole matter, he had married them then and there "to avoid greater inconveniences." But through it all shines forth the genius of Doña Josefa, who had previously contacted the friar, the groom, the various witnesses, and who very likely concocted the plot that ended in such a successful coup.

As noted in the beginning, the more pleasant features of *Romeo and Juliet* are here present. That nameless Nurse, whom Shakespeare purposely created in rough contrast to the gentlespoken protagonists and their highborn families, who minced no words when speaking or spoken to, and who was a most efficient go-between in the lovers' trysts and in arranging for the wedding with the wise old Friar Lawrence, was admirably played by Doña Josefa Baca. Fray Pedro Montaño resembles Shakespeare's famous Franciscan in his human understanding if not in his outlandish way of concluding the affair. *Romeo and Juliet* ends with a churchyard scene strewn with fresh corpses after a bit of sword-play. Although there were no killings after the wedding of Manuel and Francisca, a duel did flare up as the people poured out a second time onto the walled *campo santo* in front of the church. Two individuals by the name of Antonio de Chávez and Antonio Montoya, who had begun disputing as to whether the friar did the right thing or not, suddenly drew out knives from their sashes and began taking each other's measure. The crowd promptly disarmed them, however. Nor do we know who it was that took whose part, for Montoya was married to Francisca's sister Ynés, and Chávez was the husband of her cousin Antonia Baca.

That the Bacas in Santa Fe did not immediately approve of the marriage is shown by the fact that Manuel and Francisca did not have their *velación* (or solemn nuptial blessing with ring, coins, and candle) until two years later, when Francisca's dream came true as she knelt with her one true love before the high altar of the Santa Fe Parroquia. But in the last will and testament which Don Antonio Baca made in 1755, there appears the name of Manuel Armijo among his six sons-in-law. Doña Josefa Baca, too, drew up a will in 1746, in which she asked God's mercy for having been such a great sinner by having, though unwed, the six children who inherited her property in the order named.

Enemy Way

Enrique R. Lamadrid

Ricardo knew it would take months to get used to the silence. Back in Albuquerque the pace of his life had become so frantic that coming to the pine and sage mesa country of *Tloh' Chin To* was like stepping off into a void. Not that he had really gotten away from anything. The war and his struggle with the draft hung just as oppressively over his thoughts. Drawing a ten on the draft lottery had thrust him into the middle of a dangerous whirlwind on an unknown course. "It's the only damned drawing I've ever come that close to winning," he thought, the usual wisp of humor creeping back into his thoughts. "With luck like that something was telling me that I'd got some Asians in my future." He was glad that they would be Navajo instead of Vietnamese. He was feeling more in control of his destiny now than the night when Selective Service played TV sweepstakes with his life.

The red glow was fading from the sandstone cliffs behind his cabin as Ricardo stumbled back inside to light the lamps and start a fire. As he was fumbling with the matches he heard the bellowing and popping of Benny Chato's new GTO as it lurched up the dirt road. "God, not again," Ricardo cringed. The length of the horn blasts were the measure of Benny's drunkenness.

"*Haa t'ish ba naa ni nah*, Benny, how've you been?" Ricardo shouted tentatively.

"Hey, *Naakai*, how about we cruise some a little bit?" came the standard reply. Benny always used the Navajo word for Mexican with him, a sign of guarded trust.

"Take it easy, you want to get me killed?" Ricardo joked to ease the tension.

"Watch it, maybe I do, so just get in *Naakai*, I'm telling you."

Ricardo sank reluctantly into the front seat and Benny shoved a can of beer into his lap. Ricardo drank it slowly as Jimi Hendrix blasted out of the tape deck.

"Well, aren't you going to ask me any more about Nam?" Benny scowled. He still didn't know what to think of the outsider who had set up in his uncle's summer cabin.

"I just can't believe you signed up again, Benny, what's in it for you?" Ricardo complained, his uneasy frankness beginning to show.

"That's where the action is, you know, it's too damn quiet up here. I get too nervous hanging around."

Actually, Benny had only spoken once about Viet Nam, briefly muttering something about "those fucking Gooks and their shit smeared booby traps." It was chilling to hear the slurs coming from such a high cheeked, bronze face. Usually outspoken in condemning the war, Ricardo held back his feelings with the Navajos. They all seemed so much in favor of it, even to the point of having "Love it or Leave" bumper stickers and double eagle decals on their pick ups. It was hard enough around Chicanos, so many of his own cousins and friends had enlisted. Speaking your mind was risky business, especially when people thought you were condemning your own family.

Strangely, Benny spoke freely about his uncle in World War II, how he had been one of the famous Navajo code talkers. The silence about his own experience made Ricardo think that he must consider it in less than heroic terms. The times he asked about Ricardo's military background, Ricardo always managed to change the subject. He feared what would happen when Benny found out.

"Those bullshit hippy traitors. I wish you could've seen the one I pounded last month in Gallup," he said, slugging the dashboard. "But all you *Naakai*, you're different, more like us." He started the engine and Ricardo jumped out, relieved to see the dusty lights disappearing.

On the way to school the next morning, Ricardo felt a gnawing frustration. "How am I going to survive here if I can't tell anybody where I stand. I wish I could get it across to the Navajos what bloody mercenaries they are by joining up and going along with everything the government dishes out." Around the bend near the Chapter House, he started, braking reflexively upon seeing Benny's GTO halfway down the embankment resting square on a smashed juniper. "To think I almost went with him last night!" he sighed after making sure that nobody was in the vehicle.

At school he hurried down to the math classroom where Gloria Chato, Benny's sister-in-law, was an aide. Without even pausing to greet her, Ricardo whispered, "Is he OK? I saw his car by the Chapter House."

She made a confusing gesture, nodding and shaking her head at once, "He walked away from this one too. Didn't make it to his mother's till after midnight. Did you see him last night?"

"He came by around sundown. Gloria, I think he's really trying to kill himself." Ricardo paused, amazed they had exchanged so many feelings with so few formalities. He hardly knew her.

In his classroom, he stared out the window at the pale autumn light, waiting for the students. Ricardo had an innate sense of how to belong in a new place with new people. He felt close to what he knew of Navajo ways, but his growing awareness had its price. True differences separate peoples; there are cultural gaps that might never be bridged. Yet, his students sensed that as a *Naakai*, he was somehow more approachable, more familiar than the uptight *"Bilagaana"* teachers from back east.

It was ironic that not that long ago the Spanish had also made their attempt to dominate the Navajo. Instead, the Navajo assimilated the Spanish, taking only what they needed from them: horses, sheep, coffee and a few cultural odds and ends. Ricardo was delighted that he could communicate so well with the older people who knew more Spanish than English. Since World War II, the children had been learning English so his bond with the younger Indians was a little harder earned. Even though he taught biology, his kids were always asking himn what all their Spanish surnames meant. It was embarrassing to have to tell them that Chato was "flat face" and Cojo was "lame one," but he added that these were names used by great chiefs. Fortunately most of them had more traditional names like Martínez, Pino or García.

"Morning, Mr. Cha-Cha" the kids taunted as they piled gleefully into the room. It was only a month into classes and they had a nickname for every teacher in the school. After the class the boys cornered him with the usual questions.

"Come on Mr. Chávez, you said you would tell us about when you were in the service. Was it the Army?" He shook his head, "The Navy?" They never asked about the Marines or Air Force because of his glasses.

"All right, all right, I'll tell you but you've got to sit down first. I wasn't in the service and I won't ever be."

"Eh yah," they squealed. "Was it because you were chicken or something?" one of them laughed. A hush fell over them again as Ricardo managed an appropriate frown.

"No, I just told them I wasn't going to go when they tried to get me to. You want to know why?" They fixed their eyes on him. "Because if it was a hundred years ago and I let them take me, you know who I would be fighting with?" He paused again for dramatic effect. "You guys...and I'm not about to do that either, then or now!"

They rushed up and surrounded him, their raven heads bobbing up and down shouting, "Why us, why us?"

"Because back then you guys were the enemy, you guys were the Gooks, and Kit Carson had us killing your sheep, burning your hogans, and cutting down your peach trees." Ricardo drove his point home hard. It was they who had told him the human details of the Long Walk of the Navajos, how their parents still knew the songs that were sung by the people as they were driven with their sheep across the desert.

"So that's why I didn't go to the service. How could I shoot you guys?" he said laughing, poking them in the stomach with his finger to break the mood.

As they stampeded out the door, Ricardo stood there shaking his head, unable to believe that he had just spilled his guts to them. It was so easy and they seemed to understand the way he had made his point. "Did you say too much? Did you blow it?"

The rest of the week went by more quickly than usual. Now that the word was about him, what more could happen? His sense of confidence was gradually returning. Knowing the Navajo community as he did, he figured

his words would come back to him. "But from where?" The doubts kept rolling back throgh his mind. "If you could only explain it to the adults as easily
as you did to the kids..."

Ricardo spent a quiet weekend grading papers and splitting wood. On
Sunday afternoon he almost acted on his urge to go to town, especially since
that was Benny's favorite time to drop by. This time when he heard the rum-
ble of the souped up engine, he was ready for anything.

"*Yaa'at'eh*," Benny said, barely honking as he drove up. Not only was he
early, but Ricardo was surprised to see he hadn't been drinking. "Let's go,
Naakai, I want to talk to you." With a shrug, Ricardo jumped in.

They turned down the road towards Zuni. Benny handed him a thermos of
coffee and Ricardo poured out a cup.

"We're going to an Enemy Way over by Broken Rock. I wanted you to be
there. A friend of mine is just back from Nam and they're doing it for
him."

"What are they going to do, Benny?'

"It's a Squaw Dance, there'll be food."

"Yeah, but why your friend? Will we see him?"

"No, they'll have have him stashed away inside his hogan with the
medicine man. He got fucked up in Nam, and they're going to straighten out
his head. The action for us will be outside."

They drove part way toward Gallup and cut far west on a red dirt road.
The shadows were lengthening into rusty velvet as Ricardo's thoughts
bounded ahead of the car. Something had changed in Benny.

It was dark by the time they turned into a clearing with a hogan behind a
square log house. Already a huge bonfire was licking up into the night, making it seem even darker. An assortment of dusty pickups was parked around
the fire. People were seated in them, eating, hardly speaking, laughing
quietly. They loaded up on roast lamb ribs, mutton stew and fry bread. There
were two brand new garbage cans on small fires, simmering to the brim with
coffee. Ricardo had never seen so much coffee.

"How are these people going to drink up all that *gohweh*?" he said,
emphasizing the last word, a Navajo version of the Spanish *café*.

"They will," laughed Benny, "they will." After seven or eight cups,
Ricardo knew what he meant. The crystal-headed clarity of the caffeine

intoxication was something he had never experienced to that degree.

By then a group of singers had gathered and another bonfire was lit. Although the songs sounded serious, Ricardo noticed there were a few words tossed in to accompany the usual seed syllables of the chant. Now and then quiet laughter would ripple through the spectators.

"Are those words, Benny?" He nodded with his lips. "If this is about your wiped-out friend, why are the people giggling and enjoying themselves?"

"Listen to this one, Ricardo: 'I'm so horny, won't you let me take you home, take you home, in my one-eyed Ford, hey yanna ho, hey yanna eh!' "

"You've got to be kidding, I thought this was supposed to be serious."

"It is. They're fixing up my friend, Danny Peshlakai. Meanwhile, we're supposed to be putting in our good feelings. Hey look, there goes the sage girl. Watch what she does. You better find something to give her."

Dressed in velvet and silver, a young woman was doing a measured side step around the circle. She was clutching sprigs of sage in each hand, gently swaying them as she danced. She would pause every few steps, picking men out of the crowd with her eyes. They would come forward and do a few stately turns around her with their eyes lowered. As she dismissed them with a flick of her chin they dropped coins and dollar bills into her sash.

Ricardo was so entranced with her beauty and the pulsing songs of the chorus that before he knew it she was looking directly at him. He started slinking back into the shadows, embarrassed to be the only outsider there. Benny whispered, nudging him forward into the full glow of the bonfire, "Go on, go on, she wants you. Be sure to give her these." He dropped a handful of quarters into Ricardo's fist.

Shouts from the crowd applauded him as he circled around her. The dark folds of her dress blended with the night sky and firelight glinted from the constellations of silver buttons on her breast. Ricardo stared into her eyes for a moment too long and she brushed his face with the sage, smiling. He almost forgot to drop the coins in her sash as he stepped back into the crowd.

"Hey, *Naakai*, remember I said you would like this?" Benny said, jabbing him in the ribs.

After a few more cups of coffee, Ricardo turned towards his companion,

"Benny, did they ever do an Enemy Way for you?"

"Hell no, everyone knows I'm too crazy. Besides, I didn't bring you here to have you ask me that." A frown formed then vanished from his face.

"Why did you bring me then?" Ricardo thought, not daring to speak. They both stared at the ground.

"It's time we should go. Look how late it is," Benny said. "Besides, in an hour or so they'll start shooting off their rifles to mark the end of the ceremony. You don't want to be here for that part."

They walked back to the car and started back down the dirt road to the highway. At the turn off they both noticed a shooting star coming right out of the constellation of the seven sisters. Ricardo thought of the sage girl and everything he had experienced that night.

"I think I know why you brought me, Benny," he said, struggling with his apology. "It was beautiful. So much good energy for a returning soldier. I've never seen anything like it." He held his breath while Benny kept looking straight out the windshield. "I think I've been much too critical of your people and the war. I should shut up and learn something from you. You've been great warriors for centuries and who am I to say anything?"

"It's what you said the other day, Cha-Cha, that's why I brought you." Benny gunned the engine and spun onto the highway.

"What do you mean?" Ricardo said, alarmed at the burst of speed and the swerving of the car.

"It's my brother. Gloria told me. Gloria my sister-in-law, you know." Ricardo didn't move. "Some kids told her what you said to them." Ricardo's heart sank.

"Benny, I didn't mean any harm. I was just explaining to them why I wouldn't fight." Surprisingly the car slowed down.

"It's all right, *Naakai*, I understand. I don't want to fight you either." Ricardo couldn't believe his ears. Benny continued. "It's my brother. See if you can help him out. He and Gloria have two kids and he just got his draft notice. He doesn't want to go."

"He got his draft notice? Do they know he has a family?" Benny nodded. "That's crazy, no way those bastards can get away with that. He's got rights. I'll talk to him tomorrow."

"Thanks, Naakai, I hoped you could understand," Benny said with awkward relief. "Come on, we've got to get home and work on getting some sleep tonight after all that coffee." He reached under the seat and handed Ricardo a warm beer. They opened it and passed it back and forth silently as they sped off into the velvet and silver night.

Old Dogs New Tricks

Francisca Tenorio

Most of Rincón is urban but as you can see, here and there, many of the families have small vegetable gardens and corrals with a pig, a steer, a couple of sheep or a gallinero with a few laying hens and gallos. Esas gallinas cruzando la calle a few houses back belong to Julianita Cruz. Most of the people from the area are very understanding with her stray chickens. They are forever breaking out of the delapidated gallinero which Julianita's son, Polo, built for her a few years back. Hace tres años que se murió el Polo and now la viejita adores the tumbledown coop as a sanctuario built by her son...one of the major rememberances she has of him besides todas las cuentas que le dejó el desgraciado. Actually, Polo was a lazy good for nothing vago and that gallinero is probably the only constructive effort he ever undertook. Although the gallinero needs repairs, Julianita won't let any of the neighbors touch el monumento que le queda de su hijo que era tan huevón. There's a little story about Julianita's chickens that the gente of Rincón still laugh at today.

Unos cuantos años pasados decidió el gobierno that many of the older citizens of Rincón were wasting their human resources by sitting idly in their patios o casitas todo el santo día spinning their yarns and meditating on the

150

highlights of their past. It was decided to initiate a program using some of the agriculture students from the university. Oscar Greenly, uno de los profesores en el departamento, submitted a proposal to the federal government requesting $117,000 from the Department of Agriculture. Soponía usarse todo el dinero in a training program for Rincón's elderly. Funding was to go for renting diez acres de terreno, para comprar semillas and young plants, for farming equipment, to pay Greenly a sizable salary to direct the project, to pay the university students a small stipend for their mileage from the university to the jardincito and last but *certainly* not least, to pay thirty of Rincon's viejitos $3.00 an hour over a six month period for the time they devoted to the project.

Bueno, al oirlo the proposal sounded great. The viejitos were supposed to learn basic methods of gardening and to gain nutritional education in the process. Many of the social workers and other agency personnel from outside of the area were amazed to learn that much of Rincón's elderly population subsisted on a primary diet of frijoles, chile, papas, arroz, tortillas y café. Es que dijo el Greenly que one of the goals of the program was to educate the families on the variety of vegetables que pudieran sacar de sus jardines and a lot of different ways to prepare them.

Pues el Greenly estuvo de suerte and his proposal was funded. Thus, Government Rehabilitation in Nutrition and Gardening Opportunities...project GRNGO was born. Everything started out fairly well in the spring with evening classes conducted by Greenly and his students. Se reunían las clases allá en el community center. Casi todas las preguntas que hacían los ancianos weren't related much to the agricultural process, sinó these students were asking questions on other matters such as, would the stipend they receive interfere con sus chequesitos del seguro social? ¿Qué pudieran mandar a sus nietos en su lugar a escardar en el verano? Could the university send someone to speak to them in Spanish? Muchos de los pobrecitos no le entendían nada al gabacho Greenly.

Project GRNGO got off the ground, or should I say got "into" the ground, in April. Con poco tiempo y mucho sudor their efforts were soon yielding microscopic forms of okra, cauliflower, eggplant and turnips. Con el tiempo resultaron problemas, however. The viejitos were finding que no les valía three dollars an hour to sit in the evening classes once a week y de seguro it wasn't worth three dollars an hour para escardar el jardín in the scorching sun. Muchos perdieron interés y dejaron de vinir. Those who remained, did so mostly to visit with their vecinos...para platicar and to share cuentos and mitotes about the project and Greenly. Así se les pasaba el tiempo a los estudiantes. It was something to do, but they felt it would be considerably more worthwhile si uvieran siembrado una huerta de chile verde. They were excited about the milpa of corn, however. Le estaban poniendo mucha atención y regaban religiosamente el maíz because the men were secretly planning to use the crop to brew a gigantic batch of corn liquor they called "mula."

Another major problem facing Greenly were Julianita Cruz's chickens. Todo el tiempo he had to chase the little devils out of the broccali or rhubarb plants. Los viejitos nomás se reían and they'd shake their heads and say, "Mejor que se lo coman las gallinas. De todos modos no vamos a poder comernos esta cosecha desconosida que viene saliendo de la tierra." Greenly would chase Julianita's chickens con rabia y piedritas todos los días until one day he went too far, or I should say both he and the chicken went too far. El Greenly pescó una gallina gordita de la Julianita comiendose all the young buds off his favorite, most prized and cared for plant. He reached blindly for the chicken. Se le prendió un fuego en sus ojos y se le pararon las greñitas del cuello. Pescó la gallina de una pata and he whirled the squaking chicken over his head. La pobre gallina se surró del susto de la sacudida...right on Greenly's head. Well, Greenly had put up with all the "chicken shit" he could tolerate. Sumbó la gallina de un golpe a la tierra donde estaba él parado. Needless to say, the dearly departed chicken ya no volvió a molestar sus plantas otra vez. Well, he should never have done that.

When Julianita found out about her assasinated chicken se le salió el mero diablo. Esa gallinita gorda era su favorita que había cuidado con tanto cariño to be such a magnificent, fat, feathered beauty. Como tenía consentida esa gallina. Cuando fue oyendo lo que había pasado, la Julianita arrebató la escoba y salió corriendo de la cocina without even taking off her apron. "¡Ven acá, gringo jodido! ¡Te voy a matar a escobasos, desgraciado!" le gritaba en voz alta as she chased Greenly with the broom por todo el jardín. The viejitos sat back and howled in fits of laughter echandose en el suelo con sus carcajadas and slapping their thighs at the ridiculous sight de la Julianita corriendo detrás del Greenly.

Later, in the privacy of their own homes, they all agreed that in fact Julianita did attack Greenly, but no one would admit it después en la corte. Oh yea, it ended up in court alright, let me tell you. El Greenly fue a ver un abogado y decidió que the matter must be settled within the judicial system. He didn't want compensation for his loss, his humiliation, ni siquiera por el golpazo en la cabeza que le puso la Julianita con su escoba. No. All he was asking for was that the law force Julianita to restrain her chickens en un gallinero bien hecho or if she didn't comply with that request, that the courts confiscate her poultry.

Pues toda la gente de Rincón agreed that Greenly had pushed the issue just a bit too far. The day that Julianita received a court order to act in five days, muchos de los vecinos se enredaron el cuento de la Julianita y sus pollos. Oh, they didn't exactly like the idea of Julianita's chickens eating their flowers and leaving droppings in their yards either, but they accepted an occasional loss or sticky shoe. Besides, this was a united war against an outsider.

Where it all started, no one will admit to this day, pero la noche que Julianita recivió los papeles de la corte, typewritten neatly in English, which she couldn't read or understand, she had her revenge on Greenly. Late that night, all of the neighboring residents led by Julianita, herded their livestock out of ther trochiles, gallineros and corrales to the GRNGO garden. Cochinos, sheep, chickens, vacas y caballos all enjoyed the picnic, pero de aquellas, que duró hasta la mañanita when Greenly drove up in his brand new Volvo.

En eso marchó project GRNGO. The viejitos mourned the loss of the young corn plants and saw the gallons of mula evaporate into nada mas que un cuento to be told and relived in memories. Greenly never pushed the court order and Julianita's chickens are still running freely in Rincón. Greenly never returned to the jardincito either. His final progress report to the Department of Agriculture fue un volumen de numeros, graphs and statistics. His final summation read: "I find these elderly residents to be uneducable in modern methods of farming technology and although they are desperately in need of living skills, they are highly untrainable." Project GRNGO...a $117,000 failure? ¡Que chiste! Eh?

White Mice

Rubén Sálaz-Márquez

Mrs. Teubbes thrust her key into the knob, unlocked the door and swung it open. Her great bulk reacted against bending over to engage the stopper but the motion was completed without undue strain for a woman her size. The classroom was pleasantly quiet as she walked to her desk and set down the papers she had graded last night. She pulled out another key, the smaller one for her desk drawer, unlocked it and deposited her purse within, shoved it shut and locked it once more. She glanced at the clock. Kids would start coming in after a spell. She sat at her desk and relaxed as everything was ready for the coming day. *Two more days before Christmas vacation*, she thought. She would weather the storm of student anticipation. She was confident and all she needed now was the students. Tomorrow she would meet some of the parents for the cultural day her aide, Mrs. Archunde, had set up. Now there was a gem. If Archunde had a college education she would be a top teacher...*too*, she added quietly in her mind. These Hispanics, or Latins or Chicanos or whatever they were going by these days, had as much talent as anybody, they just didn't, well, apply themselves at the proper time or in gainful ways. There were exceptions of course, nothing being one hundred percent, but Mrs. Archunde could be excellently qualified with a degree. Teubbes wondered why she didn't go to college now, for it was never too late.

It wasn't that she couldn't speak English. She knew both languages and used them well. At least Teubbes thought Archunde used Spanish well because she taught the Spanish component for all fourth graders in the school.

Thus far Mrs. Teubbes was enjoying the bilingual component, something new for her classroom, and she was picking up the language right along with the kids. Of course, the students already had a background in it but the teachers could learn too. If the component would help the kids learn English better than Teubbes was in favor of it. She had even attended the entire bilingual conference last month in an effort to learn first-hand how to combat code switching and maybe even cultural switching, both of which her students were prone to. Her ardor cooled somewhat when she saw the conference was just a lark for a number of the participants. Some of them must have spent all their time at the lounge for they weren't seen at any of the presentations. And she had seen some of them getting rather chummy. Well, no matter. You get out what you put in. But the real tragedy was that the *bilingual* conference had been conducted totally in English. Yes, after a few "Buenos días" and such, not a word was spoken in Spanish. Kathy Teubbes had gone prepared to make a herculean effort to catch what would be said but precious little turned up in Spanish. She still hadn't decided if she was relieved or disappointed for it was her nature to take up new challenges, whether she conquered all of them or not. *After all, nobody's perfect.* But now she was quite certain the bilingual program was soft government money being put to use until it ran out. If the language wasn't going to be used all through life, including bilingual conferences, it was just as well to teach the children English and forget about Spanish in school except as a transitional tool. If these were the facts of life, and the English bilingual conference proved they were, she didn't feel badly that she had never picked up much Spanish over the years. If Hispanic adults and intellectual leaders didn't use the language, in conferences and whatever, they themselves were admitting Spanish isn't necessary in the good old USA. *Why waste taxpayers money?* Besides, mixing the two languages often trapped students in hilariously embarrassing code and cultural switching.

"Good morning, Mrs. Teubbes," said Ricardo as he bounced into the room.

"Good morning, Richard," replied the teacher as she came out of her reverie. Oh, that little imp had more energy than anyone but the only thing he could do right was say good morning when he charged in ahead of everyone else. "Are you ready for another day of learning?"

Ricardo didn't answer. Instead he sat at his desk and looked intently at his teacher.

"Well?" she said.

"Two more days of school," he said, "and tomorrow is our cultural day, huh?"

"Yes, and I'm looking forward to it. We've never done that in this room."

"You like to eat, huh?" observed Ricardo as other students began to fill the room. That impish look was in his eyes, as usual. "I'll bring something good!"

"You like Mexican food?" asked Becky.

"Of course," said Mrs. Teubbes. "Now why don't you review your vocabulary words?" What children! Ah well, at least Richard wasn't vicious. *Of course, none of the children are*, she thought as they trooped into the room. She felt most of them had very good manners, actually, and were quite nice. They were followers more than leaders but then followers were important too. She wished very sincerely these students were more interested in school work, for the sake of their future.

"Good morning Mrs. Teubbes!" rang out a happy, feminine voice.

"Well good morning, America!" returned the teacher. Now there was a jewel if there ever was one. That Martinez girl was in a class by herself as far as Kathy Teubbes was concerned. Indeed, it could almost be said the teacher was in awe of America Martinez. She scrutinized the girl as she went over to the cages of gerbels and white mice even before putting down her books. How she loved those little animals! And when there were some to give away America was sure to take them. The teacher often wondered what she did with them. They couldn't be made into hamburger. Teubbes had worked with such critters for several years but down deep she had a revulsion for rodents as a species and even the thought of "hamburger mice" almost turned her stomach. She wondered how the Martinez family could put up with them at home.

"Everybody made it through the night," said America as she went to her desk.

Mrs. Teubbes smiled at the girl. If the teacher was ever to adopt one of her students it would be America Martinez. Not that she was underprivileged or anything like that, of course. She was always clean, well dressed, polite. Her skin was a bit on the olive side but her jet black hair and pearly teeth went well with her complexion. But what impressed Teubbes the most was America's determined spirit. When she didn't understand something she'd march right up to the teacher's desk and get help. And if she didn't get it right the next time she'd come right back with another thoughtful question. She was good at language and had to work harder on her math but she was usually equal to the task. Teubbes remembered once when she had been outside on recess duty a couple of little nasties thought they were going to intimidate America. The two had each grabbed an arm but America broke loose, made a fist and whacked each one on the nose, causing them to bleed profusely. Later in the principal's office America was a picture of confidence and contentment. Lord! Most fourth graders would have been quaking in their little shoes.

"What would you do in my place?" the principal had asked.

"I'd send you back to class," America had replied matter-of-factly.

"What if those girls jump you again?"

"I'll bloody their noses again."

Heavens! Mrs. Teubbes now began to consider something she had been unable to define before. Something, perhaps bordering on the ineffable, *bothered* her about America. Was it the child's name? How could anybody name their daughter *America?* That was rather sacriligeous, wasn't it? She had heard children teasing "Miss America!" and "God Bless America!" on the playground. It never seemed to bother the little girl. Or maybe that's what disturbed Mrs. Teubbes: *nothing* seemed to bother America, such was her confidence and aplomb. Why, she could put many an eighteen year old to the blush. Somehow it just wasn't fair that a mere child, of a minority at that—

"Buenos días, señora Teubbes," repeated Mrs. Archunde.

"Oh yes, buenos días Magdalena. How are you today?"

"Fine, thank you. You seem to have been lost in thought."

"Not lost, just thinking. I'm looking forward to the cultural day tomorrow." Teubbes looked up at the wall clock just as the bell rang for classes to begin.

"You'll enjoy it," assured Archunde, "and unless I miss my guess a number of parents will be here."

"Will America's be here, do you know?"

"We can ask her."

"Yes, of course," said Teubbes. "All right children, let's take out your mathematics workbooks." There was an audible groan from the class. "Come on, borrowing is not hard and you have to learn it. How many of you worked on it at home and had your parents help you?" A couple of hands went up, including America's. "And what did your parents have to say about borrowing, America?"

"My Dad said it was what you did after you found a co-signer," replied the girl. Mrs. Archunde chuckled.

"Oh, I see," continued Mrs. Teubbes, "but that's not the kind of borrowing we mean, of course. Well let's get busy. Richard, stay in your seat. Mrs. Archunde and I will walk around then you come to the desk when you need help."

The students fell to working quickly for Mrs. Teubbes believed in discipline and no one was allowed to clown it up. After a vigilant walk around the room the teacher and her aide sat at their respective desks and tutored one-on-one. Mrs. Teubbes saw America look up with confusion wrinkled into her pretty face. "Come on up if you need help." The girl did. "Yes dear?"

"Mrs. Teubbes, can you borrow from the dollar sign?"

Now it was the teacher who broke out laughing, everyone stopping what they had been doing and staring. "No dear," said a chuckling Mrs. Teubbes, "the dollar sign just informs us we are dealing with dollars and cents. You can't borrow from it. Now let's take a look at your paper..." The problem was discovered and explained away.

After mathematics Mrs. Archunde drilled the class on vocabulary, in both English and Spanish. She reviewed the old words and carefully introduced the new. "...and what do you buy when you go to the movies?"

"POPCORN!"

"And how do you say that in Spanish?"

"Maíz,"* said Caroline.

*mah-EES

"Yes," encouraged Archunde, "that's part of it. Anybody know the rest?" No one did so she told them: *"Palomitas de maíz."*

"Pigeon corn?" asked Martin.

"Yes," encouraged Archunde further, "and can anybody tell me why they call it that in Mexico?" She could tell the kids were trying hard to figure out the riddle but no hands were up. "Now let's imagine as we think...the corn pops up and flies into the air, almost like little...white...pigeons."

"Ooooh!" chorused the class, impressed with the imagery.

"Yes, now let's review our vegetables quickly," said Archunde as she pointed to a chart on the wall. "Besides maíz, what do we have?"

"Cowcumbers!" said Martin.

Mrs. Teubbes almost interrupted to correct the code switching mistake which so many students were prone to make.

"Cucumbers," said Mrs. Archunde.

"My grandfather's are big!" explained Martin. Then to Mrs. Teubbes: "Remember those he sent you?"

"Yes, Martin." His grandfather, Mr. De La O, had sent her some very large cucumbers in September.

"He's coming tomorrow."

"Fine," said Archunde, "now let's get back to work." When all the vegetables were mentioned in English they were reviewed in Spanish, with equal gusto. "Isn't it beautiful, children, to be able to use two languages? Each one of you is worth two people if you learn both languages. Your lives will be that much richer. Now I want to teach you three new words. Maybe some of you know them, we'll see. What do you call a person who knows three languages?"

The children concentrated but couldn't come up with an answer.

"Trilingual," said Archunde then she had everyone repeat it several times. She wrote it on the board and underlined the prefix. "Remember, *tri*-means three, three." Most of the students wrote it down.

"Now who can tell me the word for a person who speaks *two* languages? You should know that one, children." But no one came up with it. "Bilingual!" said Archunde then she repeated the procedure as before. "And don't forget: *bi*-means two. Yes, I don't have to tell you to put it in your notebooks. Don't forget it over the Christmas vacation." Mrs. Teubbes walked up and down the rows verifying the notebook work.

"Now," said Archunde, "what is the word for a person who speaks just one language?" One hand instantly went up in the air. "America?"

"Gringo!" said the girl.

Archunde burst out laughing but she controlled it quickly. "No, not quite," said the aide who trembled mirthfully as she used to do as a young girl when she got the giggles in church. "The word I was looking for is *monolingual*. Mono- means one, one," she said as she wrote it on the board.

Ricardo's hand went up. "Mrs. Archunde, what's gringo?" he asked mischievously.

Archunde felt like hitting him with a *cowcumber*. She was momentarily at a loss for words.

"A gringo," said Mrs. Teubbes, "is a word used to describe someone who is of American-English descent. It is not the nicest word to use."

"My grandmother uses it all the time and she's nice," said Ricardo.

"It depends on how you use it, how you say it," volunteered Archunde. "Technically it comes from the Spanish word *griego* which means 'Greek.' *Gringo* just means foreigner. Now let's get back to our lesson so we can finish the details for the cultural day."

Other vocabulary words were introduced, written down, and drilled. When that was done the aide reinforced the cultural unit from three days before. "All right, now let's see who can lead the class in a little Christmas carol. Who wants to do it?"

"In English or Spanish?" asked a student.

"Well let me see, how should I do it?"

"I know," said Martin, "eenie, meenie, mainie, moe."

"I like the way you taught it to us in Spanish," said America.

"All right, go ahead," encouraged the aide.

America got up from her desk and turned to face the class. She pointed to a different student with each syllable she uttered: "*Tela mela, teplatí, como sal que es para ti!* Becky is it!" She sat down again.

Becky put on a persevering face, shrugged her shoulders a bit and went up in front of the class. "But which one shall we sing?" she asked in mild protestation. Other students called out a number of carols.

"You pick it, dear," said Mrs. Archunde.

"Well, let's do 'Alarrú,' but you all have to sing!"

The class was enthusiastic as Archunde picked up her guitar and everyone joined voices with the Christmas lullaby:

No temas a Herodes
Que nada te ha de hacer,
Duérmete, Niño lindo,
No tienes que temer.

Alarrú, alamé,
Alarrú, alamé, mi Señor

The class finished the carol, contentment was expressed on the children's faces. They felt good about themselves, a sentiment the two professionals had labored strenuously to achieve.

"That was beautiful, children!" said Mrs. Teubbes. "I could listen to you all day. But let's take some time to review who is going to bring what for tomorrow. I am so excited about our cultural day!" Quickly she wrote the students' names on the board then gave the chalk to Mrs. Archunde to jot down the names of the foods since she was more familiar with the spelling. When the task was completed Mrs. Teubbes said, "Children, I'm looking forward to seeing your parents tomorrow, those who can come, and everything sounds so good I'm not even going to eat breakfast at home."

"That's okay, I'll bring you some *atole*," said Ricardo.

"Wonderful, Richard," Mrs. Teubbes sighed. One never knew what that boy was going to say.

"I'm a wonderful boy," admitted Ricardo as the bell sounded for recess. "I can hardly wait for tomorrow!'

The following day no one realized how memorable the cultural day would be as the students got to class earlier than usual because of the food they brought. By the time the final bell rang to start the day, the food table was covered with all sorts of aromatic steaming crockpots, ovenware, and gaily painted dishes which lent even more personality to the foods with which Mrs. Teubbes was becoming acquainted. Indeed, this experience would do a tremendous job of broadening her cultural perspectives, as well as her palate.

The children were remarkably well behaved, especially with so much temptation at hand. Archunde put on a tape of Spanish language Christmas carols to start the festivities. *A choir of angels couldn't sound more heavenly*, thought Mrs. Teubbes. She was glad she was able to make a contribution for she had taken the time to go out and purchase the tape by José Feliciano and afterward she would play it for everyone and maybe even lead them in his "Feliz Navidad!"

Mrs. Teubbes saw Martin's grandfather, Mr. De La O, entering the room. Immediately she went to thank him for his gift from back in September. "I'm so glad you could come, Mr. De La Zero," she blurted as she shook the man's hand. "I wanted to express in person how much my family and I appreciated your thoughtfulness."

"Thank you, señora," said the old gentleman, warmly receptive to the woman's intent. "I'm glad you enjoyed our little gift."

"We have a chair for you right over here," she said as she led him across the room.

Mrs. Archunde was mixing with everyone but she went to America and her father when they walked into the room.

"I hope you won't throw us out for being fashionably late," said the man to Mrs. Archunde.

"Of course not," she replied.

"I brought the posole," chirped America. "We even grew the corn that's in it."

"Oh oh, if it's no good they'll throw us out for sure," said the father, making Archunde smile. Little wonder America had such a sense of humor. "I'll put it right over here" he said as he placed the large pot on the last remaining space on the table.

"We were saving it for you," said Archunde.

"I guess we're ready to start," said Mrs. Teubbes. "Children, you all make a line on that side of the table, with your parents, and Mrs. Archunde and I will serve from this side if you need help." A second invitation was unnecessary but everyone cooperated in orderly fashion.

Mrs. Teubbes had not eaten breakfast, usually a very large meal for her, so she was quite hungry to begin with and as she helped serve the different dishes her mouth literally watered in expectation. She controlled herself by making pleasant comments on how good everything looked but she could hardly wait to begin her own meal.

"Is this porridge or cement?" asked Denise as she looked at a white crock-pot full of light blue *atole*.

The people talked, music played, and when everyone had been through the line once the two teachers finally served themselves. Mrs. Teubbes was not shy about sampling a little of everything, starting with the items familiar to her, devouring them in as dainty a fashion as possible. Then she began with the unfamiliar dishes and this is where she got herself into a bit of difficulty. A *relleno* had some hot chile in it and the unsuspecting woman had to make a quick exit to the drinking fountain for some cold water. Undaunted, she returned to the food table and continued her adventures amid the happiness and jovial spirit which everyone shared. The good food, beautiful music, and happy people enriched the holiday season as nothing else could.

"Mrs. Teubbes, have you tasted my *posole* yet?" asked America of her teacher.

"Your what?"

"This dish over here," said the girl, "the posole."

"No dear," admitted Mrs. Teubbes, "but hand me a bowl and it will be next. I've never had such delicious food in my life!"

"Really?" said the smiling girl.

"Can you imagine that?" continued Mrs. Teubbes. "Of course, I grew up in a different part of the country. But they couldn't drag me away now." She took the bowl America handed to her and filled it generously. "Hmm, smells delicious." She was ever so slightly wary because of the chile relleno but the woman was unable to discover anything potentially deleterious to her palate as she tasted a little. "Hmm, it's good." She looked at America, put a hand on her shoulder momentarily and said, "You know my dear, I've been wondering something for a long time...I mean, I have a question for you." She continued to eat the tasty posole.

"I have always wondered, what do you do with all those little rodents you take home?"

"We put them to good use, we don't waste anything," replied America as she smiled.

"Heavens, this has such flavor!" said Mrs. Teubbes as she ate the posole.

"Quite unlike anything I've ever eaten. What do you call it again?"

After America told her Mrs. Teubbes waxed rather poetic and said happily, "One thing is certain, this taste is not a waste! What is this that gives it such flavor?"

America couldn't see the bits of white pork meat the teacher was moving about with her spoon so she assumed Mrs. Teubbes was referring to the white corn, for to her that was the best part of the posole.

"Oh, *that's* the white maíz!" replied America.

Mrs. Teubbes' eyes opened wide as saucers and an expression of terror swept into her face as she blurted: "WHITE MICE?!" She dropped the leprous bowl of posole, clamped a hand over her mouth and raced out of the room.

Las Varas De San José

Romolo Arellano

What Gregoria did not understand was that making a santo and herding a pig into a corral were both very serious business. That's why she went on a wild ride that Saturday morning Procorro was sitting in his garden carving a Saint Joseph the new archbishop had commissioned. He had started with a block of aspen and had been pounding away on it all morning with an axe until a crow landed on a pear tree and began to criticize.

"Caw, caw, caca," he said. "It looks like Abran Lincoln. It looks like Abran Lincoln."

"Maldito," said Procorro, "how would you know about San José?"

"Easy," said the crow, "I always perch on top of churches."

"So I suppose you're an expert on the Catholic religion," said Procorro.

"I can teach you catechism," said the crow. "I know as much as any nun. When you look down at a congregation from above, you see through their Easter outfits. That's why God scares you humans. You can't hide from him."

"What do you know about God," said Procorro. "You are a thief who steals from other birds."

"I only take what I need," said the crow. "So I could never run for president or be an archbishop."

With that, Procorro bent down to pick up a pear, but when he straightened up to hurl it at the crow, the bird was gone with wings flapping hard.

"He'll be back," thought Procorro, "like most black and ugly things."

Procorro went back to his hatchet, but just then he heard the screen door slam. Gregoria came toward him almost in a sprint.

"Sebastián has jumped his pen again and is heading for the cornfield. Andale, we have to bring him back."

"Maybe we should kill that pig right now. I have the axe right in my hand," said Procorro. "Just one blow on the forehead, and he'll be en el otro mundo."

"Estás tonto," said Gregoria. "You know we're saving him for Christmas. We always save our marranos for that blessed time so we can make chicharrones and meat empanaditas."

"If we kill him now, we won't have to feed him four more months," said Procorro.

"And you will eat the garbage I suppose," said Gregoria.

Procorro knew she had him there. He put down the axe and followed her to the cornfield. There was Sebastián munching on an ear of corn. Gregoria charged at him with a stick in her hands.

"Aii salvaje. I will kill you for getting in my milpa."

Gregoria resembled the angel of death ready to wipe ten civilizations off the earth with one chingaso. Sebastián looked up and saw her coming. He fled at the sight of the stick and ran through the cornfield. Gregoria followed in a fury. Procorro sat down to watch for he knew in that instant that this would be one of the grand moments of his life.

Sebastián was eight months old, well fed and easily weighed two-hundred-fifty pounds. He was fleeing for his life. He had forgotten about the corn. He ran and did not care what was before him. He only knew what was behind him: a temporarily insane human with a large stick. Gregoria followed him swinging the stick, desperately trying for Sebastián's rear end, but he was equally determined to deny her that target. He fled and she followed, one driven by the desire to live and the other by the desire to kill. They reached the end of the field, and when Sebastián saw the barbed wire fence, he turned and ran in the opposite direction. Gregoria followed hot on his heels screaming, "Animal, salvaje! I will teach you to eat my maíz."

They cut a new path across the cornfield, leaving devastation in their wake. A two-hundred-fifty pound pig and a two-hundred pound woman can wreak great damage upon a cornfield when travelling at full speed. Procorro tried yelling to Gregoria, but she was deaf to everything except the pig. When Sebastián saw Procorro, he turned back again and began a third pass across the field. Gregoria's eyes were glued to Sebastiáns rear. She made futile swings at the pig and missed.

Procorro realized at that point that everything was beyond hope. Gregoria would not stop until she collapsed from exhaustion. It would be like the time she chopped to pieces a hundred year old piñon tree because a small branch broke off and hit her on the head. Procorro sat down to view the inevitable destruction. He said a prayer for Sebastián knowing that if Gregoria got within range, the pig would die a horrid death.

Gregoria and Sebastián reached the west end of the field, and the pig fled along the fence. Then he dashed into the corn again and began a fourth pass across the field. Gregoria followed still determined to punish the pig. Procorro watched, incredulous. The two charging creatures kept up their furious pace. "God help either of them if they step into a prairie-dog hole," thought Procorro. "They will have a broken leg and maybe a broken head."

Suddenly they were charging straight at Procorro. He leaped to his feet and then they were upon him. Sebastián bumped him and Procorro fell to the right and out of the way. He was safe, but Sebastián had momentarily lost some of his speed and now Gregoria saw her chance. She leaped thinking she would grab him by the tail, but she had underestimated her leap. She fell full force on the pig's back, but he was a young, healthy animal, and he kept running along at a good clip. Gregoria grabbed Sebastián by the ears and held on. Now that the pig was out of the cornfield he could run free, and he did with Gregoria sliding from side to side but somehow miraculously holding on.

Procorro was amazed. Never had he seen anyone ride so well. Sebastián was wet with the corn dew, but Gregoria was holding on better than any bronco-buster Procorro had ever seen. Even the young Indians from the Pueblo who rode magnificent horses bareback across his land could not have

accomplished this feat. Gregoria held on when Sebastián leaped the acequia. She seemed like a spirit woman riding a mystic horse across the
heavens. Gregoria stayed on when Sebastián went through the wire fence,
although she left some of her gray hair on the wire. She held on when Sebastián made a sharp turn to escape their barking dog, Cacahuate. Gregoria
even stayed on when Sebastián went through two giant, yellow chamisos and
even when he went through a cockle burr patch.

Finally Sebastián made a very conscious decision that it was better to die
than to try to elude this demon of a woman. He headed for his pen and ran in,
and although Gregoria bumped her head on a board as he entered, she still
did not fall off. When Sebastián found himself inside the pen, he must have
felt his strength renewed. He bucked furiously and Gregoria, who had
momentarily removed her hands from his ears to protect her head at the
entrance, went flying. Next to Sebastián's trough was a large puddle which
had been formed by recent rains. It was full of black mud, manure and garbage, and that's where Gregoria fell face first. She fell so hard that she lay
there without moving for more than a minute, the air knocked out of her.
Even when Procorro arrived at the pen, she still couldn't move. It was the
saddest sight Procorro had ever seen. There lay that sweet woman he had
taken to the altar twenty years before in a state of purity now all besplattered
with black mud, her clothes torn and her hair full of cockleburrs and
chamiso. Procorro lifted her gently by one arm and led her to the house. She
was blinded by the mud. He led her into the kitchen, washed her face and
eyes. Then he changed her clothes and put her to bed. She did not complain,
resist or even say a word. She was totally defeated and seemed in shock.

Then Procorro went to the pig pen and looked at Sebastián. He too was
lying on his side, trying to catch his breath. Procorro walked to his work
bench underneath the pear tree and sat down. He didn't carve that afternoon.
He just sat and thought about what had happened. It had been a most
magnificent event. Twice he was tempted to resume carving, but he resisted
the urge. After all, he was an artist and needed time to think. Then he laughed
out loud and said to himself, "Oh, it is muy bueno to be a santero. I can loaf
when I please, and people don't criticize me. After all if I have a chisel
nearby, I could be thinking about carving their patron saint."

The next day, Procorro commenced carving. The crow suddenly spoke up behind him. Procorro had not seen him hiding in the branches of the pear tree.

"San José was a good hombre," said the crow.

"How would you know?" asked Procorro.

"I know because you do," said the crow. "I am closer to you than you realize."

"You are real," said Procorro. "I can see you in that tree. But don't start claiming to be part of my family."

"One day, you will see. But back to San José. He was Cristo's stepfather, you know," said the crow.

"Sí, I knew that."

"Think of it," said the crow. "Would God select just anyone to be step-father to his son?"

"Seguro que no. He would select un hombre bueno."

"And so he did," said the crow.

"So what are you trying to say?" asked Procorro.

"That San José had an interesting life before he married Santa María," said the crow. "You should think of that before you carve the santo."

"What do you mean?" asked Procorro. "What matters about San José is what he did after he married Mary."

"You will never know about that," said the crow, "till you sit down and think it out."

Then he flew away cawing, "It looks like Abran Lincoln. It looks like Abran Lincoln."

"Maldito," said Procorro. "If he ever returns, I will stone him."

But Procorro could no longer carve that day. The crow was right. He sat down under the apple tree and played with the ax while he thought about Saint Joseph. He allowed his mind to wander to Nazareth where Saint Joseph must have lived as a young man. He imagined St. Joseph building a house without nails by tying the lumber together with joints and wooden pegs. He pictured Saint Joseph cutting a board with a bow saw and making it into a table. And he wondered how Joseph had met Mary. Perhaps he had been building a house one day and saw a young girl walk by carrying a gourd of water to her father working in the fields. Every day she went by and every day he watched her. One day he followed her, and she came to a spring where she filled the gourd with water. While she did this, he called out, "Who do you know that drinks so much water?"

The young woman turned, startled and almost dropped the gourd.

"It is not you who has nothing better to do than to follow women around."

Next day the young woman brought him water on her way back home. It was a sweet water and colder than any he had ever tasted. She smiled as he drank.

"I see that you build houses too. Perhaps there is hope for you."

She brought him water every day after she had seen her father. One day he followed her to the spring again.

"Now what is it that you want?" she asked.

"I wish to know you better," he said.

"My name is Mary," she replied. "My father works in the fields. My mother stays home and cooks, cleans and knits clothing for us. I go to the market every day and carry water to my father."

"Yet you have time for kindness," said Joseph, "and you are happy. I have heard you sing on the way to the fields."

"My mother and father love me deeply," replied Mary. "My father always waits for me in the fields with anticipation. It is not just the water he waits for. It is to see me. I break up the monotony of his work. He tells me a story every day:

'There were three worms, you see, floating as I watered the fields' he says to me. 'One thought he was the first worm on earth and called himself Adam. The other thought he was a great prophet and preached continuously. The third was content to be a worm and went about eating the decayed husks of corn. A bird swooped down and ate all three and now the one that was Adam and the prophet are just as dead as the one who was merely a worm.'

Sometimes his stories are funny and other times they are sad, but always they are interesting."

Joseph followed Mary almost every day, and they sat and talked by the spring. He did not have to tell her that he loved her. She knew by the way he looked into her eyes. She did not mind his love and began to be fond of him in return. One day, he reached out and touched her hand. A month later, he kissed her.

Finally one day, they lay side by side on the grass. They felt the warmth and softness of each other's bodies. They spoke of getting married. Then they withdrew into the midst of some tall plants which bore beautiful, pink, flowers. They whispered again of the time they would be married. Suddenly they slept in each other's arms in the midst of the pink flowers. For two hours they slept. Butterflies and honeybees danced on the petals of the pink flowers. They buzzed about, but the couple did not wake. A hummingbird came and chased the bees away. He flitted about from plant to plant, his long beak sucking at the sweet nectar in the blooms. His humming wings did not awaken Mary and Joseph. The fragrance from the flowers rose in the hot sun. It floated over the land and permeated the air. Mary's father smelled it in the field. Then something invisible seemed to enter the place of flowers. It came from above and there again seemed to be a fluttering of wings, but larger ones now, bigger many times over than a humming bird's. The flowers became brighter. Then Mary woke with a start. She sat up crying.

"Wake Joseph, wake! I have had the strangest dream. An angel came to me. He said I would bear a child, a very special child. I do not quite understand what he meant, but he said to me, 'Hail Mary, full of grace, the Lord is with thee, blessed art thou among women and blessed is the fruit of thy womb, Jesus.' It seemed so real, Joseph. I swear it was real."

Joseph sat up and placed his hand on her arm.

"Then maybe it was real Mary. I do not understand it either, but I always felt you were very special. Why shouldn't heaven think so too? We will wait and see if there are other signs."

Procorro suddenly realized he was sitting in his garden. He must have slept. Yet he was still sitting in the same place. He could not have slept. His eyes had not been closed, he knew. But this strange story had gone through his mind. Then he smelled the powerful scent of hollyhocks in the air. It was all around him. But no hollyhocks grew in his garden. Then he remembered. Those were the tall flowers in his dream or vision whatever it had been. Those were las flores de San José. Now he knew more about this Joseph of Nazareth. Now he could carve him better.

He sat down and finished shaping the figure of the bulto with his axe. Then with the chisel and a wooden mallet, he began to carve the face and hands. He worked for three days straight as if he was mesmerized. Gregoria came outside and yelled at him. He did not respond. He seemed a deaf man. Gregoria climbed a tree and threw down rotted apples. Some of them missed Procorro by inches. He didn't see them. Next, she took the apples to the pig pen and fed them to Sebastián. Then she came back and yelled at him some more. Procorro hit the chisel with his mallet and told Gregoria to go shovel the snow.

"What snow?" she asked. "It is summer, you idiot. You make me a joke, you think. I will feed you moldy potatoes and spoiled meat. I will iron your pants with a soot covered adobe. I will put chicken manure in your bed sheets."

"See if there is corn meal in the rainbow," said Procorro. "You might need it some day if your mother comes to visit."

"Corn meal en el arco iris? Estás bien loco," said Gregoria. "You have finally lost what little brains you had carving those bultos. I always knew it would happen. You sitting here alone every day making santos when what you really are is a diablo."

Gregoria got up and left. She went to the pig pen and set Sebastián free. Then she chased him across the cornfield yelling for Procorro's attention. He ignored her and kept carving. Then Gregoria rode Sebastián up to the house determined to run Procorro down, but the pig refused to cross the acequia. Gregoria jumped off and went into the house muttering about how useless are husbands who can only sit in the garden all day carving santos.

Procorro worked for two more days carving without rest. On the fifth day, he was through. Then he put on his hat and threw his axe and saw into a wheelbarrow. He went up into the hills pushing the wheelbarrow. He spent four hours gathering plants and fruits. He gathered pieces of chamiso, coyaye and estafiate. Then he gathered yellow blooms from clover plants and the berries of the capulín, garambuyo and cirhuelas. He brought all of these home and boiled them separate and together. He made several dyes. Some were red, others yellow, and there was a brown and even a green color. Last of all, he made a pink dye. Then he began to paint the santo. While he was doing this, he heard a voice behind him.

"Finally it looks like San José."

"I'm glad you approve, cuervo maldecido," said Procorro.

"Just like a human," said the crow. "Even when you compliment them, they curse you."

"I withdraw the curse," Procorro said.

"Está bien," said the crow.

"Why do you like him?" asked Procorro.

"Because now you really know who was San José. You took the time to find it out."

"And you really think this is the way he should be done?" asked Procorro.

"Naturalmente," said the crow. "It is important that people remember he was not just a carpenter, but also a fellow who slept with the gals en las flores. Even if he didn't do anything else but sleep. And maybe that is why Dios chose him to be stepfather to his son. Because he didn't take advantage of the woman. He loved Mary, but he was willing to wait until they were married to sample her nectar."

"I never got into my woman's pants until I married her too," said Procorro.

"Perhaps that is why God chose you to carve his stepfather," said the crow.

"You think I'm special?" asked Procorro.

"Today at least you are better than other men." With that, the crow flew off.

"Wait, wait," yelled Procorro. "Tell me more."

"I would," said the crow, "but I must go bother a blacksmith who is making a plow for San Ysidro.

Chistes

Virginia Ortiz

Un día estaban estos indios platicando de que nunca habían visto una ciudad. Uno de ellos decidió irse a buscar una ciudad. Y él se había encontrao con unos traques ahí cerca. El pensó que pueda que estos traques lo llevaran a alguna ciudad.

Alistó su burro con todas sus cosas y se subió en los traques pa ver a onde llegaba. El no sabía que eran traques de un tren. Nunca había visto un tren. Empezó a caminar. Cuando iba caminando en los traques, vido esta luz, lejos, muy chiquita la luz. La luz empezó a hacerse más grande y más grande hasta que llegó a onde estaba él. Nomás en cuanto que se escapó él y brincó. El tren agarró al burro, y lo mató. El vido que era un tren, pero nunca había visto un tren.

Juntó lo que quedó de sus cosas que traiba montaos en el burro, y siguió caminando en los traques hasta que llegó a una ciudad. Cuando llegó allá, el primer lugar onde entró era una tienda de jugetes. Cuando entró, la primera cosa que vió fue un jugete de trenecitos en el suelo. Y él, la primera cosa que pensó fue de matar esa cosa. El fue y con su machete empezó a destruir ese trenecito. Cuando el dueño de la tienda vido lo que estaba pasando, él empezó a decirle que no hiciera eso, y quería parrarlo de que hiciera éso. Y el indio le dijo, "¡Ay que matar estas cosas, porque cuando crecen matan burros!"

Un día iban dos hombres andando por la calle. Uno era mexicano y el otro era francés. Adelante de ellos iba una mujer. De repente vino un viento y le voló la nagua a la mujer. El francés dijo. "C'est la vie." El mexicano dijo, "yo tambien se la vi, pero no dije nada."

Este hombre andaba buscando posada, como María Santísima y José, buscando posada. Y nadien le daba. Ya cuando se estaba haciendo obscuro llegó a l'última casa y dijo, "si aquí no me dan, pus durmiré en el viento."

Pus, le dieron posada y le dijieron en a cual cuarto durmiera. Pus ahí durmió. Pero en la noche tenía que ir pa'l toilet, y no había en esos tiempos toilet, ni le pusieron basín. Pus, el pobre ahí se estuvo. Al fin izque halló un cartón y ahí hizo su negocio y luego no hallaba que hacer con el. Antes tenían cielos de manta en las casas. So, rasgó una esquina del cielo de manta y metió el cartón pa ahí con el negocio.

Y luego, bueno, cuando se fue, y se iba a ir, izque les dijo él a la gente, "pus, munchas gracias porque me dieron posada y comida. Allá en el cielo hallaran su pago."

Una mañana, en un restaurante, estaban unos mexicanos sentaos en una mesa. En otra mesa cerquita estaban unos gringos. Los mexicanos pidieron huevos rancheros pa su almuerzo. Los gringos no sabían que ordenar. Ellos estaban escuchando lo que habían dicho los mexicanos. Cuando era tiempo pa que ellos ordenaran, le pidieron a la 'waitress,' "rancheros con huevos."

Casos

Era un hombre y una mujer que estaban casaos, de Cerrillos. Pus, izque estaban senando y partieron un pastel y lo pusieron en la mesa. No quedó más que un pedazo. El lo quería, y ella lo quería también. Y estaban peliando por el pastel. No sé a cual de ellos se lo comió, pero la mujer lo dejó (al hombre), lo divorció y todo. No más se quiso juntar con él. Decía mi tía cuando contaba el caso, "muncho cuidao comadre, sí ya hoy en día se apartan hasta por un pedazo de pastel."

ORACIONES

Angel de mi guardia
Noble companía,
Vélame en la noche,
Y vélame en el día.

Santa Mónica bendita,
Madre de San Agustín,
Echeme su bendición,
Que ya me voy a dormir.

ARRULLOS,

Duérmete mi hijito(a),
Tengo que hacer,
Barrer la cocina,
Y hacer de comer.

A la ru, ru, ru, ru,
A la ru, ru, ru.
A la ru, ru, ru, ru,
Duérmase mi hijito(a).

REFRANES

Amor de lejos, amor de pendejos.
Antes de que te cases, mira lo que haces.

Cada chango en su columpio.
Cada loco con su tema.
Cada quien sabe lo que acarrea en su costal.
Cada quien se sube en su caballo como le da su gana.
Caras vemos, corazones no sabemos.

Dios tarda pero no olvida.
Dime con quien andas y te diré quien eres.

El que más tiene, más quiere.

En boca cerrada no entra mosca.

Le dan almohada y pide colchón.
Lo de este mundo, pronto se acaba.
Lo que no miras, no te duele.
Lo que viene volando, volando se va.

No esperes a la pelona, que solita viene.
No hay mal que dure cien años, ni enfermo que lo
    aguante.
No hay mal que por bien no venga.

Ojos que no miran, corazón que no siente.
Onde hay gana, hay modo.

Panza llena, corazón contento.

Si quieres vivir sano, acuéstate y levántate temprano.

Te casates, te fregates.

Una mano lava a la otra, y las dos juntas lavan la cara.

ADIVINANZAS

Mi tía tenía una sábana,
Que no podía doblar.
Mi tío tenía muncho dinero.
Que no podía contar.   El cielo y las estrellas

Está viejito
Y saca la lengua.   El zapato

¿Qué tiene cuatro patas
Y no puede andar?   La silleta

Tenía cuatro pájaros,
Ponidos en una jaula.
¿Cuántos pájaros están   Dos (palabra: "ponidos"
En la jaula?   —poni dos)

¿Qué animal anda
Con una pata?   Un pato

Rita, Rita,
Que en el campo grita,
En la casa calladita,
Como una ratita.   El hacha.

Tú allá,
Y yo aquí   La toalla

Lana sube,
Lana baja.   La navaja

El que la hace, no la goza.
El que la ve, no la desea.
Todos la necesitamos.
Y ninguno la pelea.   La sepultura

Soy más picoso que la pimienta,
Y más quemoso que el chile colorado.
Soy el más quemoso de todos.
¿Quién soy?   Chile picante

Treinta caballitos blancos,
En una colina rosa.
Corren, muerden, están quietos,
Y se meten en tu boca.   Los dientes

En lo alto vive.
En lo alto muere.
En lo alto teje,
La tejedora.   La araña

COSTUMBRES

El casorio

Cuando un muchacho y una muchacha se quieren casar, tienen que ir los padres del muchacho a pedirle la novia a los padres de ella. Ellos llevan una "carta de empedimiento" y se la dan a los padres de la muchacha. Después de leer la carta y si la muchacha se quiere casar, los padres de ella responden con una "carta de entriegamiento" o con una visita. Durante estas visitas, es acostumbrado que las familias les sirvan bizcochitos y café a sus visitantes.

Si la respuesta es negativa, se dice que le dieron "calabazas" al novio. Si la respuesta es positiva, entonces se celebra el "recibimiento." Esta es una fiesta donde se combidan todos los parientes de la pareja para celebrar la boda pendiente y para que se conozcan las familias. En tiempos pasados, durante esta fiesta la costumbre era que les trajeran regalos a la pareja. También era posible que, como desde ese día para adelante ya la novia era la responsibilidad del novio, la muchacha se fuera a vivir con los padres del muchacho. Posiblemente sus padres le llevarían un carro de leña y provisiones. También es posible que ellos le dieran el dinero para que ella comprara su traje de novia. La novia casi siempre volvía con sus padres hasta el día del casorio. En estos tiempos, ya no se celebran estas costumbres en todas las familias. Ahora es más común que le den "showers" a la novia en lugar de la fiesta de recibimiento.

A continuación, ahora es necesario que la pareja escoga el día de la boda y que combide a sus padrinos. En el pasado no se combidaban damos ni damas. Ahora se combidan varios damos y damas, un padrinito y una madrinita y a veces hasta dos pares de padrinos. La novia pide lo que ella quiere—baile, fiesta grande, traje, etc. El novio es responsable por todos los costos.

El día del casorio, los padres de la novia entran con ella y se la entriegan al novio. Durante la misa, los padres de la pareja les ponen a los novios un rosario de lazo. Este es un rosario doble que une a los novios. Después de la misa, los padres y abuelos de la pareja les dan sus bendiciones. Los amigos y los otros parientes les tiran arroz y los congratulan cuando salen de la iglesia.

Después de la misa, se toman los retratos en la iglesia. Antes los padrinos eran responsable por los costos de los retratos. (Ahora ellos son responsable por los costos del baile—la sala y los músicos.) La fiesta es en la casa de los padres de la novia o en una sala. La comida que se sirve es lo tradicional—posole, frijoles, enchiladas, chile, tamales, chile rellenos, sopa, tortillas, pan, bizcochitos—y también las comidas americanas. Las bebidas son vino, cerveza, café y punchinello. A veces, durante esta fiesta se canta la "entriega de los novios." En esta canción se saludan los novios, sus padrinos, los damos y damas, los padrinitos, sus abuelos y sus tíos. También, por medio de esta canción, la familia les da las gracias por su presencia a toda la gente.

El baile es en la noche, dura tres o cuatro horas y casi siempre se toca la música ranchera. Poco después de que entran los novios, los músicos tocan la "marcha." La rutina de la marcha es variada, pero siempre termina con los novios en el centro y la gente en un círculo. La gente ahora puede bailar con la pareja. Los padrinos están ahí cerca para darle a la gente alfileres para que ellos les prendan dinero (uno o más dólares) a los novios en su ropa. Las mujeres le prenden el dinero en su vestido al novio, y los hombres le prenden el dinero en el manto a la novia. Algunas veces se canta la entriega en el baile, después de la marcha.

En el tiempo presente, la pareja se va en su luna de miel. En los tiempos de antes, no había luna de miel. La gente era muy pobre y frecuentemente los novios tenían que vivir con los padres del novio o de la novia hasta que pudieran hallar o hacer una casa. Ahora, muchos ya están preparados y tienen sus casas. Los regalos que reciben les ayudan mucho.

Desde el tiempo que los novios salen de la iglesia hasta que se vayan en su luna de miel, es posible que alguien se robe a la novia. La intención es de que si los padrinos pierden a la novia, ellos tienen que prometer hacer otro baile para que devuelvan a la novia. Si es la primera vez que esta pareja ha servido de padrinos, es posible que alguien los amarre hasta que ellos prometan lo mismo. Estas tradiciones son de los tiempos pasados y no se practican muy frecuente. Pero siempre los padrinos están al cuidado de la novia.

El velorio de difunto y su entierro

Cuando se muere una persona, se repican las campanas de la iglesia para avisarle a la gente que ha muerto alguien de este lugar. Este ejercicio se llama "el doble." Después de que el difunto ha sido embalsamado, se hacen las preparaciones para el velorio y el entierro.

En los tiempos de antes el velorio era en la casa y se rezaba el rosario y otras oraciones. Si la familia quería, los penitentes cantaban alabados. (Alabados son cánticos componidos por los penitentes.) Mucha gente no pedía este tipo de cánticos porque los alabados son muy tristes. El coro de la iglesia cantaba himnos de alabanza. Los parientes del difunto se estaban toda la noche con el cuerpo, hasta otro día en la mañana. Los miembros de la familia guardaban el "luto" por un año. La costumbre del luto incluye el uso de ropa negra, no escuchar música en sus casas ni participar en otros tipos de entretenimiento. A los ocho días iban todos a "la misa de ocho días." Al año se celebraba la misa de "el cabo de año."

Ahora, la tradición es de que el cuerpo del muerto se vela en la casa mortoria, en la morada (la capilla de los penitentes) o en la iglesia. Todavía se puede velar una o dos noches. Solamente en la morada es posible que se esté algún miembro de la familia con el cuerpo toda la noche. En el velorio se reza el rosario y otras oraciones y se cantan himnos. A veces, los penitentes cantan alabados.

La misa fúnebre siempre ha sido celebrada en la mañana. En el cementerio, después de que el padre da sus bendiciones y sus oraciones, alguna persona da el elogio. Después pasa la gente y les da "el pésame" (la expresión de simpatía) a los dolientes. Antes de irse, la famiia le echa un puño de tierra al cajón. Esto significa la creencia religiosa de que "de la tierra venimos y a la tierra volveremos."

Todavía se celebran las misas de "ocho días" y la del "cabo del año." Siempre continuará la costumbre de servir comidas y bebidas después de los velorios y de los entierros.

El bautismo

El nacimiento de un niño es una ocasión de mucha alegría. Pronto se comienzan las preparaciones para el bautismo.

Si el niño nace saludable, primero tienen que hacer los arreglos con el padre para el día y el tiempo del bautismo. También los padres del niño tienen que combidar padrinos y seleccionar nombre para el niño. Si el niño nace enfermo, es muy importante que el niño sea bautizado inmediatamente. Cualquier persona lo puede bautizar; no es necesario que la persona sea sacerdote. Las palabras del bautismo son muy importantes: "Aquí te bautizo con esta agua bendita en el nombre del Padre, del Hijo y del Espíritu Santo."

En tiempos pasados, el nombre del niño era el mismo nombre del santo de fiesta en cual día había nacido el niño. Los padrinos podrían añadir otro nombre al cual tenía el niño. También era la costumbre que los padrinos le compraran la "canastilla" al niño. Esto era un traje completo para el niño que incluía hasta el canasto.

El día del bautismo la madrina viene y viste al niño. Los padres y los padrinos van con el niño para la iglesia. El niño está vestido de blanco. El sacerdote lo bautiza y todos rezan las oraciones del bautismo.

Después del bautismo se repican las campanas de la iglesia anunciando la entrada de esta persona a la comunidad religiosa. Cuando llegan a la casa, los padrinos entriegan al niño a sus padres con este verso:

"Aquí te traigo esta prenda,
Que de la iglesia salió,
Con los santos olios,
Y el bautismo que recibió.

Ahora sigue la fiesta con la comida tradicional (ya mencionada) de Nuevo México. Desde este día hasta que el niño crezca, el deber de los padrinos es de dirigir su creencia en la fe católica.

The Souls In Purgatory

Guadalupe Baca-Vaughn

Si es verdad, allá va,
Si es mentira, queda urdida.
(If it be true, so it is.
If it be false, so be it.

There was once an old lady who had raised a niece since she was a tiny baby. She had taught the girl to be good, obedient, and industrious, but the girl was very shy and timid, and spent much time praying, especially to the Souls in Purgatory.

As the girl grew older and very beautiful, the old woman began to worry that when she died her niece would be left all alone in the world, a world which her niece saw only through innocent eyes. The old lady prayed daily to all the saints in heaven for their intercession to Our Lord that He might send some good man who would fall in love with her niece and marry her...then she could die in peace.

As it happens, the old woman did chores for a *comadre* who had a rooming house. Among her tenants there was a seemingly rich merchant who one day said that he would like to get married if he could find a nice quiet girl who knew how to keep house, and be a good wife and mother to his children when they came.

The old lady opened her ears and began to smile and scheme in her mind, for she could imagine her niece married to the nice gentleman. She told the merchant that he could find all that he was looking for in her niece, who was a jewel, a piece of gold, and so gifted that she could even catch birds while they were flying!

The gentleman became interested and said that he would like to meet the girl, and would go to her house the next day.

The old woman ran home as fast as she could, she appeared to be flying. When she got home all out of breath, she called her niece and told her to straighten up the house and get herself ready for the next day, as there was a gentleman who would be calling. She told her to be sure to wash her hair and brush it until it shone like the sun, and to put on her best dress, for in this meeting her future was at stake.

The poor timid girl was dumbfounded. She went to her room and knelt before her favorite *retablo* of the Souls in Purgatory. "Please," she prayed, "don't let my aunt do something rash to embarrass us both."

The next day she obediently prepared herself for the meeting. When the merchant arrived, he asked her if she could spin. "Spin?" answered the old woman, while the poor embarrassed girl stood by with bowed head. "Spin! The hanks disappear so fast you would think she was drinking them like water."

The merchant left three hanks of linen to be spun by the following day. "What have you done Tía?" the poor girl asked. "You know I can't spin!" "Don't sell yourself short," the old lady replied with twinkling eyes. "Where is your faith in God, the Souls in Purgatory? You pray to them every day. They will help you. Just wait and see!" Sobbing, the girl ran to her room and knelt down beside her bed and began to pray, often raising her head to the *retablo* of the Souls in Purgatory which hung on the wall beside her bed. After she quieted down, she thought she heard a soft sound behind her. She turned and saw three beautiful ghosts dressed in white, smiling at her. "Do not be concerned," they said, "we will help you in gratitude for all the good you have done for us." Saying this, each one took a hank of linen and in a wink spun the linen into thread as fine as hair.

The following day when the merchant came, he was astonished to see the beautiful linen, and was very pleased. "Didn't I tell you, Sir?" said the old lady with pride and joy. The gentleman asked the girl if she could sew. Before the surprised girl could answer, the old aunt cried. "Sew? Of course she can sew. Her sewing is like ripe cherries in the mouth of a dragon." The merchant then left a piece of the finest linen to be made into three shirts. The poor girl cried bitterly, but her aunt told her not to worry, that her devotion to the Poor

Souls would get her out of this one too, as they had shown how much they loved her on the previous day.

The three ghosts were waiting for the girl beside her bed when she went into her room, crying miserably. "Don't cry, little girl," they said. "We will help you again, for we know your aunt, and she knows what she is doing and why."

The ghosts went to work cutting and snipping and sewing. In a flash they had three beautiful shirts finished with the finest stitches and the tiniest seams.

The next morning when the gentleman came to see if the girl had finished the shirts, he could not believe his eyes. "They are lovely, they seem to have been made in heaven," he said.

This time the merchant left a vest of rare satin to be embroidered. He thought he would try this girl for the third and last time. The girl cried desperately, and could not even reproach her aunt. She had decided that she would not ask any more favors of the Souls. She went to her room and lay across the bed and cried and cried. When she finally sat up and dried her tears, she saw the three ghosts smiling at her. "We will help you again, but this time we have a condition, and that is that you will invite us to your wedding." "Wedding? Am I going to get married?" she asked in surprise. "Yes," they said, "and very soon."

The next day a very happy gentleman came for his vest, for he was sure that the lovely girl would have it ready for him. But he was not prepared for the beauty of the vest. The colors were vibrant and beautifully matched. The embroidery looked like a painting. It took his breath away. Without hesitation, he asked the old lady for her niece's hand in marriage. "For," he said, "this vest looks as if it was not touched by human hands, but by angels!"

The old woman danced with joy, and could hardly contain her happiness. She gave her consent at once. The merchant left to arrange for the wedding. Wringing her hands, the poor girl cried, "But Tía, what am I going to do when he finds out that I can't do any of those things?" "Don't worry, my *Palomita*, the Blessed Sould will get you out of this trouble too. You wait and see!"

Almost at once the old woman went to her *comadre* to tell her the good news, and to ask her to help get ready for the wedding. Soon everything was ready.

The poor girl did not know how to invite the Souls to her wedding. She timidly went and stood beside her bed and asked the *retablo* to come to her wedding.

The great day finally arrived. The girl looked beautiful in the gown which the merchant had brought as part of her *donas*. Everyone in the village had been invited to the wedding.

During the fiesta when everyone was drinking *brindes* to the bride and groom, and the music was playing, three ugly hags came to the *sala* and stood waiting for the groom to come and welcome them in. One of the hags had an arm that reached to the floor and dragged; the other arm was short. The second hag was bent almost double, and had to turn her head sideways to look up. The third hag had bulging, bloodshot eyes like a lobster. "Jesús María," cried the groom. "Who are those ugly creatures?" "They are aunts of my father, whom I invited to my wedding," answered the bride, knowing quite well who they might be. The groom, being well bred, went at once to greet the ugly hags. He took them to their seats and brought them refreshments. Very casually, he asked the first hag, "Tell me, Señora, why is one of your arms so long and the other one short?" "My son," she answered, "my arms are like that because I spin so much."

The groom went to his wife and said, "Go at once and tell the servants to burn your spinning wheel, and never let me see a spinning wheel in my house, never let me see you spinning ever!"

The groom went to the second hag and asked her why she was so humped over. "My son," she replied, "I am that way from embroidering on a frame so much." The groom went to his wife and whispered, "Burn your embroidery frame at once, and never let me see you embroider another thing."

Next, the groom went to the third hag and asked, "Why are your eyes so bloodshot and bulging?" "My son, it is because I sew so much and bend over while sewing." She had hardly finished speaking when the groom went to his wife and said, "Take your needles and thread and bury them. I never want to see you sewing, never! If I see you sewing, I will divorce you and send you far away, for the wise man learns from others' painful experiences."

Well...so the Souls, in spite of being holy, can also be rascals.

> *Colorín, colorado, ya mi cuento se ha acabado.*
> *(Scarlet or ruby red, my story has been said.)*

Grand Slam

Denise Chávez

Mozetta, are you there? What's the matter with your phone? Yes, it's me, Omega Harkins. As I was saying before I was so rudely interrupted, I have to tell you what happened to me this morning. Well, it all started a few days ago when my niece, Norlee, called me. Acton had called her from California. Acton, Acton Allnutt. Acton was my first boyfriend, the "first one," if you know what I mean, Mozetta, the *absolute* first, but not by any means the best, if you know what I mean. The best. Do you have a party line, Mozetta? Oh, okay. Well, it seems as if Acton called Norlee, she's down there at the State University majoring in Forestry. I don't know any woman, for crissakes, would want to go into *that* line of work, analyzing reindeer shit and whatever else you do in forests, but anyway, Mozetta, get this, Acton called. He always did like all of us, even Mother, even after she told him to leave me alone. What could I say? Poor Acton. So Acton called, get this to tell us all, especially me, well, and maybe Mother, because she never did believe he'd amount to much, that he was going to appear on a game show, that new one, on Channel 4, $50,000 Grand Slam, on the General Category and that we should all watch him, especially me. Acton? He got married about five years ago to an Italian. He was going to die in Viet-Nam when we broke up, but he got sent to Italy instead where he got some architecture student pregnant

187

and they moved to California and had a kid. What? It was a girl. Acton? He's down there at some big California university near the beach majoring in Dairy. Damn, Acton, I wrote this in my last Xmas card, why the hell are you out there majoring in Dairy? I wrote him an Xmas card that his wife never saw, it seems that he always collects the mail, but then again, it must be something European. I thought so too, Mozetta. I think you're right about that. Rock doesn't give a damn about the mail, but then again, I guess he does if it's his paycheck, only he doesn't get his paycheck in the mail, so it wouldn't matter anyway. What was I saying? Well, I ought to write Acton a letter, send him a Xmas card this year. It was about this time, around that time we met. I mean me and Rock. Xmas. I had a fever and met Rock at a Rock concert. It all fell into place, if you know what I mean. Acton's action wasn't anything like Rock's, where was I? Oh, okay. Norlee didn't know who the hell Acton was, but then she remembered. I'd told her all about him late one night when we were in bed at Mother's and we couldn't sleep. You know, for a freshman in Forestry, Norlee is pretty advanced, if you know what I mean. You do? Okay, so Acton called to tell us to call all his friends. Porky Hartzo...Corney Hawkins...Little Dickie...to call them all and tell them that he, Acton Allnut, was going to be on a game show in Los Angeles, California, in the General Category, with a special emphasis in Dairy and the New Testament. This was a few days ago, Mozetta. Well, Norlee finally got a hold of me at work. I was stamping a new price on the LeSeur's. They've gone up. Can you believe it? What is this world coming to? It's a good thing I don't eat LeSeur's. Me, I just buy the Town House variety. They're just as good. There's something suspicious about the baby size of those peas, they don't seem real. Give me a mouthful of pea, I say, not a—you like that joke about the pea soup...hold that chicken and make it pea? Huh, Mozetta? Well, Pres came up to me as I was sixty-fouring those LeSeur's and told me that I had a long distance call from my niece, Norlee, she's a freshman at State. I couldn't believe it! So I ran down the aisle and into the office. Wences was in there eating his lunch and I said, will you excuse me, I have a long distance call from my niece, Norlee, she's a freshman at State majoring in Forestry, maybe someday you'd like to meet her. I said all that you know, to make it seem like a very important call. No, I wasn't going to introduce, what for? Him? But he wouldn't move out and I

said, come on, Wences, you can eat your lunch in the back just like everyone
else. The plucky kid likes to eat in Mr. Hedvale's office. Old Bunny is his
great uncle or something like that. Can you imagine having a name like
Wences Hedvale, for crissakes? I mean, it's out of season. That Wences,
he's a pain! I can never get him to take out anything, all he does is hang out
near the magazine rack and breathe on the Oui's and the Cavalier's. I mean, I
don't believe this kid's fixation. Well, he's about sixteen, blond with frizzy
tangled hair. A real pimply kid from the nose down, the rest of his face as
smooth as a baby's rear. Wences, do you mind, I said, this is long distance.
Privately long distance. It's my niece from State. It's an emergency. Okay,
he said, I'm gonna tell my uncle about this, you know what you can do with
that phone. I said, I'm gonna tell Mr. Hedvale on *you*, Wences, I've been an
employee of the Stop and Save for going on six years, to which he said, Tell
Bunny to...by this time I could hear Norlee saying, he called you, he called
all the way from Los Angeles, California, to tell you about his great appearance on the Grand Slam. The program will be on this next week, meaning
this week, he lost the twenty thousand, she said. He did, he did, but how?
How, I said, that Acton's sharp as A and even more, what happened? He
won a car but he doesn't like it, so he's going to sell it, Norlee said. He lost?
He lost? How? How? He couldn't remember the name of Napoleon's dog.
For crissakes, I said over the phone, he lost for *that*? What was the category?
Famous dogs of history, she said. For crissakes, what kind of car was it? He
didn't say, she said. Where is it now? When did he call? How did he sound?
He asked about you, Omega, and I told him you were fine. I told him you
were "engaged." Engaged? Hell! Now what'd you want to say that for? Me
and Rock have an understanding, that's all. Did Acton say anything else?
Tell me, Norlee, what did he say? The program is on this week, I gotta go
now, Omega, I have practice. Practice for what, Norlee? I almost yelled, the
kid had built up my excitement and now she was leaving me to the LeSeur's
and that aisle staring me in the face, #15, Canned Vegetables, and to Wences, to that plucky kid. I could tell he was outside the door listening. What
practice, Norlee? I'm a Caperette, she says. What's a Caperette? Omega,
she exclaimed, it's only the top ranked girls' sword drill team in the West!
Give it up, Norlee, I said, it's a radical organization. I don't believe in
swords. Don't be silly, she said, and hung up. I was crushed but I went back

to the pea pile, past Wences and sat down on my little stool, my stamper all inky all over my hands, my head full of thoughts and my heart full of lost feelings for Acton. Where did we go wrong? Why didn't he die and end our mutual misery? Now he was alive and well and driving a Vega or Camaro in Los Angeles. Acton, I sighed. Acton, where did we go wrong?

Mozetta, there I was sitting next to Rock and he was sliding on his pants, yawning himself awake, half of him in the daylight and half of him in the night, it was the craziest thing. I turned on the t.v., and Rock says, what are you doing now? And I told him a friend of mine, stressing the *friend*, was going to be on the Grand Slam. Rock, I said, we gotta watch this. Who is this dude, he says? He's a *friend* of mine, we're just *friends*, that's all, we grew up together, I said to him aloud, but to myself: Acton, Acton, where did we go wrong?

He's going to be on the Grand Slam, Rock, we have to watch this. Then the t.v. flashed several faces in front of the bed, that's where we were, on the bed. I had on my bathrobe, the fuzzy one that Mother gave me, and Rock was there next to me. I saw Acton's face all of a sudden. Mozetta, I couldn't believe it, he looked like his daddy! I was so shaken up. Rock kept saying: Is that him, is that him? Where did you meet him, who is he, stuff like that. I met him in a play, I said, in high school, kinda whispering, he was my alcoholic husband, it was a melodarama. Sure, Rock says, you the actress, uh huh. You're fulla it, and we watched Acton play, and he won! He won $15,000 today, this was this morning, I'm talking about, Mozetta, and the questions were real hard. Like who is the Beatles' manager and about Dolly Madison. But anyway, the thing about all this is that I simply could not believe how much Acton looked like his daddy, and I've met the man. He's tall and fat and has a bald head with some swirly hair. He looks like a crayfish. And he has beautiful blue eyes, just like Acton, and Mozetta, to tell you the truth, I felt sick, nauseated almost. Another thing, here it was today, and yet it was last week and tomorrow. By today I mean today, and by last week I mean last week when it was filmed, and Acton won and lost and by tomorrow I mean...I don't know what I mean. It was simply weird and nauseating and I thought I would die to see Acton in a suit, smiling and sighing in that funny way he used to sigh. He looked so scared and small and defenseless and fat...Mozetta, I fell in love again, or maybe I fell in love for the first time.

Only this time, I saw Acton as his daddy, fat, balding, and old, and I felt sorry about that and that made me love Acton. Like never before. I never did like Acton too much but he hung around me all the time and liked me so darn much, I had to pretend some. It was all a lie, but I didn't know that until later. But at first, he was fine, Mozetta, attentive, my first real boyfriend, if you know what I mean. The first. I like that, a man being attentive. But to show you the kind of person he really was, well, when we broke up, he figured out how much he spent on me all those years, and told me. How do you like that? Oh. About $1,500. I mean, it wasn't too much was it, after all *I'd* given him. I mean, here he's got $15,000 for knowing who the Beatles' manager was...not to mention a new Camaro. But anyway, what does it all mean? It means Acton was there in a suit, smiling and sighing, sighing and smiling, and I was in my living room sitting next to Rock, and him putting on his pants and me in my bathrobe. That's what it means. Then Rock said, who is this guy to you? And I said back, what do you mean, who is this guy to you, you have terrible English! And I suppose Ackburn is a Shakespeare, Rock said. Acton, I yelled, Acton! He's a friend, he's a friend, that's all!

And there I was Mozetta, there on the bed, and Acton was on the t.v., and he had just won the $15,000 and I couldn't stay tuned to see what his decision would be tomorrow because that's my shift at the store, and it really didn't matter cause I knew he'd already lost. It seemed like such a lie to me, all of it, me in the robe, Rock there, scratching himself, and Acton, on the t.v., answering questions about the Beatles. It was too strange. The part that really got me was the part about time. Here it was today and Acton's today was yesterday and mine's was today's and he won and lost and tomorrow what would he decide? Well, Mozetta, I just can't stay tuned. I can't. Acton looks too much like his daddy. Afterwards, I went into the bathrooom and looked at my face and felt sad. All day I felt sad. I did crazy things in the soup section. I got lost and put asparagus in the chicken noodle and when Wences came up to tell me about listening to my phone conversation, well, I just started to cry, there in the soup section. It seemed like such a lie. All of it. Oh, I...you have to go now...Tosty's back from work and wants his supper...oh, okay, I'll call you tomorrow. Oh, Mozetta, I tell you, it was too...too...I don't know you know what I mean? I just can't find the words. I told Rock that we'd met in a play, that he was my alcoholic husband...now why'd I say *that*, I wonder? Mozetta, you there?

El Correo

Arturo Sandoval

Mosco Trujillo swerved to avoid the pack of dogs fornicating in the middle of the only paved street in Pueblo Chico, hit several potholes that caused his hubcaps to sail into the nearby ditch, and finally coasted to a landing in front of the village post office.

Dragging his heavy mail bag behind him, he entered the combination post office and living room of Abrán Saavedra, shaking his fist at the dogs, at the potholes and at his rotten luck in being the mail carrier for the village.

"¿Que tal?" Mosco shouted to Abrán, who was sitting in front of his wood-burning stove, rocking and humming alabados under his breath.

"Aquí está el correo," he added. "There's a lot this week." Abrán just kept rocking and humming, oblivious to Mosco. His son, Sonny, as blind as his father, but with good hearing, responded instead.

"Ven a tomar un café, Mosco. Hace mucho frío. ¿Como está la carretera?" he asked.

"Resbaloso. Si no tienen que ir a Las Vegas, no vayan," Mosco responded. "Bueno. Gracias por el café. Nos vemos la semana próxima, ¿que no?" He picked up his bag of outgoing mail, slung it over his shoulder and left.

"Ven, papá, llegó el correo."

Abrán eagerly shuffled over to the kitchen table, then furiously began opening every package and letter before him. Sonny grabbed a cup of coffee and joined his dad at the table and the task at hand.

Sonny was 55, and had spent all his adult life helping his father run the post office. Like his father, Sonny had inherited the eye disease that had afflicted all of the male members of the Saavedra clan since time immemorial. His eyesight grew progressively worse, until Sonny lost all of his vision at the age of 16. Abrán had lost his eyesight a month after his high school graduation, at the age of 18. On weekends, Sonny joined his friends to play saxophone in a ranchera band that played at one of Las Vegas' seedier cantinas. Sonny was famous for his sax playing, and the local dives were constantly after him to perform at their establishments.

Though his cut of the payment for playing was peanuts, Sonny looked forward to his weekend gigs. He always got free drinks and his pick of the women that congregated in Las Vegas from the outlying ranchitos on weekends. To him, every one of his amorous conquests was as beautiful as Lucha Villa. With his practiced fingers, Sonny found the beauty in each of his weekend paramours. Ay, que suave, he thought. Tengo la vida regalada.

Sonny's mother had died of complications from her second pregnancy and Sonny had been raised by his father, mostly at the post office. Abrán Saavedra was already suffering from poor eyesight when he had been named postmaster, and he had counted on his wife's pair of good eyes to make the post office job a going concern. After her death, Abrán's blindness had cast the Pueblo Chico post office into chaos. The chaos had slowly evolved into an intricate social system that was now supported by all of the villagers.

Because of his blindness Abrán had been forced to guess which package or letter belonged in which villager's box. Try as he did to learn each villager's idiosyncrasies, Abrán always guessed wrong. Try as he did to feel and smell every letter by opening everything delivered by Mosco Trujillo, Abrán always got the wrong letters in the wrong boxes. Since his wife's death, Abrán had never been right once.

Because he never received a complaint, Abrán thought he had fooled the villagers. He thought he had an infallible nose.

The mail usually arrived on Thursday morning. It took Sonny and Abrán three hours to sniff and paw their way through the packages and letters, then slip them into one of the 250 active boxes in use.

Villagers from outlying pueblitos began arriving just before noon, sitting in the back of their battered pickups, and making a small picnic of it in front of the post office. Sonny would usually break out his saxophone, someone else would bring their guitar, and everyone would have a wonderful time mitoteando while they waited for the post office to open after lunch.

It was clear the villagers had adapted to the blind man's bluff mail delivery system pioneered by Abrán and perfected by Sonny. Though no one would admit it publicly, the villagers had grown to secretly love the excitement generated by receiving someone else's mail. They took the mail home, read it over and over, then spent Friday returning it to its rightful owner.

There were few secrets in Pueblo Chico.

Everyone knew Sonny had sacrificed his enormous talent as a musician to stay with his father in Pueblo Chico. He poured his heart and soul out through his saxophone at his weekend gigs. Women could feel his loneliness and passion flowing through his saxophone. All of them wanted to make Sonny feel less lonely. They tried. Sonny accepted them all. He still longed to make it to California, but as the years passed, he settled into his routine of weekend gigs and weekend women.

His job as assistant postmaster took at most a half day on Thursday and an occasional sale of stamps or money orders to one of the villagers. The rest of the time, Sonny spent practicing his saxophone, listening to his large collection of jazz records, and anticipating the weekend.

Sonny and Abrán also spent a lot of time together talking. They talked endlessly about the villagers, about the weather, about the sound of things changing in their rural enclave. Abrán told stories he had learned from the old borregueros when he was a boy. Tale after tale about diablos y muertos, brujas and unfaithful husbands and wives.

Abrán was mother and father to Sonny and they both enjoyed each other's company. After drinking a bottle of Jim Beam on a cold evening, Sonny would regale his father with his weekend conquests. What they wore. What they said. How surprisingly willing they were to try new positions. How they smiled. How they felt.

At first, people thought the two men at Georgia Halverstrom's general store were Mormon missionaries. Every Spring, the Mormons sent young men out proselytising in the villages around Las Vegas and Santa Rosa.

Usually, they wore dark, ill-fitting suits, with white shirts, ties and white socks showing because the pants were always high wawas. They rode around the village on bicycles, and usually left frustrated, not because the villagers were adamant Catholics, but because most of the villagers did not speak English and the Mormons knew no Spanish. The encounters normally ended with the Mormons leaving each family a bible, which the villagers later used to start fires in their fogones each morning.

Word soon spread, however, that the two Mormons were actually government agents, sent from Albuquerque to investigate Pueblo Chico's post office. Though Georgia Halverstrom denied it, everyone in the village was certain she had called the feds to oust Abrán and Sonny from their jobs. Georgia was determined to get her own son the post office job, and she was tired of the village's unspoken convention about reading everyone else's mail.

She had finally decided to call in the federal investigators when word spread throughout the village that she was jacking up her grocery prices beyond the limits of decency. Her billings ended up in Onofre Martínez's hands one day, and the village schoolmaster spent an entire week teaching his seventh and eighth grade students the evils of price gouging in civics class, using Georgia Halverstrom's practices as an example.

The Monday following the weeklong civics class, Georgia placed a long distance call to Albuquerque and reported that Abrán and Sonny were violating federal law by opening people's mail prior to placing it in boxes.

It took the feds two weeks just to locate Pueblo Chico on the state map and another two weeks to find two junior sleuths to assign to the case. After one particularly frustrating afternoon of knocking on doors only to find the villagers denying that anything was amiss with their mail service, the federal sleuths ended up at Halverstrom's store, bitterly sucking on beer and complaining to Georgia.

"Why are all these people protecting those two blind mice?" one asked Georgia. "Don't they realize they can go to jail for lying to federal investigators?"

"They're tontos," Georgia replied. "They're proud of the fact they stick together against all outsiders. It's all they have, really. Look at this place. The last time the street was paved was during the Depression when the WPA came through. Look at the school. We get all the alcoholic teachers, all the malcontents, all the Republicans from Santa Rosa. No, Pueblo Chico isn't a place that has much to brag about. So the people here react the only way they can, by shutting out outsiders, by protecting their own against all things. Heck, just last week we had a knifing at a wedding dance and when the Sheriff showed up, no one wouuld talk. No one. They'll settle it among themselves, but they will never take it to outsiders."

"That's just great, Mrs. Halverstrom. How are we supposed to prove the blind men are opening mail illegally, then?"

"Simple. I've got several of the old widows who will testify that is the case. They owe me their lives. They owe me more here at the store than they will ever be worth. They'll do as I say," she smiled knowingly as she spoke.

Mosco Trujillo dropped the mailbag on the kitchen table and sat down across from Sonny, who had already pushed a cup of coffee in front of him.

"How's Abrán taking it?" Mosco asked.

"Not very well, I'm afraid," Sonny replied.

"Damn that Georgia, hija de su..."

"Well, it had to happen, sooner or later."

"No, it didn't. We were doing just fine hasta que metió la pata esa Georgia. She had to go and drag all of us to Albuquerque and make a spectacle of us. I swear, she's going to pay for what she did to Abrán."

Sonny just shook his head. "No hombre, that's life. ¿Que vamos hacer? My Dad will just have to get over it, that's all."

"Where is he? It's not like him not to be sitting in his chair, waiting for me."

"He's in his room, just sitting there, staring at the walls. He said he couldn't bear to face anyone after the trial y todo, ¿sabes?"

As he said the last words, Abrán came shuffling into the kitchen, headed straight for his chair and sat down heavily.

"¿Que tal, Don Abrán?" Mosco shouted. "Aquí está el correo. Como siempre."

Abrán didn't answer, just waved his hand feebly in Mosco's direction.

"Come on, Don Abrán, you've got to get over the trial. Todavía tiene mucha vida por 'delante."

"¿Que dices?" Abrán said, his voice rising. "I have a lot of life ahead of me, is that what you said, Mosco?"

"Sí."

"¡Que pendejadas! Do you think I can show my face around here again? Do you think I'm not the laughingstock of the entire county? Did you know I had already written a story for Ripley's Believe It or Don't about my infallible nose?"

Mosco just stared at his coffee cup.

"That's right. And I was even thinking about sending the Pope a letter about my infallible nose, about how I had never been wrong with the mail for all these years, how no one had ever complained about me getting a letter in the wrong box. Never! And then they put me on the stand and they ask me if I knew I had never been right. Not once! ¡Nunca! ¡Que vergüenza!"

Abrán's thin shoulders shook as he wept silently. Mosco stood to go to him, but Sonny called him back.

"Ya deja de llorar, Papá," he said. "You are so upset over losing your infallible nose, you haven't seen the real miracle in all this."

Abrán stopped crying. "Miracle?"

"Sí, Papá. You've been so hurt because you learned you weren't infallible and you're mad at la gente here for not telling you for all these years. Pero, piénsalo, jefe. They all got on the witness stand in Albuquerque and protected you. They told the judge you had never been wrong. As far as they knew, everyone got his mail okay. Everyone in Pueblo Chico swore to that, except for the two viudas Georgia forced to help her."

"Why did Georgia do it, hijo?"

"It doesn't matter, Papá. What matters es que la gente stood behind you and behind me. They forced the judge to dismiss the charges. Isn't that a miracle, jefe?"

"I hadn't thought about it that way, hijo."

"Well, do, jefe, because it's the truth. You and me, we're just two old blind mice with no wives and no kids. But we're not alone, jefe. Everybody here loves us. Everybody here is our family. As long as we are here, we are safe, we are home, Papá."

Abrán pushed himself out of his chair, walked through the silence to the kitchen and pulled out a bottle of tequila. Carrying three glasses with him, he returned to the table, filled the glasses and said, "A toast. To Abrán Saavedra's almost infallible nose and to my family, la gente de Pueblo Chico."

Man Of Honor

Ronald P. Chavez

Juan Pablo Nieto was the first Santa Rosa soldier killed in the war. From all points of the rural county, people arrived at the rosary wake with a hushed sense of urgency, as if to miss it would be disrespectful and possibly even sacrilegious, so far from the ordinary was this wake.

It had been a dry, bitterly cold day. As evening fell, a wintery dusk dropped its curtain of half-light down on the little town, shrouding into dimness the thick, white-washed walls of a converted old adobe now serving as a chapel.

Still, a flood of people came. The huge wooden door squeaked and creaked, groaning annoyingly at each opening as people entered, stamping their feet stiffly on the wood-planked floor, vigorously rubbing their hands, seeking a sense of warmth. Inside the fast-filling chapel the mourners waited and watched in reverent silence.

Many came in sorrow, but a few came only to gawk and stare at their first military wake; it had a certain air of pomp and pageantry, novel to many. There was the bright and colorful American flag draped neatly over the army-gray casket; there was the crisp, sharp appearance of the honor guard standing at parade attention, their rifles gleaming in polished splendor. The aura of all this could not help but be impressive.

But for most the wake was a terrible, heavy burden, like a tragic black-ening cloud hanging over them, sinister, storming, threatening. There was in the room a feeling of unbearable pain, a pain mixed with almost reverential love, a love coming forth from a people who felt entirely unworthy, by com-parison, to the lone survivor, Emilio, the grandfather. The people who knew and understood the distressing circumstances surrounding the death of this boy-soldier felt an extreme but painful sense of respect and admiration for that grim-faced old man who sat alone up front. Stoically, stately, rigidly, he sat next to the flag draped casket. The casket dominated the front of the chapel that now was filled with streams of sad-eyed mourners who took turns standing before the old man. They wept; they embraced; they stared blankly into the old man's eyes, saying nothing, as they choked with emotion.

His eyes welling with tears, Emilio sat silent and erect, dressed in a double-breasted striped black suit which set off his bold bearing and sharp, massive features which appeared to have been chiseled from hard stone, so distinctive was his head and face. Tall, with huge, calloused hands that spoke of earth in their veins, Emilio was a man few dared reckon with. And not many men did or would in his lifetime.

But now Emilio's face suddenly turned stern and unemotional; his con-trolled countenance did not betray his inner thinking, but his mind raced to memories of his grandson, who lay dead in the casket. He sought comfort, even joy, by recalling the boy-soldier as a child.

"Papo!" the little two-year old called out, "come get me. Me cold."

He had been wading and splashing in the shallow part of the river below brush dam where the overspill from the irrigation ditch flowed into the river, cold and clear and swift. The time was fall and the air was dry and crisp and the sunlight bright with sharp colors as the eye pleasantly caught sight of the low-lying salt cedars in regal red and rust and the towering cottonwoods shimmering in yellow, the brilliant gold contrasting to the deep blue of the sky. Such was New Mexico in the fall along the verdant Puerto de Luna Valley. Such was the scene Emilio was now experiencing, somewhat absentmindedly, failing to respond to the boy immediately.

Again the boy yelled out, this time sharply, "Papo! Papo! Come get me!" Naked and shivering, his sun-bronzed skin glowing from the sheen of drip-ping river water, he repeated, pleadingly, "Papo, Papo, hurry, me cold."

Fondly and hurriedly, the old man tossed him in the air and caught him with out-stretched hands and arms. He hugged the boy and carried him to a clear patch of river beach and partially buried him in the warm sand, smiling broadly and reassuringly at him and thinking to himself how this little boy with the dark face and reddish streaked hair, who was fatherless, had given him so much pleasure, so much love; not the love of affection alone, but of peace, a peace more wonderful than the human mind could every fully understand, a peace that kept his thoughts still and quiet and his heart at rest. This love for the little boy was unmatched and unbroken by anything or anyone in his life. Theirs was a bond of trust.

Kicking away the sand, the boy squealed with delight. "Let's go. Me not cold now, Papo. Let's throw rocks in river." He paused. He looked up, his eyes big and brown, "You want to Papo?" the boy asked.

"You bet I do," the old man replied, overcome with emotion, hardly containing his enthusiasm to do the boy's bidding, for he delighted in and was totally intrigued by the boy's intellect, so quick for such a young age, his boundless energy, his joy for living, the way he called out, "Papo!" in confidence, in dependence, in constant love and interest. The boy was fast becoming his only reason for living.

"But gimme a big hug first," the old man said as he drew the boy up and held him close, "and gimme a big smacker."

The boy flung his tiny brown arms about the old man's neck, kissed him loudly, whispering, "We go play now?"

"Yes, we go play now," the old man said, then added, "but first hug me again, tight, very tight, so you'll never forget me."

The little boy squeezed tight. "Papo, Papo, me never forget you. Never!"

By now the chapel had filled to overflowing.

All the pews were full and people stood at close quarters along the side walls and others were packed clear to the back. There was nowhere else to sit or stand. All was solemn and still and the thick air was heavily laden with grief.

Except for one.

At the farthest corner, opposite the military metal gray casket, sat a tall young man, flaxen-haired, with curious blue eyes. But he felt no grief. Next to him sat a short, white-haired man, grim-faced. The young man drew close to the old man and spoke in a barely audible whisper, "Sir, pardon the intrusion, please. But something very special is happening here, is it not?"

The white-haired man turned, half startled at such a direct question. He thought for a moment, then answered in a whisper, "yes," covering his mouth with his hand, not hiding his annoyance for being distracted from his private thoughts.

"What is it?" the stranger asked.

"Perhaps not really special," replied the old man. He did not want to talk about it yet he tried to avoid being rude out of courtesy. He obliged the young man curtly but politely. "Just tragic," he said, "and painful, to me personally." Disdainfully he looked the other way, and with his hand brushed his white hair abstractly, obviously expressing his wish to be left alone.

"Not so!" the stranger pressed. "It is something. I can feel it. The air is thick with it," he exclaimed. "How can you deny that?" he challenged openly, almost brashly.

What the white-haired man did not know was that this young man was a newspaperman, an outsider. Against his will, his editor had dispatched him to this remote little town on a hunch that an interesting hero-story could be gleaned from the death of this boy-soldier. But instead of hero-stuff, the outsider had stumbled onto something deeper, something perhaps even sublime, certainly something uniquely tragic, something beyond his cultural understanding. But what? That question fueled his curiosity and fired his imagination. So he pressed on. "What are the facts here?"

Still the old man ignored the prodding.

"Please speak to me," the stranger said, pleadingly, again in a soft, convincing whisper. "I want to understand what is happening here." His instinct for a story was aroused.

Again, the old man turned, sighed, reconsidered, touched a trembling finger to his lips, and spoke, half choking, "Not special," he repeated with strong conviction. He paused, then said haltingly, "Much more like privileged." He paused again. "For us, perhaps even supernatural. What ever it is, it is something you cannot understand, not being one of us. To truly understand you have to be close to that old man up front, like me." He thought for a long time, then said, "No! No! This is not for you. You are an outsider. A stranger. What need have you to probe into this thing? Yes," he said as if to himself. "Yes! Yes! Very rare, indeed," he concluded sadly, almost tearfully, dropping his eyes, wanting desperately to be left alone, and whispering, "you have no share in this. You can only be bad for it."

"What?" asked the young man with arrogance, not touched by the old man's distress. His newspaper instincts flared openly: "What are you calling rare? How rare? Answer me. I'm a writer. You must not leave the story hanging."

"I'm sorry. That's all I have to say," the white-haired man replied, unimpressed by the man's credentials.

Up front Emilio sat straight-backed, pensive, in deep concentration.

"So you know him well?" the stranger pursued anxiously, but less demanding, not wanting to lose his story source, pointing to Emilio at the front of the altar, his voice rising above a whisper. "Why is this thing rare? What did he do?"

The white-haired man looked the stranger straight in the eyes, coldly, speaking with disturbing but delicate finesse, needing to end the matter, he said evenly, "He gave his word."

"So?"

"And he kept it."

"And?"

"And it killed his grandson."

Just then a disciplined hush settled over the crowd and the rosary started, "Our Father, Who art in heaven..." Everyone dropped to their knees, repentent and regretful, and the cantor repeated prayer after prayer in a sorrowful, soulful cadence.

Young Juan Pablo Nieto had been killed in action his very first time in battle. He had taken a direct hit from a Viet Cong mortar shell. They shipped his body home in a gray metal box.

In a flash! At the blink of an eyelid, it was suddenly and quickly over, just like that.

But to Emilio, it was not suddenly and quickly over, just like that. The inner shock waves he felt were still crashing and slamming against his fractured soul!

Yet he sat, concentrating, silently. The praying droned on and on, rising and falling in pitch only at the changing of stanzas at work in the beaded rosary..."Holy Mary, Mother of God..."

His mind drifted. He was hearing echoes of the boy speaking excitedly. It had been a special day to remember. The boy was fourteen years old then.

"Look! Look, Papo!" The boy was beaming proudly, waving his report cards in the air. "Papo, check out my grades! All A's!" he boasted. "Now does that make me smart or not? Or what?" the boy asked brashly.

"It could," the old man replied sagely, stroking the boy's head. "And it could not," he stated, frowning slightly. "By boasting and bragging it could mean not."

"And why not?" the boy queried with feigned surprise, not wanting to hear the old man's subtle admonishment. "Papo, you know how I need and want so much to be smart," he said ardently, then deadly serious, he observed aloud, "You said, a man's mind is the master over all things, when properly motivated. True?"

"True," Emilio quickly agreed, knowing he was boxed in by the boy's keen and perceptive retort. He gave a long thoughtful pause, knowing he had to respond logically and avoid preaching, for lately the boy had taken to challenging him intellectually, always at the ready with instant opposite viewpoints. He settled for an unshakeable truism: "Only when properly motivated by God. Then and only then!" he concluded, self-satisfied with his response.

"Then I shall cram all there is to know into my brain as fast and as well as I can," the boy conceded. "Then it shall be my brain, my mind, that shall be master over all things, properly motivated by God," he qualified teasingly, "right?"

"Yes, if you will it," Emilio answered, then added highly pleased, "And on you shall the sun rise, my son, rest assured, of that I will make certain."

Outwardly, Emilio roared with kind laughter at the boy's obsession with worldly knowledge. Inwardly he recalled God's warning to man: But about going further than words given by one shepherd, my son, be warned; of making many books there is no end, so do not believe everything you read, and much study is a weariness of the flesh.

"After all has been heard, the end of the matter is: Fear God!" That bit of wisdom would come later, the old man thought. Yes, but not much later.

"Then why do you laugh at me," the boy asked, his high spirits sagging.

"Only at your innocence," he reassured the boy, "not at your intentions. Time will tell. There is much to life. Much more!"

"But you agree it's possible?"

"Of course," Emilio exclaimed with optimism, not wanting to dash the boy's moment of triumph over his studies. "And Papo will make it possible. Continue to study hard. You will go to the best schools..."

The rosary concluded. In the far corner, the stranger resumed his whispered but intent interrogation of the white-haired man. Final condolences began. Once more the people paraded before the closed casket, stopping briefly where Emilio sat. His correctness of manner and his moral strength were like a bright beacon in the dark; and the people felt it. Their grief only intensified, but few words were spoken. The all merciful unspoken word prevailed, for the pain of grief was becoming unbearable. More so to those few who truly knew why the loss of the boy was so complete, so final, so tragic, and so exclusive to Emilio.

Finally all the people walked past, tight-lipped, heads dropped, hands clasped, crying muffled sobs.

"What are you saying?" the newspaperman was now asking frantically, aware the ceremony was ending, "that he killed his own grandson? But why? How?"

"No more questions," the white-haired man pleaded. "Now I must go to him."

"Wait!"

Vexed but wanting to end this incessant probing, the white-haired man relented. "Yes. He killed the boy. Indirectly." He started to pull away.

"How? For God's sake, tell me how!" His mind was wild with curiosity concerning this strange but compelling relationship between the old man and the boy. He pressed on: "How?"

"By virtue of his position," he said sadly, "that's how he killed the boy." He went on as if to himself in a monotone voice. "Not directly, mind you.

Because he was prepared to take a position consistent with his values, he lost the boy. Because he is a man of his word. Because he is a rock of a man." Then with rancor, "But you could never understand that!"

"Try me," the newspaperman pleaded, "Tell me, how was the old man responsible?"

"Because of the draft," he said, his voice weak with emotion. "The old man was chairman of the draft board. And in public, fearlessly and boldly, he gave his word of honor that always he would be fair and impartial to rich or poor, brown or white-skinned, kin or no kin. He gave his word...and he kept it."

"He drafted his own grandson?" the stranger asked, with incredible disbelief.

"Yes."

"And now he has to bear the guilt..."

"Yes, now excuse me." The white-haired man stood, slowly walked up to Emilio. Emilio stood for the first time and embraced his close friend warmly but firmly. There stood two old friends in time of desperate need. Both were recalling how the white-haired man had angrily objected to Emilio's drafting of the boy. Emilio heard the echoes of his desperate pleas, "Emilio, Emilio, *hombre*, my hard-headed, dear, dear friend, must you be so stubborn," he had begged. "After the boy there is no one left." Then he tried to use reason: "Tell me, my friend, who will work the farm? Who will tend to the ranch? Nobody, right? Emilio, no one can fault you for not drafting the last of the line...no one!"

Now inside the dim-lit chapel, each stared directly into the other's eyes, both stricken with grief and sorrow beyond measure. There was no anger. No vengeance. Only the unspoken question: Why? They just stood there, two men, two friends, agonizing, silently dealing with that terrible question that warps the human spirit: Why?

No answer came.

Again Emilio's mind drifted.

"Papo, Papo!" the young Juan called out. "Look," he beamed, proudly waving a ribbon-tied college diploma over his head. "With honors, Papo," he emphasized. "Now are you proud of me?" he teased, with a twinkle in his eyes.

"To overflowing," he said eagerly, a happy smile firmly fixed along his entire face. Barely able to contain his joy, he bear-hugged the boy, saying, "You earned it!"

Soon afterwards, Emilio drafted young Juan into the army.

That memory now haunted his mind, soul and body.

"Don't pity me," Emilio asked his friend, the first words he had spoken in the chapel. His voice quavered, "Not here." He lowered his head, his chin to his chest, tears welling in his eyes, "Not now."

His friend touched him on the shoulder knowingly, and said nothing. He walked away. Heavy-hearted and weary, thinking, remembering, he said to himself, "What a rock of a man, my compadre is a man who speaks little but understands much. At a time when every wind of doctrine bent and swayed the minds of men every which way, here stood a man who held to his word. And paid the price!"

The white-haired man shook his head, stepped out into the cold and wept.

By now all the people had left the wake, save Emilio. He sat motionless beside his grandson. He was recalling how the boy had rationalized his situation and what he concluded would forever remain implanted and rooted in his mind.

"Papo," young Juan had said, "listen and understand. It is not you who does this to me. Somethings are of necessity the way they are. Not by chance but by fate. Look how our ancestors, those brave Spanish souls, came to New Mexico, to a far away strange new world. Here the hail fell, to rain ruin and destruction. Here the lightning struck suddenly, frying a man in his tracks. Here the wild March winds blew and the dust storms raged across the *llano*, drying up the last bit of winter moisture. Yet we did not attempt to tame the elements nor the *llano*, nor did we seek to subdue the land. To this day all this remains the same, unchanged. Simply put, we found the life of the vast *llano* lonely and primitive and especially harsh. Yes, but lonely and primitively and harshly we survived. They had to be strong, they had to have courage. So, strong and courageously they also went off to war. My ancestors, those brave souls, did it. Now...so must I do it. Or my future, my life, my hopes, my beliefs will prove false and futile. Understand clearly, Papo, what ever happens in that future shall have to be compared and tested to what happens today,here in my heart, in my mind, in my total consciousness. I must do my duty. So I go. For this also cannot be changed. Now give me your blessing, Papo, that I may go into battle strong and courageously."

With this thought, finally, his grief was reconciled. Comforted and cheered by the knowledge that his only grandson, the last of the line, had lived and died by honorable standards, not because they were popular or unpopular, whether the opportunity seemed favorable or unfavorable, or whether it was convenient or unconvenient. Instead, he had kept his sense of urgency, gone into battle, fought, and was killed.

There, and then, the boy's life had been stilled, with honor.

At last the old man stood up, privately bid the boy a long farewell, left the chapel, and walked out into the cold night.

"No Es Hablar De Su Vida, Sino Su Muerte"

Estevan Arellano

—Si ésto hubiera pasa'o hoy día en lugar del '59 todo hubiera sido diferente; siete muertos en un año, CUATRO TENDIDOS A LA MISMA VEZ y ni ruido. Ningún editorial o comentario; de la investigación oficial ni una palabra en la prensa, ni que hubieran sido animales los que dieron su vida fuera por su propio descuido o lo que fuera; el gobierno era el responsable; pero no, con $20,000 trataron de tapar sus injusticias. ¿Qué estaríamos todos durmidos? es uno tan tonto que de nada se fija, ni quien le advirtiera de nada. ¿Qué pensaríamos? luego tu tío Antonio estar tendido al mismo tiempo. ¿Qué no taparía el gobierno me pongo a pensar ora? Por fin me carcomia...(suspiro)...como ha cambia'o todo desde entonces.

DEL CAÑON DEL RÍO BRAVO (cual fue rajado como un rayo que le pega a un pinabete, así éste fue abierto por las aguas turbulentes del norte), de repente, de ese llano cubierto de chamiso pardo donde sólo las víboras y el borreguero en su silencio pasan sus días oyendo el sonido del sincerro, de ahí, igual que hinchazón, brotan las montañas de la Sierra Madre pero que ahora se nombran las Sangre de Cristo. Por promover el turismo, como parte de la estrategia del ferrocarril en los 1890s, un periodista de Chicago las nombró así porque el nombre sonaba más romántico para poder atraer asmáticos por el clima. Al norte del valle de la Española se alcanzan a ver las montañas azulejas de Taos y al este la majestuoza Jicarita, la guardián del norte, y abajo queda el valle de la Peña de donde se ven, como dedos huesudos de la Comadre Sebastiana tocando el harpa, las montañas más bastas y toscas en el estado. De arriba de las costillas, de los lomos de estos cerros bruscos, se ven todos los pueblitos como en un sueño, calladitos y tranquilos y nada enseñan del remolino y ansia que sienten los corazones palpitantes y heridos de estos lugares antiguos. La frontera del noroeste está fortalizada por el Pedernal, el "cerro vagabundo," como le dicen los "Tofes," cual ocupa un lugar único, como rey de la frontera más solitaria; escultura ambiental dominando el paisaje. Todos estos cerros están al mismo punto de altura; cuando andan las nubes rodeando la Jicarita, cruzando por los dedos de los camellones de los picachos de Truchas, hasta que se llega el momento que todo el cielo oscurece como borrego negro recien lavado; en un instante está el cielo en tribulación; son los dioses peleando con sus espadas relampaguiantes y sólo los crujidos del hierro se oye. Los indios reclaman que es Moctezuma luchando contra Cortez; la plebe de hoy día dice que son los "low-riders" al tamboraso con los "hippies."

Ahora, abajo de las cordilleras, donde antes estaban los valles aforrados de ganado, trigo, aveno y papas, todo lo que se encuentra son vehículos que parecen ser casas modernas con todo adentro y con placas de Tejas; tratando de huirle a los inviernos del llano, dicen, pero sólo es la última conquista del norte. —Los gueros de Tejas quieren nuestras tierras y agua—, lamentan los ancianos. Desde el centro de esa región atraviesan los llanos estacados donde los cíboleros iban a arresgar sus vidas para traer alimento a sus familias y pueblo; desde allí viene esta plaga de turistas peor que chapulines, mientras en los pueblitos andan los diez uñas de los tecatos que no dejan casa que no ventanean y de todos lados sigue el cancer cundiendo. Dentro de esta enfermedad, hay locuras y gente que todavía están vivos dentro de un capacete muerto.

Esta es una gente muy curiosa—pues, quiero decir, muy extraña—el santo día trabaja y no se les hecha de ver nada, como luego decía el tío. En la mayoría de las situaciones el marido trabaja como pendejo y la mujer gasta el cheque como agua a lo loco. Siendo que la pasan el maldito día sin quehacer de bonitonas delante del maldito tubo mirando las fantasias de una realidad que no existe, hasta el ceso se les está secando como ratón volador muerto en estero seco, reseco igual que caspa; tela para pescar moscos muribundos se les está volviendo el ceso pinineo.

A veces no sé quien será el pendejo, si yo o la gente; ha llega'o a tal punto que me siento como el dinosauro cuando empezó el alimento a acabarsele; aquí estoy tirando monoteadas de ahoga'o. Después de durmitar un rato—¿dónde te conocí? ¿en la pinta o el asilo? pues ¿dónde estoy? ¿es sueño o pesadilla? ya ni durmir puedo de tanta fiebre que tengo—recuerdo con la misma tentación: los frega'os son la gente. Hasta vergüenza me da ser de la misma especie. Los animales están más agusa'os, ellos no nos reclaman, nosotros queremos salvarnos con ellos.

Ya que saben de que pata cojea el penco, como decía tu tío, abajaremos al plan para encontrar la gente que aquí habita: ahí podemos aterrizar. La gente que dice que el diablo es mexicano (el infeliz cabrón) y la muerte es española (la comadre sebastiana), son los habitantes de esta región. A esta gente de tanto trabajo ya se les acabó la fiesta en sus vidas; después del jale todos se encuentran en las mismas cantinas, contando los mismos chistes secos y la misma plática aburrida de tan sin sabor.

No sé que son estas voces que oigo o de donde vienen:

—*¿Qué hay de nuevo?*

—*Nada, ¿y tú qué tienes de nuevo?*

—*Nada, lo mismo...pura calor; puro "preschure;" y esta calor que no se aguanta...*

—*¿Jalando?*

—*Jalando; dale y dale y en lo mismo...cada día peor...*

—*Ya hacía tiempo que no te miraba; ¿de nuevo? ¿nada?*

—*Nada, pisteando aquí; ando más crudo quel infierno...*

—*También yo; anoche me las conete; ya mero no me dejaba la "queca" entrar; tú sabes como son las rucas...puro darse uno en la madre, jalando como pendejo y todavía no quieren que tire uno poco party.*

—*¿Enque no tienes nada de nuevo?*

—*Ni naranjas...*

¿Qué voces pa' molestar! De la esquina de La casa de mi ruca, como se llama esta maldita cantina, se oye la vitrola cantar "...la vida no vale nada..."

¿Qué les digo? Hasta la música lo dice. Pásenle, llegen a echarnos un traguito aquí con el Diablo. Solo que escuchen pa' reflejar esta gente. De aquí de esta esquina nada se pasa y ni quien moleste de suerte; a mí no me conocen y a usté tío no lo ven. De vez en cuando se me invitara la ocasión y le ofrecere un comentario como chile rescolda'o en las brazas siendo que ya no conoce la famosa Cuerda y sus habitantes. Para no enredarlo o encuerdarlo, vamos a pistear y observar. Uste en su lugar y yo aquí en mi condenada esquina; aquí tratando de escribir una novela que no debo escribir; al govierno no le va a gustar; así son los federales. De modo que para no escribir esta novela que no me dejan escribir, me tengo que entretener platicando lo que hubiera de escribir en papel. Pero donde voy a encontrar papel; ora ni lápiz tengo; dicen que estoy loco pero no estoy; ellos son los locos, yo estoy bien pero me están queriendo relajar. Como es una labor tan difícil la de escribir pa' un público que nada aprecia, por eso sólo voy a contar lo que traigo en mente; eso o me pueden quitar. Posible más allá si escriba ésto pero ahora no es tiempo. Siendo que yo soy sus ojos, boca y oidos en ésto, escuchen con mucho cuida'o porque no lo puedo repetir; no me deja el gobierno; por eso tengo que jugarla de loco. Hay están esas malditas voces de vuelta; como friegan, no me dejan concentrar en lo que tengo que escribir.

—*Cuida quien entro, ¡orale bro! ¿quéciendo?*

—*Del jalisco...*

—*¿México?*

—*No; ojala que viniera de Jalisco; vengo del Jalisco, de quitarme el yugo, luego nomás llego al chante sale la vieja toda emperrada, echándoseme al pedo porque llego a la barra...no quiere que me le desprenda de las naguas...¿qué están pisteando?*

—*¡Chales! yo l'agarro; Diablo, danos una, dos, tres, cuatro...o, danos un round a todos. Lo que estén pisteando. Ya es viernes y mañana no hay jale; durmir tarde...*

—*¿De nuevo?*

—*Nada; ¿contigo?*

—*Dale y dale y que no se alcanza uno.*

—*Así estoy yo. ¿Ónde jalas; todavía 'onde mismo?*

—*Sí; en el Árbol...todavía cortando...jale; a toda maquina, no hace*

uno nada; nunca ha pasa'o ningún pedo aquí..........
¿NO? ¿CÓMO QUÉ NO: qué de los cuatro en el S-Site en el '59?
¿tú?
—*En la misma, en el "jureniam," como le decía tu tío al uranio. Ora
que hay jale obliga'o a entrarle; la vieja quiere TV de color nuevo y
una dish washer y yo quiero sacarme una Four-Wheeler pa' ir al
vena'o; ora le estoy poniendo hasta sesenta horas con el martillo
blasteando polvora...*
PRECISO; eso es lo que está haciendo el vecino (—Gracias por la cerveza, bro...); lo que nos va a volver polvo ora, y el inocente sin saber que está
haciendo. Y él puro echarme de conta'o que yo como escritor sin papel ni
lápiz, vivo de puros programas; en otras palabras que soy un mantenido de
los pagadores de tasación. Lo que él no se da cuenta es de que es él al quien
mantienen los pagadores de tasación siendo que él trabaja por el departamento que llaman defensa y yo muerte. Pero el muy contento trabajando
sobretiempo por la muerta y la "huesuda" desmorecida de la risa; cuando
llega a la casa, en lugar de tortillas y frijolitos pintos le asisten pan blanco de
la tienda, masudo peor que chicle—el de la "Bettybubbles"—y empalmado
de a dos con una poca de breca entremedio...(Ésto me recuerda de un chiste
de Don Cacahuate; escuchen porque no lo voy a escribir ni repetir: izque en
una vez estaba el huerco llorando porque no quería la tortilla sola; siquiera
una mantequita con sal pal sabor. Ya izque le gritó Don Cacahuate a Doña
Cebolla, —Pues si no la quiere sola, empalmale de a dos—.) Y dije, "lo asisten" como el choclo—el perro—que el pobre animal que culpa tiene que no
le den huesos; ni a él le gusta la comida de la tienda porque a esos revoltijos
no se les puede llamar refín, ni siquiera pipirín. Cuando más breca se le
puede nombrar, apenas detiene el hambre; muy apenas acincha poco "las
grandes" pa' que no se coman a "las chiquitas." Nomás el delirio queda aunque llene el tubo de lástico de tantas hamburgesas perrodas y perros calien-
tes secos.
    Que extraño es el mundo pero que le vamos a hacer; ya estamos en este
tren pasajero-carguero y tenemos que darle hasta el fin y luego quien sabe
después; nadie sabe. Este mundo es un carnaval donde nosotros somos los
titires (de algo así quiero escribir la novela que no puedo escribir; no me
dejan), recordando solo con el sonido hueco no del duende sino la feria; un

sonido que penetra hasta el fin del oído y la punta del dedo gordo en el pie izquierdo. Curioso, o posible no sea curioso, el poder que tiene este sonido; es un sonido que repica hasta la mano vuelta plato del cura mendigo; hasta al más garrudo lo dobla, igual que al que dice que el capital es la raíz más dañosa del mundo. Hasta el huaino de peso se evaporizó de la tierra porque ya ahora no piden peso, sino peso y cuara: —el inflation, coño—, como dice el vecino Mage.

No les digo como es la gente, esta plaga de pordioseros; luego están todos los "salvadores" nuevos, o sean los consejeros de amontones a todos niveles; desde los tapa'os en salú mental que están más sierras que un jarro sellado pero que los tienen ahí por lambe roscas, hasta les ole la boca a fundio; luego los "testigos de Jehova" que a todos andan platicando sus confesiones de como eran ellos allá por los "tiempos de upa" cuando bebían en canastos, robaban al vecino y andaban en la jaina, perdidos en las delicias de la vida. Todo tengo en mente de poner en mi novela si es que algún día la escriba; ¿les podía apostar que la gente me va a decir que soy majador? ¿Quién era peor que Zacarias? hora mirenlo, nada se parece a aquel que iba para El Paso por carga y grifa; más bien ahora anda bien vestido del pleito que ganó izque porque se lástimo el espinazo (esta enfermedad nomás a los huevones les da) y así se maderea con sus dedos llenos de diamantes. A todo que le pone oreja le dice de como era él antes; de cuantos pesos perdió en la parranda; cuantas cosas él pudiera tener si no hubiera sido pendejo. ¿Ya para qué sirven piedradas al sabinto después de que el conejo ha huido? Es inútil recordar el pasado que uno mismo labró; es una tontería lamentar los años que se fueron en la "canilla." Pobre hombre, no se puede dar cuenta que lo pendejo es herencia que llevará al sepulcro. Dijo JesuCristo cuando se iba a ir del mundo, "—Aquí los dejo, para que el vivo se haga rico de los pendejos—." Recuerden que los perros abren los ojos a los quince días, pero los pendejos nunca. ¿A quién quiere engañar esta gente? ¿Qué no se darán cuenta de las cicatrices que atraviesan su cara embalsamada? aunque poco borradas por los cosméticos aplicados en sus más-caras como caldo espeso; no puede uno cambiar de máscara nomás quiere porque bajo esa falsedad brilla el verdadero ser como un cuerpo radioactivo.

¿Qué no piensa que la gente, a veces, no se porta como gente? Además de una corta resolana o una larga sombra, depende en el tiempo del año, el mejor lugar para saber como piensa (o no piensa) la gente, es una cantina como ésta. Aquí hasta el gallo más capón tiene huevos, aunque estrellados. Antes que se me olvide, dejen contarles lo que le pasó a un amigo en una vez que llegó a vender fruta en una casa. Si estuviera escribiendo mi novela contada, entonces no pudiera desviarme por estas veredas. Como creo que sabe, a lo que le teme uno más cuando anda en la frutiada de vendedor son los perros; pues anyway para recortar el cuento, cuando aquel se apió de su troca alcanzó a ver al dueño del lugar y al mismo tiempo un perro cascarrillento levantó las orjejas. Al camarada de una vez se le fruncieron las corbas, y le gritó al dueño, "—Cuideme el perro, no me vaya a morder—." Y ya le respondió el viejito, sin fijarse, "—No le hace nada, si está capón..." "—Si no tengo miedo que me joda, sino que me muerda—," le contestó el camarada.

Deberas que se tiene uno que cuidar más de las mordidas que le tiran de todos lados que de las nalgas. Por eso es tanta la necesidad por consejeros; no es que está la gente tan fregada, es por la mordida de tener a la gente empleada y creyendo que están haciendo bien; nada tiene que ver por ayudar a los arrastrados. Todos tenemos que ocuparnos en algo, más que sea en hacer mal. Usté se que me quiere preguntar como lo hicieron mis sobrinos el otro día, pero ellos son mi sangre, y tienen derecho, "—¿Cuál es mi oficio—?" Qué arrogante de usté quererme hacer tal pregunta o preocuparse en que me ocupo yo cuando apenas nos estamos conociendo. Ni el maestro que la otra noche estaba preguntándole a un camarada que trabaja por el estado, que si que hacía, cuanto ganaba, etc.; en otras palabras estaba preguntando lo que no le importa y así está de maestro. Todavía yo que pregunte, pues para eso estudié, para ser periodista y al escritor le pagan por ser mitotero pero ese no es el oficio del maestro; mi oficio no es de enseñaries, es de informarlos. Podía decirles como dice un primo chisteando, —Todo lo que hago es matar, robar, y no hacerle mal a nadie—, o podía decirles semejante a como dice el camarada Morgan, —¿Pa' qué fui a la escuela? ¿Saben pa' qué preguntones? Pa' no trabajar y pa' que les arda a ustedes *sanamacuiches*—, pero creo que pensaran que les estoy dando carrilla cuando les estoy hablando en serio. Pero la verdad es que mi "oficio" es el de no tener oficio para poder venir todos los días a este mismo banco, en esta misma esquina maldita, que desde que me acuerdo nada ha cambiado, ni la telaraña han quitado hace años, se conoce; sólo para venir a este púlpito a escuchar un pueblo adolorido, herido, lastimado, maltratado; a escuchar un espíritu agonizante buscando cuerpo; despertando a otro amanecer sin conocer la cama ni la mujer y sin saber donde está uno. Este mi oficio es el más difícil; no crean ahora que quiero presentarles mi moralidad porque posible no tenga, como los del "*Moral Majority*," que todo es que salen de la iglesia cruzan la calle a la casa de putas, y es por la simple razón de que todos quieren hacerme aceptar su moralidad pudrida de después de darle la carne al diablo, ahora quieren darle sus pobres huesos cateados a Dios. ¡Cómo son hipócritas! Por eso es difícil mi oficio de sin oficio, de observador; ahora saben porque no tengo el tiempo de escribir mi novela prometida.

Ya nadie me pone atención porque la gente piensa que estoy loco y borracho; hace tantos años que no me quito de esta maldita esquina que hasta los granos en la madera los tengo contados y si tuviera el tiempo, que deberas si lo pudiera tener pero no quiero, yo personalmente les dijera como se llama cada uno de estos infelices. Lo que si les puedo decir es quien son aquellos infelices que se ven cantando por fuera y llorando por dentro. Aquel chinchonte es el "Aguila Negra," luego está el Foncho; 'mano Pacomo es el viejito malcriado que por sobrenombre le dicen el Veneno; luego sentada está la María—si no crean, también mujeres llegan; también ellas tienen el alma en el cuerpo; algunas están más locas que los hombres; hasta libros pudiera uno escribir de ellas, pero no hay tiempo—y después está Tarugo y el "predicador" es Inocencio, hablando por el vino. Pues no sé ni para que les estoy contando sus nombres, al cabo que no los conocen y más poco les ha de importar quienes son. Esta es la rechola que se redondea por estos *pules* diario; ellos como yo, somos parte de los muebles.

Me dispensa, se oye el teléfono; ¿podía apostar qué es para mí? no es que estoy esperando llamadas; ven, ¿qué les dije? hasta medio brujo soy; sí es para mí. ¿Pero quién me estará llamando aquí? Nadie sabe que aquí estoy, verdad que no salgo de aquí; pero no tengo ni amigos, ni parientes; nadie quiere a los anarquistas como yo; pero además, también soy existencialista porque "el que no piensa tres veces al día que se va a morir, no puede vivir una vida completa." Nadie me conoce aunque todos me miran; caras vemos, corazones no sabemos. No creo que haiga computadores para que la policía sepa donde estamos todos los borrachos a todo tiempo. Luego, pues

yo no soy borracho siendo que no tomo ni consejos; cuando más dos cer-
vezas al día me bebo y es porque me las compran ¡Nomás miren! que raro
que sonará el teléfono por mí; tan demañana, en cuanto iba a "tirar el miedo"
(de miarme en los calzones) por primera vez hoy. Y anoche que iba en rumbo
de la casa, pensando de lo que pasa en este santo hogar, las confesiones y tes-
timonios de los demonios, me citó la placa por ir diez millas, ¡fíjense! sólo
diez millas arriba del limite y me multó quince pesos o diez días de carcel. Y
los criminales libres. Lo que él no sabía es que yo conozco al juez y es como
dice el primo Rafael, "—Es mejor una pulgada de juez que cien de
abogado—." Pero me dispensan porque alguien me espera del otro lado de la
líñea telefónica (en el mitotero, o "el chucho," como dice Goñito) y luego,
pues, tengo que ir al Juez de paz; ustedes saben, al escusado.

Suerte que no era nada ni nadie; solo una de mis viejas que miró mi troca
afuera; que para no mentirles tengo de todas en mi atajo, "viudas, solteras, y
una que otra casada," como dice la canción. Me fascinan las mujeres; los
hombres tan aburridos, tan serios y pendejos; pero las viejas todas tan
parecidas y tan diferentes; todas tan buenas en la cama, el único lugar donde
todavía hay caridad y el dinero no cuenta; también es la única vez donde el
hombre admite aunque sea a si mismo en la obscuridad del cuarto de que la
mujer es más poderosa. Ni puedo recordar con cuantas reinas desde Juarez a
Wáshington (y que a mis "putas" yo sólo tengo el derecho de decirles así;
para ustedes son "señoritas," y no se equivoquen), no he pasado las horas y
las noches enteras en sus brazos que a medio mundo han acariciado. Lo
bueno de una que lo vende por el sonido que baila el chango, es que no son
"vagabundas" sino unas mujeres tan sabidas, pasiadas, y las únicas que
deberas saben como amar. Ahí, está la Toña, ¿cuántas veces no hemos dor-
mido juntos sin ninguna vez cobrarme por sus placeres? más bien ella me ha
dado dinero, cuando no me ha dado estampas, y comprado no se cuantas
copas de café. El cura no hace eso; más bien él todos los días me pide para
tratar de salvar a gente como la Toña que al pobre nunca le cobra; ella sabe
bien a quien aplanarle la tecla y empelotar. Pero no sólo la Toña; parte de mi
vida y para ésto la mejor parte, la he pasado con mujeres del mundo que
nunca me han cobrado nada nada, ni siquiera que las ame; más bien muchas
de mis viejas me pasan *bicoca* y me tratan a mí, este pobre infeliz arrastrado

y olvidado, como si fuera rey. Pero también conozco mujeres que dan las nalgas a gobernadores, senadores y a los "meros gallones" sólo para tener más poder; para hacerse más mandonas y cabronas; estas para mí son las verdaderas "putas" aunque anden con la cruz en el pecho.

La única friega es que mis viejas no se pueden ver unas con las otras; cada una dice que me quiere más que la otra y al momento tratan de probarme sea en la calle, atrás en cajón de la troca, o donde sea, hasta abajo del agua. Yo les digo que por mientras no arrebaten, hay para todas pero todas me quieren—"chingar," dijera el primo solteron que murió el año pasado a la edad de ochenta años, sin nunca gozar de una mujer. Si por ellas fuera no estuviera aquí en esta maldita esquina platicando mientras nos tomamos unas heladitas; cada una tiene un nicho ya hecho para mí, pero como no soy santo, en ninguno quepo. Hasta temblor y escalofrío me da nomás pienso de lo que mis amantes, y tanto que me quieren, tratan hacer conmigo. Siempre les hecho achaque, pero como no son pendejas, ellas saben que yo soy como un pajarito que prefiero el frío de la nieve en enero, a la jaula más lujosa del mundo en julio. No me gustan palacios porque el día que me muera no me lo voy a poder llevar, ni mujer bonita para que no me la quiten. ¿Para qué? para un hombre "sin nombre" y "sin oficio" como yo, dondequiera lavo y plancho y cualquier nabo me sabe a pastel. Por eso quiero a mis viejas por-que saben que ninguna puede decir que soy de ella; en realidad no pertenesco a nadie, hasta me vida está prestada; de todas soy igual aunque ya los años se me enreden en los pies; todavía puedo con una de quince, sabiendo que ya los quince son al revéz.

Medio siglo y un año más, esa es mi edad. He visto mucho y todavía todos los días sigo mirando, mirando cosas que en mi vida había reflejado. Cosas tan chiquitas que antes no me daba el tiempo de mirar; "una piedra en el camino me enseñó que mi destino era," como el della, "rodar y rodar." De joven anduve por dondequiera, todo el mundo me pasié; todas clases y colores de mujeres me platicaron de sus maridos celosos que les pegaban después que ellos eran los vagos; de sus queridos impotentes tanto en la vida como en la cama y nunca encontrar una virgen. Posible sea una de las ilusiones peores de la juventud; idealista, buscando lo perfecto, el amor que dure los "noventainueve" del contracto. El primer tropezón, un fracaso en la mente juvenil. Viví aquí y allá y ahora no se si vivo allá o vivo aquí; pero continuaremos después de este traguito. Como dicen en la televisión, "este es un anuncio pagado." ¿Han tenido los teleles? O, ¿nunca se han puesto muy turilailos? Yo sí, pero ya no tomo tanto; no puedo, no quiero ir al Embudo con el camarada Lencho, al museo de los huainos; si quieren saber que parece un huaino sobrio deben de venir aquí siendo que es uno de los pocos lugares donde puede ver tal maravilla.

Sí, estos ojos que se los va a comer la tierra han visto mucho; tanto que ni me quisiera acordar. A veces posible hasta de más, posible cosas que no hubiera de haber visto, pero el destino me puso en ese lugar a ese tiempo (yo no pedí estar ahí presente); muertes de camaradas, parientes, por lumbres, lluvias, piedras de relices. Como he visto ésto, también tengo recuerdos papables que nunca se borraran de amantes que jamás volveran, montañas bruscas cuyos picos rascan al cielo, bailes llenos de gente desconchiflada, y niños inocentes con su sonrisa que nada saben que los espera al dar la vuelta los años engañadores. De mi niñez muy poco me acuerdo, quizás por la simple razón de que cuando uno está mediano se preocupa más en vivir que en pensar sobre la razón por vivir; vivir aquí en esta esquina maldita que no se mueve, ni platíca, ni mira; nada hace más que marcar los minutos y segundos de mi vida que se están yendo para jamás volver. Pregúntale al más huevón su oficio y siempre les va a decir que "muy ocupa'o." ¡Qué embustera gente! lo peor que sabe uno la verdad, y siempre mintiendo que buscan la verdad. Eso dicen todos, la verdad y única verdad, entonces se vuelve el dinero. "Si no hay dinero, no hay amigos," me decía mi madre cuando estaba yo creciendo pero no la creía. Ahora comprendo eso, cuando tengo dinero me sobran amigos, cuando ando "brujas" ni quien se arrime a preguntarme si ando crudo; bien que saben que ando tronado. La verdad, ¿por qué dirán todos que andan buscando la verdad? ¿descubriendo la luz de vuelta? es que todos buscan la plata; hasta los profesores que dicen llevan a pecho el bienestar de la "comunidad," la comunidad que no conocen si el color no es verde o no tiene sonido hueco. Todos, menos estos que están aquí, tratan de salvarse por el dinero, por eso están aquí; no quieren ser falsos. No tenemos que condenar al dinero, él no tiene la culpa; la gente lo que ha hecho bajo su nombre, igual que bajo el nombre de Cristo. ¿A cuántos infelices predicadores no habrá hecho Cristo ricos y la gente más pobre? El cristiano le llama bendiciones, ¿será bendición robar al pobre y tomar ventaja del pendejo? ¿Y Marx, el dios de muchos chicanos vendidos? La misma gata pero revolcada. No les digo, curiosa que es la vida.

Tan suave la vida, no te agüites; "no te apures pa' que dures," echate otro jalonazo de agua bendita. —Cantinero, mira...dame dos frías—;como es liviano este cantinero, en tanto año no he visto este señor hacer un equivoco. Al fin cantinero, igual son los matanceros, pues una es para mí y la otra para *usté* amigo ausente, que todavía no conozco y platicándole, y posible nunca conozca; ¡qué importa! Pero va a tener que perdonarme si quiere saber de que va a tratarse la novela que pienso algun día escribir; si quiere saber va a tener que venir a escucharme todos los días para este lugarcito, o por lo menos cuando tenga chanza y yo le platico; ésta es mi casa. Solamente aquí; para mi casa no lo invito porque no tengo techo, sólo el sol y las estrellas. Es que tengo tanto que podía platicarle pero hay despacio le cuento; todo es que nos conozcamos mejor siendo que no quiero darles todos los secretos de mi novela y luego resulte escrita por otro como me ha pasa'o. Y no piense que lo estoy corriendo, no la agarre por mal, y quien sabe si yo lo esté aburriendo; usté bien vestido y oliendo a perfume caro y yo en este traje con sudor de pobre. Pero así es la vida, los dos tenemos diferentes oficios, el mío es matar el tiempo, y posible el suyo sea de aprovechar el tiempo. Yo quiero parar el tiempo, detenerlo, y usté estirarlo; lo quiere hacer lástico.

No sé, posible esté mal como luego sucede, pero a mí quizás me gusta mejor matar el tiempo; es más honorable matar, que aprovechar. Un aprovechado es un "sinvergüenza" y traicionero, pero no es pícaro; un pícaro está muy quemado para el comal. No digo de que es aprovechado pero el *sute* y la corbata me hacen afirmarme y poner el pie en el suelo. Y posible no entienda ni mi idioma, ni le importe un pito, pero le doy gracias por prestarme su oreja como amplificadora, para que retumbe por dondequiera. Y todo lo que yo quería ser cuando estaba mediano era mayordomo de la acequia...pero nunca fui; no pude. No sé como se cambió el guante y aquí estoy, tomándome una fría y apenas son las diez y media de la mañana. Y ni se ni que mañana; todas las mañanas son iguales mientras recuerde uno; si no recuerdo pues ni que decir. Como son largos los días a veces; otros no se acabala uno de tiempo, con ser que este es mi oficio y lo ha sido por los últimos veinte años. Todos aquí tenemos el trabajo de "sin oficio;" es el mejor trabajo, la única friega es que no pagan nada, más bien gasta uno lo que no tiene. Los mineros, pues ellos llegan con cheques de mil bolas por semana; para que vean, que tan malo no será el trabajo donde pagan tanto por hacerlo. Pa' comer, cojer, beber, no tienen que pagarle a uno nada. Hasta yo tengo jale de "sin oficio." Mi nombre nomás no se los doy, todavía, y posible nunca, porque no quiero que llegues preguntando por mí. No quiero que nadie sepa que nos conocemos. Yo no conozco a nadie y nadie me conoce a mí; así me gusta a mi vivir. En veinte años el cantinero no me ha preguntado por mi nombre y yo nunca le he dicho como me llamo. ¿Qué importa el nombre? él me conoce y yo a él; hasta me fía, pero me detengo, nunca le he debido más que quince pesos en un mes. Ni él nunca me ha fiado más que quince; así es el combeño. Cheques me cambiara, pero no tengo dinero en el banco; para que tener el dinero guardado agarrando mojo. Aquí todos me conocen de vista pero no por nombre. Este es el costumbre de los indios. Yo soy yo, y no me paresco a nadie porque nadie soy, y solo mis huellas saben por donde me redondeo pero lo bueno es que ellas no hablan. Así hubieran de ser los verdaderos amigos. De todos los que he conocido en este vida, incluyendo las mujeres que en mis brazos se han durmido después de gozar de sus delicias, a nadie le he tenido confianza como a mis huellas. Ellas son los únicas que nunca me han entrega'o, aunque muchos sus huellas si los entriegan; se vuelven traicioneras. Es porque soy nadie y nada, y saben que existo porque les he platica'o de los pasos por donde he anda'o. Es todo. y se que estoy vivo porque me voy a morir. Y cuando se volaron cuatro de un fregaso que nadie hizo caso, nada; pero eso era un cuarto de siglo atrás, en la antiguidad. Veintiuno quedaron huerfanos.

Aquí en el polvo este puedo escribir con mis dedos la fecha, hoy 14 de octubre del 1984, el tiempo está lluvisnado.

—*Medio siglo atrás en la antiguidad de los 50s tu tío se voló en el Árbol y nada hiciste, ni te importó ni a ti ni tus primos...* ¡YA CALLATE VOZ! ¿QUÉ IBA A HACER? ¡YA DEJAME EN PAZ! *...es decir, si lloraron, lamentaron, se consolaron unos a los otros pero no le siguieron los baños al gobierno; encuanto le cayó bien; todo barrió pa' bajo el piso como basura. Nadie cuestionó lo que pasó; todos lo tomaron como la mano de Dios cuando era un ACTO DIABOLICO, negro, tramado..al cabo que eran mexicanos, alguien tiene quehacer el trabajo peligroso por penes; que era vital para la seguridad de la nación; ellos fueron los que empezaron la* guerra de Vietnam y los que acabaron con la numero Dos; fueron los primeros casualidades pero sus nombres no aparecen en la tumba de marmol negra en Wáshington, en ninguna tumba, ni en la conciencia de los familiares, conti más en la del país, sólo en la mente de sus seres queridos que todo le dejaron a dios...DEJAME VOZ COBARDE; SAL DE DONDE TE ESCONDES.....

In Search of Epifano

Rudolfo A. Anaya

She drove into the desert of Sonora in search of Epifano. For years, when summer came and she finished her classes, she had loaded her old Jeep with supplies and gone south into Mexico.

Now she was almost eighty, and she thought, ready for death, but not afraid of death. It was the pain of the bone jarring journey which was her reality, not thoughts of death. But that did not diminish the urgency she felt as she drove south, across the desert. She was following the north rim of El Cañon de Cobre towards the land of the Tarahumaras. In the Indian villages there was always a welcome and fresh water.

The battered Jeep kicked up a cloud of chalky dust which rose into the empty and searing sky of summer. Around her, nothing moved in the heat. Dry mirages rose and shimmered, without content, without form. Her bright, clear eyes remained fixed on the rocky, rutted road in front. Around her there was only the vast and empty space of the desert. The dry heat.

The Jeep wrenched sideways, the low gear groaning and complaining. It had broken down once, and had cost her many days delay in Mexicali. The mechanic at the garage told her not to worry. In one day the parts would be in from Calexico and she would be on her way.

But she knew the way of the Mexican, so she rented a room in a hotel

222

nearby. Yes, she knew the Mexican. Part of her blood was Mexican, wasn't it? Her great grandfather, Epifano, had come north to Chihuahua to ranch and mine. She knew the stories whispered about the man, how he had built the great ranch in the desert. His picture was preserved in the family album, at his side, his wife, a dark haired woman. Around them, their sons.

The dry desert air burned her nostrils. A scent of the green ocotillo reached her, reminded her of other times, other years. She knew how to live in the sun, how to travel and how to survive, and she knew how to be alone under the stars. Night was her time in the desert. She liked to lie in her bedroll and look up at the swirling dance of the stars. In the cool of evening, her pulse would quicken. The sure path of the stars was her map, drawing her south.

Sweat streaked her wrinkled skin. Sweat and dust, the scent commingling. She felt alive. "At least I'm not dry and dead," she said aloud. Sweat and pleasure, it came together.

The Jeep worried her now. A sound somewhere in the gear box was not right. "It has trouble," the mechanic had said, wiping his oily hands on a dirty rag. What he meant was that he did not trust his work. It was best to return home, he suggested with a shrug. He had seen her musing over the old and tattered map, and he was concerned about the old woman going south. Alone. It was not good.

"We all have trouble," she mumbled. We live too long and the bones get brittle and the blood dries up. Why can't I taste the desert in my mouth? Have I grown so old? Epifano? How does it feel to become a spirit of the desert?

Her back and arms ached from driving; she was covered with the dust of the desert. Deep inside, in her liver or in her spleen, in one of those organs which the ancients called the seat of life, there was an ache, a dull, persistent pain. In her heart there was a tightness. Would she die and never reach the land of Epifano?

She slept while she waited for the Jeep to be repaired. Slept and dreamed under the shade of the laurel in the patio of the small hotel. Around her Mexican sounds and colors permeated her dream. What did she dream? That it was too late in her life to go once again into the desert? That she was an old woman and her life was lived, and the only evidence she would leave of her existence would be her sketches and paintings? Even now, as weariness filled her, the dreams came, and she slipped in and out of past and present. In her dreams she heard the voice of the old man, Epifano.

She saw his eyes, blue and bright like hers, piercing, but soft. The eyes of a kind man. He had died. Of course, he had died. He belonged to the past. But she had not forgotten him. In the family album, which she carried with her, his gaze was the one that looked out at her and drew her into the desert. She was the artist of the family. She had taken up painting. She heard voices. The voice of her great grandfather. The rest of her family had forgotten the past, forgotten Mexico and the old man Epifano.

The groaning of the Jeep shattered the silence of the desert. She tasted dust in her mouth, she yearned for a drink of water. She smiled. A thirst to be satisfied. Always there was one more desire to be satisfied. Her paintings were like that, a desire from within to be satisfied, a call to do one more sketch of the desert in the molten light before night came. And always the voice of Epifano drawing her to the trek into the past.

The immense solitude of the desert swallowed her. She was only a moving shadow in the burning day. Overhead, vultures circled in the sky, the heat grew intense. She was alone on a dirt road she barely remembered, taking her bearings only by instinct, roughly following the north rim of the Cañon de Cobre, drawn by the thin line of the horizon, where the dull peaks of las montañas met the dull blue of the sky. Whirlwinds danced in her eyes, memories flooded at her soul.

She had married young. She thought she was in love; he was a man of ambition. It took her years to learn that he had little desire or passion. He could not, or would not, fulfill her. What was the fulfillment she sought? It had to do with something that lay even beneath the moments of love or children carried in the womb. Of that she was sure.

She turned to painting, she took classes, she traveled alone. She came to understand that she and the man were not meant for each other?

She remembered a strange thing had happened in the chapel where the family gathered to attend her marriage. An Indian had entered and stood at the back of the room. She had turned and looked at him. Then he was gone, and later she was not sure if the appearance was real or imagined.

But she did not forget. She had looked into his eyes. He had the features of a Tarahumara. Was he Epifano's messenger? Had he brought a warning? For a moment she hesitated, then she had turned and said yes to the preacher's question. Yes to the man who could never understand the depth of her passion. She did what was expected of her there in the land of ocean and sun. She bore him a daughter and a son. But in all those years, the man never understood the desire in her, he never explored her depth of passion. She turned to her dreams, and there she heard the voice of Epifano, a resonant voice imparting seductive images of the past.

Years later she left her husband, left everything, left the dream of southern California where there was no love in the arms of the man, no sweet juices in the nights of love pretended. She left the circle of pretend. She needed a meaning, she needed desperately to understand the voices which spoke in her soul. She drove south, alone, in search of Epifano. The desert dried her by day, but replenished her at night. She learned that the mystery of the stars at night was like the mystery in her soul.

She sketched, she painted, and each year in spring time she drove farther south. On her map she marked her goal, the place where once stood Epifano's hacienda.

In the desert the voices were clear. She followed the road into Tarahumara country, she dreamed of the old man, Epifano. She was his blood, the only one who remembered him.

At the end of day she stood at the side of a pool of water, a small, desert spring surrounded by desert trees. The smell in the air was cool, wet. At her feet, tracks of deer, a desert cat. Ocelot. She stooped to drink, like a cautious animal.

"Thank the gods for this water which quenches our thirst," she said, splashing the precious water on her face, knowing there is no life in the desert without the water which flows from deep within the earth. Around her, the first stars of dusk begin to appear.

She had come at last to the ranch of Epifano. There, below the spring where she stood, on the flat ground, was the hacienda. Now could be seen only the outlines of the foundation and the shape of the old corrals. From here his family had spread, northwest, up into Mexicali and finally into southern California. Seeds. Desert seeds seeking precious water. The water of desire. And only she had returned.

She sat and gazed at the desert, the peaceful quiet, mauve of the setting sun. She felt a deep sadness within. An old woman, sitting alone in the wide desert, her dream done.

A noise caused her to turn. Perhaps an animal come to drink at the spring, the same spring where Epifano had once wet his lips. She waited, and in the shadows of the palo verde and the desert willows she saw the Indian appear. She smiled.

She was dressed in white, the color of desire not consummated. Shadows moved around her. She had come home, home to the arms of Epifano. The Indian was a tall, splendid man. Silent. He wore paint, as they did in the old days when they ran the game of the pelota up and down las montañas of the Cañon de Cobre.

"Epifano," she said, "I came in search of Epifano." He understood the name. Epifano. He held his hand to his chest. His eyes were bright and blue, not Tarahumara eyes, but the eyes of Epifano. He had known she would come. Around her other shadows moved, the women. Indian women of the desert. They moved silently around her, a circle of women, an old ceremony about to begin.

The sadness left her. She struggled to rise, and in the dying light of the sun a blinding flash filled her being. Like desire, or like an arrow from the bow of the Indian, the light filled her and she quivered.

The moan of love is like the moan of life. She was dressed in white.

Contributors

Rudolfo A. Anaya is the author of *Bless Me, Ultima, Heart of Aztlán, Tortuga, The Silence of the Llano, A Chicano in China* and various other works. He is the editor of *Voces*.

Marcella Aguilar-Henson received her Ph.D. in 1982 from the University of New Mexico. Presently, she is a free-lance interpreter and writer in Los Angeles. She has published *Figura Cristalina*, a book of poetry and the *Multifaceted Poetic World of Angela de Hoyos*, a book of criticism.

Estevan Arellano is the author of *Palabras de la Vista/Retratos de la Pluma*. He is also a sculptor and a photographer. His work may be viewed at his gallery, Chimplín, in Dixon, New Mexico.

Romolo A. Arellano was born and raised in Taos, New Mexico. He received a B.S. degree from New Mexico State University in 1970. His poetry and fiction have been published in *Puerto Del Sol, New America, Conceptions Southwest* and *De Colores*. His plays, *Tito* and *Penitencia*, have been presented in New Mexico.

Jimmy Santiago Baca is a native of New Mexico. He teaches creative writing in the Continuing Education Program at the University of New Mexico. He is the author of *Immigrants in Our Own Land, What's Happening* and *Swords of Darkness*.

Guadalupe Baca-Vaughn is a retired school teacher and former Director of Education for the Kit Carson Foundation. She has translated and published *Memorias del Presbitero Antonio José Martinez*.

Fray Angelico Chavez is a native of Wagon Mound, New Mexico. He is a retired Franciscan missionary, poet, painter and historical researcher. He has written more than twenty-five books and numerous journal articles. *La Conquistadora: the Autobiography of an Ancient Statue* and *Origins of New Mexico Families in the Spanish Colonial Period* are among his well-known works.

Denise Chávez is a native of Las Cruces, New Mexico. She has a degree in Fine Arts from Trinity University and an M.A. degree in Creative Writing from the University of New Mexico. Her collection of short stories, *The Last of the Menu Girls*, was published recently by Arte Público Press.

Ed Chávez is a native of Albuquerque, New Mexico. He graduated from St. Michael's College in Santa Fe. He is employed by the federal government. He is working on a trilogy on New Mexico, from its territorial days to the present.

Jaime Chávez lives in Albuquerque, New Mexico. He graduated from the University of New Mexico. Presently, he is associated with the Atrisco Land Rights Council as a community organizer. He is a poet and a media writer.

Ronald P. Chavez was born in Puerto de Luna, New Mexico. He is owner of the Club Café in Santa Rosa, a community near his birthplace. His works have been published in local newspapers.

David Fernández, born in Albuquerque, New Mexico, lives in Taos. He attended the University of New Mexico. He was a journalist in Santa Fe and Taos in the 1970's. Presently, he is a water consultant and president of Tres Ríos (Acequia) Association of Northern New Mexico.

Robert Gallegos lives in Grants, New Mexico. He is a sculptor and a poet. His latest book *Pie Town Diary* was published by Bludgeon Press in 1986.

Cecilio García-Camarillo is from Laredo, Texas. He received his B.A. in literature from the University of Texas at Austin. He founded and edited *Magazín, Caracol* and *Rayas*. He has published several books of poetry: *Calcetines Embotellados, Double-Face, Winter Month, The Line, Hang a Snake* and *Borlotes Mestizos*. He currently lives in Albuquerque, New Mexico, and is the host of a public affairs program at the University of New Mexico radio station.

James Gonzalez is from Albuquerque, New Mexico. He is a former school teacher. Currently he devotes his time to writing and is the proprietor of the Barelas Coffee House Café in Albuquerque.

Erlinda Gonzales-Berry is a professor of Spanish and Chicano Literature at the University of New Mexico. She has published numerous articles on Chicano literature and has just completed her first novel, *El Tren de la Ausencia*.

Francisca Herrera Tenorio, currently residing in California, is a native of Albuquerque, New Mexico. She was a host for a public affairs program for the University of New Mexico radio station—KUNM.

Enrique Lamadrid is a professor at the University of New Mexico, where he teaches New Mexico folklore, Chicano and Latin American literature. He has written scholarly articles on Chicano literature. He specializes in "indita ballads" of the Navajo borderlands.

Elida Lechuga was born in Albuquerque, New Mexico. She has degrees in English from New Mexico State University and the University of New Mexico. "Bitter Dreams" is an excerpt from her novel, *I Just Don't Know*.

E.A. Mares, from Albuquerque, New Mexico, is a poet, playwright, fiction writer, and essayist. He has a Ph.D. in European History and research interests in the Southwest and in the History of Science.

Demetria Martínez was born in Albuquerque, New Mexico. She received her B.A. from the Woodrow Wilson School of Public and International Affairs at Princeton University. In 1984 she wrote *Only Say the Word*, a play for three actors. Her freelance articles and reviews appear in the *Albuquerque Journal*. She also writes for the *National Catholic Reporter*.

A. Gabriel Meléndez is a professor of Spanish and Latin American literature at Mills College, California. He received his Ph.D. in Spanish from the University of New Mexico. In 1985, he received first prize for his poems, which were published in *Palabra Nueva: Poesía* by Texas Western Press, at the University of Texas at El Paso.

José Montoya was born in El Gallego, a ranch in Escaboza, New Mexico. He attended City College in San Diego, California and the California College of Arts and Crafts in Oakland. He has exhibited his art work nationally and internationally. His poetry has been published in numerous anthologies. He is the author of *El Sol y Los de Abajo*.

Joseph M. Olonia lives in Albuquerque, New Mexico. He is a student in creative writing and literature at the University of New Mexico. He has published in *ViAztlán*.

Virginia E. Ortiz was born in Springfield, Massachusetts. She is a student and an employee at the University of New Mexico.

Rosalie Otero was born in Taos, New Mexico. She received her Ph.D. in English from the University of New Mexico. Recently, she received a Mellon Fellowship to study modern women writers at Rice University in Houston, Texas.

Juan José Peña is from Las Vegas, New Mexico. He received his B.A. and M.A. degrees from New Mexico Highlands University. Currently, he serves as interpreter and translator in the federal courts. He has published *The Question of the Socialist Workers Party* and *The Politics of San Miguel County* among others.

Leroy V. Quintana was born in Albuquerque, New Mexico. He received degrees in English from the University of New Mexico and New Mexico State University. In 1978, he was awarded a National Endowment for the Arts Creative Writing Fellowship. He is the author of *Hijo del Pueblo: New Mexico Poems* and *Sangre*.

Leo Romero lives in Santa Fe, New Mexico. He is the author of *Celso* and *Agua Negra*. He is also an artist, working in mixed media, etchings, and sculpture. He is employed by Los Alamos National Laboratory in its science education program for the public schools.

Orlando Romero is a native of Santa Fe, New Mexico. He is a former National Endowment for the Arts recipient. He has published numerous articles on the Southwest. He is the author of *Nambé Year One* and *The Day of the Wind*.

Gustavo Sainz of Mexico City served for ten years as professor and chairman in the Department of Journalism and Communication Sciences at the Universidad Nacional Autónoma de México. He taught at the University of Texas, San Antonio, and the University of Wisconsin, Madison. He is now teaching at the University of New Mexico. He is the author of *La Princesa del Palacio de Hierro*, *Gazapo*, *Obsesives días circulares*, *Compadre Lobo*, *Fantasmas aztecas* and *Paseo en Trapecio*.

Rubén Salaz-Marquez lives in Corrales, New Mexico. He is the author of *Cosmic: the La Raza Sketch Book*, *Heartland: Stories of the Southwest* and *I Am Tecumseh*.

Arturo Sandoval was born and raised in Española, New Mexico. He currently lives in Albuquerque, New Mexico where he is active with La Compañía de Teatro de Albuquerque as a playwright and tour director.

Michelle Sedillo was born in Albuquerque, New Mexico. Her grandparents' storytelling has been inspirational for her writing. She studies creative writing at the University of New Mexico.

José Luís Soto, originally from Juárez, Chihuahua, Mexico, lives in Albuquerque, New Mexico. He is a member of Taller Literario del Museo de Arte e Historia de Ciudad Juarez (INBA). He is on the editorial board of *NOD*, the museum's magazine.

Sabine R. Ulibarrí was born and raised in Tierra Amarilla, New Mexico. He received his B.A. and M.A. degrees from the University of New Mexico and his Ph.D. degree from UCLA. He is a professor of Spanish at the University of New Mexico. He is the author of *Mi Abuela Fumaba Puros y Otros Cuentos*, *Tierra Amarilla* and *Al Cielo se Sube a Pie*.

Lorenzo J. Valdez is a native of northern New Mexico. He attended the College of Santa Fe and New Mexico State University. He has been writing for several years.

Catherine Vallejos Bartlett received her M.A. degree in English from the University of New Mexico. She has been published in *Imagine: International Journal of Chicano Poetry* and *Confluencia: Revista Hispánica de Cultura y Literatura*.

Enriqueta I. Vásquez, born and raised in Cheraw, Colorado, is an artist and writer. She has been active in community activities in Colorado and New Mexico. Her work has been published in several anthologies. She co-authored *Viva La Raza*.

Cleófes Vigil, born and raised in San Cristobal, New Mexico, is a rancher and folk artist. He is well known for his reptoire and singing of alabados. "Mother of all Life the Earth," one of his many poems was published in *La Raza* by Stan Steiner.